A WILD LIGHT

"Written in flowing, at times poetic, prose, *A Wild Light* reads like a languid, surreal dream, punctuated by fierce, sudden, and often unexpected action . . . a superlative series." —*The Miami Herald*

"Truly one of the most darkly intense and spellbinding series in [urban fantasy] today! Every Liu book should be an autobuy!" —*Romantic Times* (4½ stars)

"This pivotal book in the Hunter Kiss series proves Liu's dark side is a haunting place to be as she pushes Maxine to the brink as a sharp-witted, uncompromising defender, not immune to self-doubt but tempered and made stronger for it." —*Booklist*

"[Liu's] depth of imagination and her talent for creating unforgettable characters is masterful." —*Night Owl Reviews*

"The third Hunter Kiss urban fantasy is a terrific entry that contains a powerful story line while also moving forward on the overarching theme . . . With a late great twist, fans will enjoy Marjorie M. Liu's dark *A Wild Light*." —*Genre Go Round Reviews*

DARKNESS CALLS

"Ms. Liu has an eloquent writing style and gives readers a story where the secondary characters are every bit as fascinating as the leads. *Darkness Calls* is vividly described and full of paranormal action from beginning to end." —*Darque Reviews*

"[Liu's] ability to deliver kick-butt action and characters whose humanity resonates, even when they're anything but human, is a testament to her outstanding storytelling skills. Liu's imagination is an amazing place to visit." —*Romantic Times* (top pick)

Romantic Times (4½ stars)

continued . . .

"*Darkness Calls* is one riveting book and Marjorie Liu is one great writer. The desperation Maxine feels as she deals with her past and unknown future is one that will keep you reading and anxious for the next terror Maxine will have to endure."

—*Fresh Fiction*

"Liu has done an excellent job of developing and expanding the mythos she created in *The Iron Hunt* . . . I look forward to reading the further adventures of Maxine Kiss."

—*SFRevu*

THE IRON HUNT

"I adore the Hunter Kiss series! Marjorie Liu's writing is both lyrical and action packed, which is a very rare combination. Heroine Maxine Kiss and her demon friends are wonderful characters who are as likable as they are fierce. You'll want to read this series over and over."

—Angela Knight, *New York Times* bestselling author

"Liu is one of the best new voices in paranormal fiction."

—*Publishers Weekly*

"Marjorie M. Liu writes a gripping supernatural thriller."

—*The Best Reviews*

"From the imagination of one of today's most talented authors comes a mesmerizing, darkly disturbing world on the brink of apocalypse. With her new Hunter Kiss series, Liu has created a uniquely tough yet vulnerable heroine in Maxine Kiss . . . Through Maxine's eyes, readers take a heart-stopping ride where buried secrets could change the fate of the world."

—*Romantic Times*

"Readers who love urban fantasies like those of Charlaine Harris or Kim Harrison will relish Marjorie M. Liu's excellent adventure. This is the superb start of a dynamic-looking saga."

—*Midwest Book Review*

"A stunning new series . . . The mythology is fascinating, the characters complicated, the story lines original. I'm a big fan of Liu's Dirk & Steele series, but this one surpasses even it."

—*Fresh Fiction*

"An incredibly complex, engrossing story that will stretch your imagination and broaden your ideas of what is and what could be."

—*Romance Junkies*

THE MORTAL BONE

MARJORIE M. LIU

ACE BOOKS, NEW YORK

THE BERKLEY PUBLISHING GROUP
Published by the Penguin Group
Penguin Group (USA) Inc.
375 Hudson Street, New York, New York 10014, USA
Penguin Group (Canada), 90 Eglinton Avenue East, Suite 700, Toronto, Ontario M4P 2Y3, Canada
(a division of Pearson Penguin Canada Inc.)
Penguin Books Ltd., 80 Strand, London WC2R 0RL, England
Penguin Group Ireland, 25 St. Stephen's Green, Dublin 2, Ireland (a division of Penguin Books Ltd.)
Penguin Group (Australia), 250 Camberwell Road, Camberwell, Victoria 3124, Australia
(a division of Pearson Australia Group Pty. Ltd.)
Penguin Books India Pvt. Ltd., 11 Community Centre, Panchsheel Park, New Delhi—110 017, India
Penguin Group (NZ), 67 Apollo Drive, Rosedale, Auckland 0632, New Zealand
(a division of Pearson New Zealand Ltd.)
Penguin Books (South Africa) (Pty.) Ltd., 24 Sturdee Avenue, Rosebank, Johannesburg 2196,
South Africa

Penguin Books Ltd., Registered Offices: 80 Strand, London WC2R 0RL, England

This is a work of fiction. Names, characters, places, and incidents either are the product of the author's imagination or are used fictitiously, and any resemblance to actual persons, living or dead, business establishments, events, or locales is entirely coincidental. The publisher does not have any control over and does not assume any responsibility for author or third-party websites or their content.

THE MORTAL BONE

An Ace Book / published by arrangement with the author

PRINTING HISTORY
Ace mass-market edition / January 2012

Copyright © 2012 by Marjorie M. Liu.
Cover art by Craig White.
Cover design by Judith Lagerman.
Interior text design by Laura K. Corless.

ISBN: 978-1-937007-18-8

ACE
Ace Books are published by The Berkley Publishing Group,
a division of Penguin Group (USA) Inc.,
375 Hudson Street, New York, New York 10014.
ACE and the "A" design are trademarks of Penguin Group (USA) Inc.

PRINTED IN THE UNITED STATES OF AMERICA

10 9 8 7 6 5 4 3 2 1

For J.D.
El futuro está lleno de luz.

ACKNOWLEDGMENTS

I'd like to thank my editor, Kate Seaver, for her constant support and kindness. And to my copy editors, Sara and Bob Schwager, I send you warm wishes and a great deal of appreciation. Lucienne Diver . . . a huge thank-you, as well.

And to my readers . . . oh, you lovely readers . . . what can I say? I love you all.

To learn more about my books, please visit my website at www.marjoriemliu.com—or follow me on Twitter at @marjoriemliu.

The wound is the place where
the Light enters you.

—RUMI

CHAPTER 1

WHAT happens in Texas, stays in Texas. Except when demons are involved.

I was sitting on the sagging porch of the old farmhouse, sipping an ice-cold ginger ale, when a red pickup truck appeared around the last bend of the long, curving driveway. I stood, shielding my eyes against the late-afternoon sun noticing, as had become my habit, the gold glimmer of my wedding ring standing out in stark relief against the obsidian, mercury-streaked tattoos that covered my entire left hand.

Dust kicked up behind the truck, but not much. The driver was taking a slow approach.

I hadn't lived on this land in years. Maybe it was a nosy neighbor coming to visit. Or a social worker who had heard that a teenage boy was in residence and not attending school. Could be someone lost—but the driveway was almost three miles long and blocked by a heavy gate. A bit out of the way, just to ask directions.

I felt a tug against my tattooed skin. A persistent ripple that traveled like a small shock wave from my toenails to

1

the base of my neck, as though an electrical pulse was moving through Zee and the boys.

I set down my drink. Against my neck, the tip of Dek's tattooed tail thrummed, like the quiet warning of a rattle-snake. When I flexed my fingers, the organic silver armor covering my right hand tingled. Everything, coming alive as that red truck rolled and rumbled down the driveway.

The driver parked in front of the barn, surrounded in a swirling cloud of pale, hot dust. I couldn't see much behind the tinted windows, so I listened to the engine pop and groan as I stepped off the porch.

The door opened, and a foot dangled out. Fortunately, it was attached to a leg. I wasn't always that lucky.

I saw a simple white sneaker with a thick sole, and an equally thick ankle that was so swollen the flesh seemed to sag over the top of the shoe. I walked sideways, peering into the truck to see what else that limb was attached to.

What I found was a demon having a heart attack.

That's what it seemed like at first. The unfortunate host was a woman well over three hundred pounds, who wore a sleeveless blue sundress that clung to her round stomach and heavy breasts. Her arms were thick and wide, as was her soft neck, which was almost lost in her sagging jaw. She had pale skin—around her hands—but the rest of her was pink and red as a lobster, and dripping with sweat.

Soaked brown hair clung to her face, along with a thun-derous aura that marked her as demon-possessed. Some-where, deep inside, a human soul still resided . . . but it was impossible to tell just how long it had been buried beneath that seat of darkness. Some demons, the young ones, clung with only a light touch, a whisper. Others dug in, latching onto the flesh, sliding into lives, and pulling every string.

Those clinging shadows rose and fell off the woman's shoulders with each heaving breath, and she sat—half-in, half-out of her truck—with her eyes closed and mouth open, panting and clutching her chest.

It would be easy for me to exorcise the demon. Even a year ago, I would not have hesitated. Those gutter rats who regularly escaped the prison veil had no business possessing humans and feeding off their pain. Nothing had changed my opinion about that.

But I'd learned a thing or two about demons—and myself—that blurred the lines between good and evil. I could no longer cast stones. Not without asking questions first. Any demon looking for me was very desperate—or coerced—and that was bad news, in more ways than one.

So I waited, silent. Wishing I had gum to chew. The aftertaste of that ginger ale had gone sour, right along with my stomach. I hated this so much. All the possibilities of all the bad things this demon might tell me, crowding my head, making my pulse thicken.

The possessed woman finally caught her breath and opened her eyes to look at me.

She didn't seem to know where to settle her gaze, which flitted above and around, and on me, with such rapidness it made me dizzy. Finally, she settled on my eyes, then danced down to the tattoos covering my arms: an unbroken tangle of obsidian muscle and scales, knotted, curling, shimmering with veins of mercury that caught the light—though not nearly as much as the glinting crimson eyes that always remained open and staring.

I'd found some of my mother's old white tank tops in the closet and hadn't seen much point to leaving them there—or hiding the boys. I had few, if any, secrets from the people in my life. Which was another dazzling departure from the way I had been raised.

"Boo," I said to the possessed woman, and felt sort of bad when she flinched from me, like I'd hit her.

Silent, and with agonizing stiffness, she reached sideways into the passenger seat and dragged a red plastic bowling bag across her stomach. Her breathing roughened again, and sweat dripped off the ends of her thin hair.

"Take it," she whispered. "Hurry."

Licking a bad case of herpes sounded more appealing than taking a gift from a demon. Safer, too.

I did not move. "Why are you here?"

"Come on, it's fragile." Her demonic aura twitched and fluttered, tendrils of shadow flirting with escape. "Please. I was told to come."

"Who told you?"

She flashed me a hard, frightened look. "A voice in a dream. I was ordered to give you something that belongs to my host."

I frowned. A voice in a dream? *Really?*

Unfortunately, it sounded too strange to be a lie. And that demon was genuinely terrified.

I reached for the bowling bag. I wasn't worried about its being a bomb. I'd survive a nuclear blast—or bullets, knives, fire. Sending me to the bottom of the ocean wouldn't

4

kill me, either. Not while the sun shone, somewhere above me.

The possessed woman snatched back her hand before I had a full grip on the oversized handle, and I almost dropped it—partially because it was unexpectedly heavy. The shape as it bumped my leg felt round and hard.

"This better not be a human head," I muttered.

She shuddered. "Close."

I flashed her a hard look and unzipped the bowling bag.

No hair or bone inside. No blood. The afternoon light gleamed off a round, smooth surface—clear as glass. I reached inside, bracing myself as the armor encasing much of my right hand and forearm began tingling again, like pins and needles.

Nothing happened, though. The armor quieted. I slid my hand under the cool, hard object—and lifted it from the bowling bag.

I stared, for a moment unsure what I was looking at. I saw depressions for eyes, a hard jaw and rows of teeth . . . but it was all wrong, and eerie.

Yes, there was a head in the bowling bag. A skull.

But it was carved from crystal. And it did not look human.

"Groovy," I said. "But what the hell?"

The demon tore her gaze away, trembling. Moments later, I also started quivering—unable to help myself as a tiny tsunami rolled over every inch of my skin. Zee stretched and rippled, as did the rest of the boys, all of them tugging, pulling, struggling toward the crystal skull in my hand.

The truck's engine roared. I jumped back as the vehicle

jolted forward, spitting dust in my face. The driver's side door was still open, swinging wildly, but the possessed woman had pulled her leg inside and was twisting at the steering wheel, her aura flaring wild and dark. I dropped the skull inside the bag, and ran after her.

Too slow, too late. The front bumper hit my knee as she accelerated past, but the boys deflected the impact. I tried to grab the door, but all I caught was air—and a glimpse of her determined, terrified expression.

I stopped running and watched the truck tear down the driveway in a choking cloud of dust. Bewildered, feeling stupid. Would that possessed woman have been able to pull off the same escape a year ago? Was I *that* sloppy?

Or am I getting too used to letting demons go?

I hated both possibilities. Might as well stick one foot in the grave. I was losing my edge.

That, or the edge had shifted sideways. Demonic possession didn't mean the same thing anymore. It didn't feel like the same threat I'd always thought it to be—not now, not after being exposed to far more immediate, and terrible, dangers.

I had lived my life believing that I was supposed to kill demons—*all* demons.

But the truth was worse.

I was the very thing that needed to be feared most. My body, a prison for five of the most dangerous demons ever to exist.

Reaper Kings. Devourers of worlds.

And I was their Queen.

CHAPTER 2

I was back on the porch, sipping that ginger ale, when Grant and Byron came home. I heard them coming before the dust started rising. My mother's station wagon hadn't been driven in close to fifteen years, and the engine had a complaint for every half mile—grumbling and coughing, spitting like it was some cranky old man. The wagon had been old before its retirement: one of those gas-guzzling tanks that whole families could camp inside on summer road trips into the mountains. Like a Disney movie, or something.

My mother and I had lived in that car for years. Comfortable. Lots of windows. Always an interesting view.

I felt strange every time I heard the engine. Too many memories. But that seemed to be what I needed right now, because I had Johnny Cash playing on the other side of the open window, his thunderous rumbling voce filling the warm air, and there was nothing like his music to inspire some deep contemplation of my mother and magic, demons, and murder.

That, and what we were going to have for supper. I was hungry.

I ambled down to meet the station wagon. Byron was behind the wheel, a nervous half smile on his face. He looked like a city kid with his floppy black hair, and the kind of pale skin you could only get from living in a place that never saw the sun. Like Seattle.

He was skinny, strong, all his fingernails painted black. An earring dangled, shaped like a feather. He'd had it for three days, bought from a local at a farmer's market, and I was pretty sure it was his favorite thing.

Byron braked too hard, slamming him—and his passenger—against his seat belt. Dust flew. Creaks and pops filled the air, like settling bones. I bit back a smile, tapping the hot hood with my dark fingernails, and made my way around the bumper to the other side of the station wagon where Grant leaned out the window like he was thinking of crawling free.

"Save me," he mouthed. I laughed out loud, and he reached out to hook his fingers inside the waist of my jeans, pulling me close until he could kiss the part of me that was closest to eye level—which just happened to be my hip. Heat spread through me, along with tenderness so big, I didn't know why my heart wasn't beating outside my body, maybe in the same spot where his mouth pressed against me.

"Welcome back, Mr. Cooperon," I murmured, running my fingers through his thick brown hair. I felt, inside me, a tug—right below my heart—and inside my head saw a vision of golden thread burning bright.

Our very real bond, linking us, soul to soul. My strength, his. His strength, mine. Married, in more ways than one.

He made a small, contented sound. "Good to be alive, Mrs. Kiss."

Byron, mostly out of sight on the other side of the massive station wagon, murmured, "I didn't drive *that* bad."

"Even the *road* tried to get out of your way," Grant retorted, and opened the door with a groan. I grabbed his cane before it fell out, and held it for him as he swung his bad leg from the car. A hammer-wielding schizophrenic had crushed those bones some years back, but even with that old injury, my husband kept up with me better than anyone else in this world.

My husband.

Two words that made me warm and goofy. I had never imagined I would have this kind of relationship. It was not done. It was not safe. No woman in my family, to my knowledge, had *ever* tried to make a life with a man.

Of course, there was a lot I didn't know about my ancestors. My bloodline was ten thousand years old. Assumptions were stupid. People fell in love. My grandmother had. So had my mother. But neither of them had stayed with her man, for better or worse.

For better or worse, I *had*.

Grant winced as he got out of the station wagon. Tall, broad, dressed in jeans and a white T-shirt that strained against his hard chest and shoulders. He radiated warmth and light, in ways that everyone felt, from young to old. He had a strong, masculine face, and eyes that could see right through a person. Or a demon.

Grant could see souls.

Souls, which were nothing but energy. Energy that could be manipulated, altered . . . and transformed.

With nothing but his voice.

My mother would have killed him, just for that. No hesitation. No second thoughts.

Byron slid from the driver's seat and walked around to the station wagon's rear hatch. I saw grocery bags inside and began to go and help him. Grant, though, touched my arm. The boys stirred beneath his hand, straining to be closer to him.

"Something happened," he said, with a slight frown. "Your aura is . . . tense."

I didn't know what a tense aura looked like, but that possessed woman had been terrified—her demonic shadow fluttering like hummingbird wings. I could only imagine Grant was seeing something slightly more low-key around me.

"We had a visitor," I told him quietly, while Byron wrestled with plastic bags. "She left a gift. It's on the porch."

Grant's frown deepened. I kissed his cheek and went to grab some groceries.

Byron was still trying to load up on bags, like he was aiming to carry all twenty at the same time. I nudged him aside with my hip and a grin, and he smiled back, shyly.

"See any cute girls?" I asked him, watching from the corner of my eye as Grant limped to the porch.

The boy shook his head and touched the dangling earring. "I'm not sure I quite fit in, anyway."

"You miss Seattle?" We still had a home there: a warehouse loft that sat above a homeless shelter that Grant operated out of his own deep pockets. It had been a month since we'd left it behind. There was too much death inside those walls. We needed time, not just to let the memories fade but to air out the stink of blood.

"Maybe." Byron hesitated. "But this is nice. I like it away from the city. It's . . . quiet."

"Quiet feels safe," I murmured, wondering if that was why my mother had made us live here after years on the road.

"Yeah." He gave me a thoughtful glance. "How safe are we?"

I hesitated a heartbeat too long. Byron blinked, and looked away. I nudged him again and ruffled his hair.

"Safe," I said. "You're safe with us."

He didn't say anything, wrestling instead with grocery bags—jaw tight, eyes dark and far away. I wondered, sometimes, if he remembered *anything* of all the lives he had lived—those thousands of years lingering somewhere in his cells, despite all attempts to keep him ignorant of his true, immortal nature.

Byron was no ordinary teenager. I was no ordinary woman. Grant was probably the most human of us all, but even *he* wasn't from this world.

Our little family. Crazy and wonderful. And that was even without Zee and the boys.

Byron grabbed some bags, and I took the rest. Looked like vegetables and fruit, and baking materials. I spotted a lot of frozen dinners, too, along with motor oil, a dozen bottles of rubbing alcohol, and about that many family-sized bags of M&Ms. Good eats.

We lumbered to the house. Grant sat on the porch, staring at the crystal skull. I had set it out on a chair, nestled on a tattered red cushion. Johnny Cash still rumbled, this time about the apocalypse—which seemed incredibly appropriate.

Byron paused, staring at the skull. "Wow."

"Yes, wow," Grant muttered, and gave me a piercing look. I shook my head and went into the house just long enough to dump the grocery bags and put away the frozen dinners. Byron opened the cabinets, unloading rice and cans. I patted his shoulder on my way out, and he only flinched a little. It wasn't personal. He still had trouble, sometimes, being touched.

Outside, I found Grant sprawled in his chair, staring at the hill where my mother and grandfather were buried. He was humming beneath his breath, less a melody than a rumble, less music than power. His flute was in the house, but he'd been using it less, learning instead how to rely on his own voice to twist at the threads of energy around him.

"What's the verdict?" I asked him.

"Who brought it?" he replied, instead of answering my question.

"A possessed woman. Terrified. She said that she was . . . ordered. In a dream."

"That makes me feel *so* much better."

I snorted and leaned against the rail. "It's not shaped like a human skull."

"No," he said softly, "it's certainly not."

The cranium was wide, with three ridges across the brow and a similar protruding crest at the cheeks. The eye sockets were huge, and the carved jaw thick. The upper and lower rows of teeth were sharp as dagger points, jutting at odd, uneven angles that reminded me of a piranha's mouth.

It should have been ridiculous. But it wasn't.

It was disturbing as hell.

My first view of the skull, out in the driveway, had been too quick. I had not appreciated, then, just how unsettling it really was—but I'd been sitting with the thing for over an hour, and it was pretty much getting on my last nerve.

"I assume you've heard of crystal skulls," Grant said.

"New Age bunk," I replied. "Signs of alien life. Hosts of supernatural powers. Ancient computers. I spent a lot of late nights watching bad hotel television before I met you."

His mouth twitched. "Pre-Columbian fakes. At least, that's what one camp says, while others believe . . . well, everything you just said."

"Uh-huh," I said, rubbing my tattooed arms, soothing the boys. "But I bet demons didn't deliver up *those* skulls in a bowling bag and red pickup truck."

"No, you're special," he replied dryly. "This skull, sweetheart, isn't from earth."

CHAPTER 3

A lot of things weren't from earth. Including humans.
Life had been a lot easier before *that* little discovery, which I tried not to think about all too often, given that it involved genocide and quantum highways, and aliens that could—and did—manipulate human DNA like it was nothing but silly putty. Those same aliens had imprisoned five demons on my ancestor's body in an attempt to stop a war, and those same aliens had played God on this earth and on other worlds, creating monsters, *becoming* monsters, using humans as a living dolls in games meant to ease the burden and boredom of being immortal.

They were called the Aetar, or Avatars, and only one—that I knew of—still resided on earth. The rest had been gone for thousands of years, off to other worlds accessible through a network of quantum roads called the Labyrinth: a place outside time and space, a nexus where the infinite was possible across a universe that might only take a heartbeat to traverse.

I didn't understand any of it . . . not as much as I needed to. A war was coming, and if it wasn't fought, if I couldn't find a way to stop the Aetar . . .

. . . *this* world would be lost. Humans would find their own bodies turned against them. If they were lucky.

Of course, there was *another*, even *worse*, possibility.

Six billion people could end up penned like cattle and *eaten* by the vast and starving demonic army currently locked away on the other side of a crumbling interdimensional wall.

A month ago, some of those demons had broken free. Humans had died. Next time, the break in the prison wall would likely be permanent.

Maybe I'd be able to control that army. Maybe not.

Up shit creek. No paddle.

But at least I had friends.

❦

FIVE minutes until full sunset. Grant went inside to start dinner, and I took a walk, carrying the crystal skull inside the bowling bag. Neither of us wanted it in the house, and I had questions that couldn't be asked around Byron, no matter how much weirdness the kid had been exposed to.

All that big sky hanging over the horizon was pale and golden and held the promise of shadows. I walked toward the hill where the oak tree stood over my mother's grave. Even from here, I could see the green leaves shimmering with that same last light, nature turning to gold like some Midas touch of evening.

Birds sang, and insects hummed in the tall, dry grass. I inhaled deep, savoring the summer heat in my lungs, heat that I could not feel beneath my sleeping tattoos—and the warm wind blew, and was sweet, and so was the world.

I had almost reached my mother's grave when the sun set below the horizon. I felt its last ray of light wink out in my soul . . .

. . . and the boys woke up.

Happened in a heartbeat. A hurricane of knives, skinning me alive. Every inch of my body, from nails to breasts, between my legs, and the soles of my feet—ripped away in one hard blast of pain that still, after all these years, almost dropped me to my knees.

I kept walking, though—staggering, bent—focused on reaching my mother's grave. Tattoos peeled, shadows tearing off my skin and pouring out from beneath my clothing—gathering in a knotted dance of darkness and flicks of lightning. Hard. Fast. Whispers bent through the air, twisting into soft growls and laughter that dropped into hisses. I heard singing, brief and lilting.

Shadows coalesced. Claws gleamed. Razor-sharp spines of hair flexed against chiseled skulls. Muscles rippled beneath skin the color of soot and shadow, and in those shadows, smears of silver and throbbing veins, and jutting bones sharp as knives. Red eyes glinted.

I reached the grave and fell down on my knees. I felt the impact. I felt the sting of a pebble beneath my left palm. The wind was hot, even blistering, against my skin. Dry grass scratched my wrist. I felt it all, my skin tender, raw, and new. Totally human, without a single tattoo.

I was mortal. Until dawn.

"Maxine," whispered Zee. "Sweet Maxine."

I smiled for him, still trying to catch my breath. The little demon was vaguely humanoid, with spindly arms and legs, claws instead of fingers, and rakish, angular features: like the love child of a dragon and wolf, parts of his body caught in limbo between the two. He tended to crouch when resting, which meant he rarely stood higher than my knees.

Zee sat back, eyeing the bowling bag as Raw and Aaz bumped against my arms, trying to crawl into my lap. The spikes jutting from their spines flexed with pleasure as I scratched behind their flattened ears, and I reached up to pat another set of sleek heads: Dek and Mal, who coiled their serpentine bodies over my shoulders. Purrs rumbled.

My protectors. My family. My friends.

Bound to my blood until I passed them on to the daughter I'd one day have—just as they had been passed on to me and every woman in my line, reaching back to the first of us—a human bound to demon flesh, bound forever, bound by heart and spirit. Bound, always, until the world tumbled down—and then, even, still together, perhaps.

I could not imagine life without them. I had never *known* life without the boys.

Zee had *delivered* me. If that wasn't close, I didn't know what was.

"How were your dreams?" I asked him, as Raw and Aaz tumbled off my lap and began prowling around my mother's grave. Her headstone was a giant slab of rock that had been carved from the ground by little demon hands. My grandfather was buried alongside her, with a similar headstone. The dirt hadn't yet settled. His body had only been dead for a month.

But he'd be back. Once he found someone else to inhabit.

Along the edges of those stone slabs were shadows—deep, lengthening—which Raw reached into with one long arm, as though sticking his hand into a bag. A magician's bag, maybe, where doves and rabbits hid and where you might disappear if you weren't careful.

Raw pulled nails and candy from the shadow—suspiciously like the ones Grant and Byron had brought home from the store. Aaz giggled, reached into the same shadow, and dragged out a six-pack of beer—which definitely was *not* from the house. He tipped back his head, pushed an entire can into his mouth, and closed his eyes with a sigh.

Zee edged closer to me, raking claws across his belly, drawing sparks.

"Bright," he said, narrowing his eyes at the bowling bag. "Long and bright."

I tipped out the crystal skull. I didn't want to touch it again with my hands.

Zee tensed when he saw it. Dek and Mal stopped purring, their tails tightening around my throat. Raw and Aaz made choking sounds, and spat out the nails and chocolate bars they were stuffing by the fistful into their mouths.

"What?" I said to them, with unease. "What *is* this?"

A shudder raced over Zee. Raw spat on the ground. Aaz reached into the shadows, pulled free a teddy bear, and hugged it so tight the seams split and stuffing spilled. Dek and Mal began strangling me with their tails. I had to reach up, and hook my fingers between their bodies and my throat.

"Okay," I said. "It's not good. I get that."

"Not good," murmured Zee. "Should not still exist."

I saw movement at the bottom of the hill. Grant, making his way, slowly, toward us. A thin black strap crossed his chest: his flute case, slung around him. Each step was careful, controlled, much of his weight on the cane. This hill was hell on his knee. He looked up, caught my gaze. I stared back, unease deepening in my stomach.

"Zee," I said. "No riddles."

"Riddles are safe," he whispered, edging closer to the skull. Raw and Aaz joined him, eyes glittering, slinking on their bellies with hot, fluid grace. Dek remained wrapped around my throat, but Mal slithered down between my breasts, and coiled in my lap—quivering, ready to strike.

I pushed him aside, trying to stand. Forcing myself to breathe. Unclenching my right hand. Golden light was fading from the sky. Shadows, lengthening. Night would be here in the blink of an eye, and the unease in my gut was growing.

I wanted to put that skull away. Bury it inside a mountain. I had a bad feeling about all this. My simple case of the creeps was becoming a wail inside my head.

A wail accompanied by a pulse, deep in my soul: an infinite darkness, a presence not my own stirring, waking, cracking open one vast, hungry eye.

Ah, it sighed. *Ah, Hunter.*

Go back to sleep, I told it, with a firm mental shove—and snapped my fingers, trying not to wince when my voice cracked. "Answers."

"Those eyes," Zee whispered, edging sideways, never once looking away from the crystal skull. "Those eyes are the lock. The mind is key. We remember. We remember the dawn, our last dawn, burning in light. We screamed. We screamed, but none heard. Drowned, our voices. Drowned, in knots and pieces."

I stepped toward him, but Aaz leapt close, blocking

me—putting his back against my legs. Like Zee, he did not look away from the skull. When I reached down to touch his head, he shivered. So did I.

"Zee," I said. "Tell me what it is."

"Lock and key," he murmured again, and tore his gaze from the skull to look at me. "One of thirteen. Thirteen hammered vessels. Thirteen minds. Thirteen, to bind."

"Bind." I tried again to step forward, but Aaz continued to hold me still. Raw grabbed my hand and rubbed his cheek against it. Mal coiled around my ankle, and a keening sound rose from his mouth. Dek buried his sleek head against my throat and made the same high, mournful cry.

"Bound," rasped Zee, looking at me. "To our first old mother, bound. To her flesh, bound."

I stared, taking in those words, knowing what they meant—but too stunned, bewildered, to accept the truth.

Grant had almost reached us. Limping faster, his jaw tight. Warning in his eyes. He looked at me, but also the crystal skull—and my right hand tingled, the organic metal embedded in my skin shimmering with heat.

I pressed my hand to my stomach, heart pounding—but not because of the armor.

"Zee," I croaked. "You're talking about my ancestor. The first woman you and the boys were imprisoned on."

He drew in a deep breath and closed his eyes. "She screamed, too."

I swayed. Grant took his final steps up the hill, and stopped—leaning on his cane, breathing hard. A fine sheen of sweat covered his brow, and a narrow line running down the front of his T-shirt was dark, soaked. I saw the faint bulge of his mother's amulet beneath the white cotton. He had not been wearing it earlier. That he had it on now meant only one thing.

We were going somewhere.

He gave me a hard stare. "You're all hurting. What happened?"

Zee looked away. All the boys did.

So did I, after a moment. I stared at the crystal skull, at its large eye sockets and sharp teeth, and wondered what the hell it was doing with me now. Why, after ten thousand years, had it surfaced in Texas, in a red bowling bag, delivered by a terrified demon in a pickup truck?

Who was the voice in the dream?

I needed to talk with that demon.

"Long story," I said to Grant. "You don't look happy, either."

He limped closer, worry in his eyes. "Just got a call from Rex. He found something during the cleanup of those burned apartments at the shelter. He's calling it a message in a bottle."

I gave him a sharp look. So did Zee, and the rest of the boys.

"Message?" I said. "What does that mean?"

Grant's voice dropped, so grim. "He thinks it came through the Labyrinth. A note, of sorts. For you."

I didn't move because I knew him too well—and even though what he had just told me was bad enough, there was something else, in his eyes.

"And?" I said to him, carefully.

Grant drew in a sharp breath. "It's from your mother."

CHAPTER 4

M Y mother had been dead for over six years. That was a fact. I was sitting at the kitchen table in the old farmhouse when a demonically possessed man shot her in the head with a shotgun. It was on my birthday. She had made me cake.

I still blamed myself. I couldn't help it. She had died because Zee and the boys abandoned her for me. That was the way it happened, for every woman in my bloodline. One day, when I had a daughter of my own, when she was old enough . . . the boys would leave me for her. No warning. No apologies.

And then, I would be murdered. Just like that. Something would be waiting. Something was always waiting.

On the day I became pregnant, the clock would start ticking. I might have sixteen years, or twenty . . . but not much more than that. I was almost certain I would not live to see fifty. Which was something Grant and I didn't talk much about. He was convinced I'd die old, of natural causes.

If he wanted to believe that, I wouldn't stop him. For him, for any child we had, I would fight. I would fight to my last breath to stay alive and be with them.

My *mother*, however, was dead and buried. Dead, *now*. In the present.

But not in the past.

And the Labyrinth was slippery when it came to matters of time.

WE could have taken a plane, like normal people, but the airport was two hours away, and the flight we needed left in an hour. If we had been normal, we would have waited until the following morning—to sit in a metal box at thirty thousand feet, contending with airsickness, pressure sickness, and the uncomfortable suspicion that I might be claustrophobic.

We were not, however, normal people.

Byron was waiting for us on the porch when Grant and I walked down off the hill. He did not comment on my missing tattoos. He never had though his gaze skimmed my pale arms and lingered on the two serpentine demons coiled over my shoulders. Dek and Mal gave him toothy grins, and started humming Heart's "The Road Home."

Byron cleared his throat, and in a voice that was only slightly strained, said, "Grant told me we're going back."

"I thought you'd stay here," Grant told him, with the same reluctance and conflict I was feeling. We had talked about what to do in moments like this and never come up with a good answer. "I'll ask Killy—"

"No." Byron shook his head, and gave us a hard, grim stare. "No."

"Okay," I said, struggling not to argue with him. I could

just leave without the boy, but he would never forgive me for abandoning him. It wasn't some teen-thing, wanting to be in on the action. I wished it were that simple.

He had been abused, so deeply, for so long, that he felt safer, and more normal, with *us*—in the middle of all our craziness—than he did on his own. Like the monsters, the demons, were *safer* than humans.

Grant and I shared a brief look—and then I suffered a soft pang as Byron reached behind him on the porch chair and handed me my leather jacket—which was really my mother's. Like armor, inherited after her death. In his other hand were my knives: a shoulder rig, modified to sheathe a dozen razor-sharp blades, meant to be handled by someone whose skin could not be cut. Good weapons for daylight hours.

I dressed—all of us quiet, tense. Behind the boy, Raw and Aaz lingered in the farmhouse doorway, watching with big eyes. Somewhere, they had found baseball hats and were wearing them backward over their heads. Spikes poked through the cotton. Little punks. I tried to ignore them as they poured motor oil down their throats. The plastic containers followed, crunched and swallowed in seconds.

When Raw reached into the shadows and pulled out an ax and a squeeze bottle of chocolate syrup, I had to look away. Watching him nibble nervously on a candy-coated blade was making *me* nervous.

Zee stood beside them, staring at the bowling bag in Grant's hand. Then he looked at me. Red eyes blinked once, filled with old, hard memories. Not for the first time, I wished I knew what went on in his head. Just a glimpse of the fire that made him burn.

My boys. My heart, wrapped around theirs. Once, I

would have said that I knew where I began and ended, but not anymore. Grant, even Byron, others who were not here—all of them, holding my heart, giving it a home after years without one.

Home, I thought, flexing my right hand, with its quicksilver shimmer of armor buried in my forearm like a ragged cuff. I wondered how much of my body I would lose this time.

"Hold on," I said, grabbing the front of Byron's shirt. Grant stepped close, and I wrapped my other hand around his waist, meeting his solemn gaze. The bowling bag bumped my leg. Dek and Mal purred thunder in my ears. Zee, Raw, and Aaz hugged us, releasing their hot breath in three long sighs. I smelled chocolate and burning metal.

I rolled my right hand into a fist, and the armor tingled.

A moment later, we slipped sideways from the porch and Texas dusk—into the void *between.*

Between space. Between the cracks of reality. Between, in a place of infinite crushing emptiness. My soul stretched to the breaking point, stretching to accommodate that terrible void, flying apart until all I was, all I would ever be, was one lost, endless scream.

When we stepped free, I was still screaming—inside my head. I tasted blood. I had bitten my tongue.

Seattle was two hours behind Texas, which meant the sun hadn't yet set. The moment we left the void—even before my foot touched the hardwood floor of the warehouse apartment—the boys surrounded me, settled, flexed upon my skin. Five heartbeats, thundering. Five bodies, embracing mine. Pale flesh gone, covered entirely in tattoos: sinuous, tangled bodies etched in shadow, glimmering with veins of throbbing silver. Scales, claws, teeth, tangled black tongues: covering every inch, except for my face.

Mortal at night. Immortal by day. Until sunset, nothing could kill me.

Being scared to death was another matter entirely.

Free of the void, Byron fell on his knees—gasping. Grant leaned on his cane, jaw tight, breathing hard through his nose. I pressed a deep kiss to his chest and rested my forehead there. When I looked down, I saw the bowling bag on the floor, flipped on its side.

"Wasn't this bad last time," he murmured.

"It's been a while. Maybe you're not used to it." I hoped that was the truth. I hated slipping space. It felt no less horrific to me now than it ever did.

Grant turned over my right hand. Black nails, hard enough to cut steel, glimmered like an oil stain. Even the armor had changed its appearance—cut with knots that resembled roses. Red eyes stared from my palms: Dek and Mal, sleeping on each hand.

A new thread of armor crisscrossed my palm, joining an entire web that traveled from the base of my fingers to the underside of my wrist. Couple more jumps, and my entire hand might be made of organic metal.

"Some price," Grant murmured, and kissed my hand. I closed my eyes, then forced a faint smile.

"I hate planes," I told him, crouching to check on Byron. "Security lines. Body scanners. Smelly air filled with icky human germs."

His mouth twitched. "What a diva."

"That's right." I pushed Byron's hair out of his face, very gently. "I am a totally bodacious bad girl."

Grant smiled and bent over his cane to look at the boy. "You okay?"

"Sick to my stomach," he muttered, and took another deep breath. "But fine."

I glanced around. The loft was just as we'd left it. Rare late-afternoon light streamed through massive windows, making the floors glow. Long shelves crammed with books lined the exposed brick walls, and the old grand piano had a light layer of dust on it. Grant's red motorcycle, which he had ridden before the injury to his knee, still stood in the corner. His worktable, covered in handmade flutes, had not been touched.

My grandfather's body had been murdered in this room, but I no longer smelled his blood—and the stain was gone from the floor. That relieved me more than I cared to admit.

I walked to the kitchen, ran some cool water over a rag, and brought it back to Byron who looked about two seconds from vomiting. I pressed the rag to his brow and held it there. He touched my hand, and all the boys tugged toward him, rippling warm.

"Stay here," I said, quietly. "Relax. When you feel better, go down and say hi to the volunteers. We'll be close."

He raised his head and gave me haunted eyes. "We didn't come back here, like this, because you'll be staying *close*."

I stared. Grant reached down and rested a gentle hand on his shoulder. The teen tensed—and then, after a long moment, nodded and looked away.

I wondered if I'd ever made my mother feel this shitty.

Grant and I left the loft. I carried the bowling bag. Clouds scudded across the blue sky, covering the sun. A cool, salt-scented breeze washed over me, and somewhere distant, I heard the horns of the shipping yards. We were in the warehouse district, south of Seattle's downtown. Concrete everywhere. Skyscrapers crowding the horizon. The only color surrounding us was gray, in all its limited variations.

I missed Texas. Quiet and safe, where I could pretend to be a mother to a teenage boy. Where I could be a new wife in an old house and imagine that I was a normal woman with a normal life, who did not have five of the most lethal creatures in the world living as tattoos on her skin.

When I touched Grant's hand, he tangled those long, lean fingers around mine and pulled me close.

"Byron will be okay," he said quietly.

"Promise?" I said, knowing it sounded childish and not caring.

He was silent a moment. "I almost . . . calmed him. If I'd said a single word, I would have."

"It wouldn't be the first time," I reminded him. "If you'll recall, you've done a lot more than just 'calm' people at this shelter."

For years, he had conducted morning sermons and impromptu flute concerts, using those opportunities to cure attendees of addictions or abusive behavior, or to transform despair into hope. But it was without their knowledge and against their will.

Therapy or control. Such a fine line. Grant called it playing God—and for a former priest, like him, that was a moral quandary difficult to reconcile.

He grimaced. "This time it felt different. I'm not sure I would have just calmed Byron down. I didn't even stop to think about whether it was necessary. The power was there. I barely stopped myself in time."

"You make it sound as though you would have hurt him."

"Maybe. I know my potential now, Maxine. I could be like the Aetar." Grant gave me a concerned look. "I didn't feel in control."

"But you *did* stop."

His jaw tightened. "I didn't want to."

I held his hand, tight. I would never know what it felt like to manipulate the living energy of another person, but it was a power that made him, quite possibly, the most dangerous individual in the world—besides me.

He was also, likely, the last of his kind. Last of the Lightbringers, the most hated enemies of the Aetar—who had destroyed them all in a long war that amounted to little more than genocide, and the enslavement of an entire race. The *human* race, to be exact, which the Aetar had commandeered as their playthings.

If the Aetar learned Grant existed, nothing would stop them from trying to capture him. It was only a matter of time. They had already sent one investigator—a genetically enhanced slave, descendent of a Lightbringer. We had managed to turn her to our side. I didn't think we'd be so lucky a second time.

But this . . . Grant's struggle with his power . . .

"I trust you," I said. "You know that."

"You're the only person in this world I can't affect with my voice."

"That's not why I trust you, and you know it."

Grant shook his head. "Now, when I speak, every sound

I make . . . there's *more* waiting. More power. More . . . *potential*. It feels as though I'm plugging the Hoover Dam with my finger."

"It's not the same finger you use to touch my—"

"Maxine."

"I'm just saying, it's a *magical* finger. I'm not surprised it can—"

Grant bent and kissed me hard and sloppy on the corner of my mouth. I held up my hands in surrender.

"Listen. Don't be like me, all gloom and doom, and full of self-doubt. You feel like you're on the verge of losing control and doing something awful? Been there, done that." I stood on my toes, gripping the front of his shirt and staring hard into his eyes. "Accidents will happen. Accept that now. You are going to screw up."

"You always make me feel *so* much better."

I kissed his chin. "You are my best friend. Nothing you do will change that, ever. Whatever you're dealing with now? Don't be afraid of it." I placed my hand over the amulet hanging beneath his T-shirt. "You're not alone."

Grant dragged in a deep breath and placed his large, warm hand against the back of my neck.

"You," he said, "are my miracle."

"Dude, I am a miracle *machine*." I honked his nose. "Face it, you can't live without me."

"I can't," he said seriously, and smiled. "Really."

I placed my hand on his chest, savoring the familiar tug between us—like a vein connecting our hearts, pumping life, and light.

Our bond. Lightbringers linked with others as sources of power, but for most of his life, Grant had managed on his own—not realizing he needed to bond with someone in order to survive the full use of his gifts. Fortunately, I had an almost limitless amount of energy to spare.

I couldn't live without him either, though. But if I admitted that out loud—something he already knew—I'd be more of a mess than him right now.

Gooey. He made me so gooey.

I cleared my throat. "Just remember, if you ever step over a line? I'll crush you like a bug. That's my miracle to *you*."

"You wouldn't go soft? Not even for your *husband*?"

I tried giving him a grumpy look. "You just like saying that word."

"I have a *wife*." Grant wrapped his arms around me in a massive hug that I felt even through my tattoos. "And she can *crush* me like a *bug*."

I hugged him back, and that ever-present light sparked into a glow that burned like sun-fire.

I needed that light when we finally rounded the outer corner of the homeless shelter—and I saw the blackened remains of the burned apartments. Once they had been homes for families who needed a last boost to get back on their feet. No rent. No one breathing down their necks. Just responsible folk looking for reliable work.

A month later, the apartments still looked awful. Worse than I remembered. A smear on all the good things that had been growing here.

The bowling bag felt heavy. My chest hurt. "You're sure Rex isn't just pulling a prank?"

Grant's hand tightened.

We entered the southern entrance of the homeless shelter, closest to where the fire had burned, and an area that had been cordoned off by safety inspectors. Convenient for us—given that structural damage wasn't the only reason we didn't want people in that part of the building.

Rex met us at the door, and his demonic aura was almost as thunderous as his face—so huge and wild, I didn't know how normal humans could look at him and not see that he was *other*. His possessed body was dark-skinned, older, maybe in his fifties. A red knit cap had been tugged low over his forehead, and he stood straight in a green Windbreaker and jeans.

When I saw his eyes, I knew my answer.

Not a prank. Whatever he had found, it was deadly serious.

"Took you long enough," he said, with disdain and fear. "The words *Labyrinth* and your *mother* weren't enough?"

And then he looked down at the bowling bag and frowned.

"What," he said slowly, "is in *there*?"

Grant grunted. "Later. Where's the message?"

"Upstairs." Rex backed back, still staring at the bag. "I didn't want to move the thing or touch it once I realized what it is."

I followed, wanting to ask him what he thought was in the bowling bag. "Why do you think it's from my mother?"

A scowl flitted over his face. "You'll see."

A new staircase had been built, the timber raw and unpainted, and a chain-link wall, erected across the hall, blocked off the burned-out area. I smelled food from the cafeteria, which was on the other side of the shelter, and heard low voices and laughter. Music playing. Ella Fitzgerald.

But here, no one. No other footsteps but ours. The click

of Grant's cane was loud on the floor—and then, the new stairs. Rex pulled ahead of us. I lingered, taking up the rear, filled with dread. On my skin, the boys rumbled in their dreams, five hearts beating in unison with mine. It felt like thunder. It felt like I lived inside a storm.

You are *the storm,* my mother would have said.

The fire had ravaged the entire second floor. Late-afternoon light trickled through the gutted windows and walls, and most of the roof was gone. There was hardly a floor, but a construction team had fixed a walkway that led from the stairwell to the end of the hall. The firm hired to build it had objected, saying there wasn't much point: That whole side of the warehouse needed to come down.

True. And it would. Once we were certain there was no longer a rip in the fabric of space—just outside the door of the last apartment on the right.

Which wasn't something we could explain to an architect.

Rex walked halfway down the hall, then stopped and pointed. I didn't need him to explain. I could see the thing in question. The message.

It was a rose.

CHAPTER 5

THERE was something my mother used to say, from a book she loved . . . that you are responsible, forever, for what you have tamed.

You are responsible for your rose.

But a rose, she would say, *is never truly tame.*

It wears its armor. It is always ready to fight.

For it has much to guard.

I pushed past both men and walked down the hall. I put down the bowling bag and removed my mother's jacket. I left both on the walkway. I wanted my arms free.

Crystal skulls. A rose. I suffered the same itch of dread, a rising tension in my chest that made me want to jump out of my skin. The boys felt it, too, shifting over my body, rearranging themselves in a slow liquid burn of muscles and scales, and flexing claws that shimmered and flowed with disconcerting, dizzying effect. Red eyes glinted against my arms. Teeth gleamed.

34

My boys, watching in their dreams.

I stopped a short distance from the rose, studying it with more care than I would a bomb. I'd never met a bomb, after all, that made me afraid—but this was something different. No human had crafted this rose. No human could have.

Not grown in a garden. Not organic, in any earth sense. Crafted instead from a quicksilver metal that appeared slick and fluid—so wet, it was as though it were made of water, or perhaps mercury, fixed in some dream of roses.

Perfect and unreal.

I crouched, edging closer. Runes covered the petals: knots and tangles of coiled lines that perfectly matched the etched, shifting designs that decorated the armor embedded on my right hand—which tingled, and tugged toward the rose, and grew hot. I curled my hand into a fist and tucked it against my stomach.

Words had been engraved on the stem.

Grant's cane echoed dully on the walkway and stopped behind me.

"What do you see?" I asked him, my voice little more than a whisper.

"A heartbeat," he said, just as quietly. "A heartbeat like the one in the crystal skull. That thing is from the Labyrinth."

I nodded, unsurprised. Just one look was enough to know the truth, after living the past two years with the armor on my hand.

The skull in the bowling bag had been crafted from a fragment of the Labyrinth itself. Now this rose.

Dangerous. Very dangerous.

I moved closer. The letters written on the stem curved

around its long thorns. I reached for the rose and deliberately used my left hand.

"Careful," Grant said.

"Sure," I lied, and then held my breath as I touched the rose.

Nothing happened. No explosions. No disappearances. No time travel.

I half expected the metal to slip away beneath my fingers, but it remained firm, surprisingly soft, and warm. Almost like human flesh.

I let out my breath and heard Grant do the same. Rex muttered, "Shit, I hate this."

Me, too, I thought, trying to stay calm as I brought the stem into the faint light shining through the burned roof. I frowned, peering at the tiny words etched into the metal. A delicate script, but irregular, as though written by hand.

A queer, unpleasant nausea hit me: cold, rippling through my chest, down into my stomach. I swallowed, dizzy. On my skin, the boys tensed, drawing every inch of my body close and tight until I had to hunch like a turtle trying to withdraw into its shell.

I recognized that handwriting. It looked like mine, except for the *e*'s.

My mother had written this. Even the words sounded like her voice.

Remember where your heart rests, I read. *Remember who you are. No one can take that from you. You are strong alone.*

I turned over the rose, studying the other side of the stem.

Forgive your father. He loves you. But it is all a matter of time.

Your mother, Jolene Kiss.

I leaned back, staring.

"Shit," I said. "Shit."

Grant said my name, but I hardly heard him.

My father. I didn't know my father. But a month ago, I'd learned that my mother had entered the Labyrinth in her youth . . . and returned to earth, pregnant.

That alone had stunned me. But then Grant and I had shared a vision of a man.

A man who loved my mother.

A man who had given us the information we needed to close the prison veil.

My father.

But what did *this* mean? Who the hell sent messages on a fucking rose? Who would go to the trouble, for what I had just read? Not that it wasn't wonderfully strange to receive a message from my mother . . . but writing a letter and leaving it in a safety-deposit box would have been a hell of a lot easier.

I could read between the lines. This was trouble.

"Maxine," Grant said, and his voice was so sharp I blinked, coming back to myself. He was reaching for me, but his gaze was on my left hand—and his urgency made me look down, fast.

The rose was melting. Petals drooping, oozing sideways, all those runes sliding down into the heart of the bloom. My mother's handwriting, sinking into the stem like little twigs consumed by water.

I tried to drop the rose, but it stuck to my fingers. I stood, shaking my hand, but it wouldn't come off my skin. Grant reached for the rose. I leapt away, afraid for him to touch it, and wrapped my right hand around the stem.

The armor sparked and twisted—recoiling. I gritted my teeth and held on, pulling with all my strength. It was like trying to yank off my own arm. The rose would not budge.

But it continued to melt—right into my skin.

I stared, horrified, as that liquid metal oozed into my tattoos, soaked up, disappearing as the stem collapsed against my fingers—followed by all those slinking petals that fell into my hand and faded like melting snowflakes.

The boys screamed.

Their voices slammed into me all at once: a hard, rising wail that did not falter, but only grew stronger, more frenzied, slicing through my soul like a falling sword. I staggered, clutching my head, breathless and dazed. Grant shouted my name, but I barely heard him. All that mattered were the boys, filling up my mind with their voices, tearing me apart—not with rage—but with pain and terror.

Then I screamed with them.

Every inch of my skin heaved and ripped, as surely as if some giant hand was grabbing my toes and pulling me inside out, taking parts of my soul with the flesh. When I staggered forward, bracing my hands on the burned wall, I saw the boys writhing on my skin—clawing at their faces in a knotted tangle of limbs, and throbbing veins, and glowing red eyes that oozed tears of blood. Blood that rolled down my arm, and dripped onto the floor.

Arms wrapped around me, but being touched felt like razor blades and acid. I struck without thinking, taking another step forward and falling on my knees. I came down too hard, though. The floor beyond the door was nothing but a charred husk, boards burned through, weakened.

I fell through.

Time slowed down. Every moment, stretching. My body flew apart, taking my soul with it, and my heart. I felt my body die. I believed it. I believed I was dying. All the times I'd felt close to death were nothing compared to this. Everything that mattered was leaving me.

Shadows gathered. I saw lightning. I heard screams.

I hit the floor. Face-first.

The impact lasted a split second, but felt like a mountain was crushing me. I shouldn't have felt it, but I did—and then, nothing, except a terrible spreading pain in my face, and head. I lay still, absorbing that pain, breathing hard, heart pounding. Mind totally, blissfully blank.

Until I heard whimpers all around me.

I cracked open one eye, and found myself staring at Zee. We were both on our sides, cheeks pressed to the cold tile. His red eye leaked tears of blood.

I tried reaching for him, but my arm wouldn't move.

"Maxine," he breathed.

I tried to speak, but my jaw wouldn't move. I tasted blood.

A hot tongue licked my ear, and I heard a broken purr that ended on a sob. Raw dragged himself into view, pulling Aaz's still body with him. Mal flopped onto the floor, limp as a sock, eyes closed. Dek, still wrapped over my shoulders, grabbed my ear with his tiny claws and pulled—like he was trying to make me move. I would have been thrilled to oblige, but nothing worked.

I couldn't feel anything below my shoulders.

Zee managed to heave himself closer, claws digging through the tile like butter. I heard distant shouts, but all that mattered was the grief and stunned shock in the little demon's eyes. That, and his weakness.

My boy was never weak. Never.

"Maxine," he whispered again, finally reaching me. His palm rubbed my cheek, so gently. I tried to lift my head, but the effort was too much, even with Dek's help. The slightest attempt sent a slicing, mind-fucking pain through my entire skull, so much I thought I would pass out. I *hoped* I would pass out.

But I didn't, and I rolled my gaze upward, trying to see Zee better.

What caught my attention was the shaft of sunlight hitting the wall on the other side of the room.

Sunlight.

Sunlight.

No, I thought. *No.*

The boys and I had been ripped apart.

CHAPTER 6

I knew I was paralyzed before Grant found me.

I had a minute—a full minute, a hundred years, a thousand—to think about why I couldn't move. I'd had worse falls. Figured there was a grim, horrible joke in my breaking my spine from plummeting just ten feet.

Terror slammed me. The most profound, destructive horror of my life. It consumed me for that same infinite moment, filling every cell of my body with poison. Igniting me with a pale fire more terrible than any conjured hell.

Zee touched my cheek with his claws, razor claws that could dig through stone like water, that could eviscerate with just a glancing blow. He touched me, and his caress was gentle, light as air. He wept blood.

Dek was making mewling sounds, and so was Mal, flopping on his side, trying to orient himself with a pitiful, shocking lack of control. Raw had dragged Aaz into his lap and rocked back and forth, sucking his claws. All of us, traumatized.

"Broken," whispered Zee, voice cracking with grief. "All of us, broken hearts."

I'm sorry, I wanted to tell him, unable to speak, screaming, screaming on the inside. *Baby, I'm sorry.*

I heard the quick, rhythmic slam of a cane. Grant, shouting my name. Footsteps pounded, but not his. Someone faster.

"Damn," said Rex, behind me.

Zee snarled. Raw stopped sucking his claws and leapt over my body, teeth bared. Aaz, pushed to the floor, twitched his tail—but otherwise remained unconscious.

Mal tried to growl, but it sounded weak. Hisses poured from Dek's throat, and his long body coiled even tighter over my head. I wanted to tell him he was too heavy. I was pretty certain my nose was broken, and it was getting difficult to breathe.

"Damn," said Rex again, but his voice was weaker, and he sounded farther away.

"Maxine," Grant said, then—but he choked on my name, and I knew he stood frozen, staring. I wished I could turn my head to look at him. I wished I could tell him I was okay, even if it was a lie. I wished. I wished so hard.

"Severed," Zee whispered to him. "Hurry."

Grant limped close. I saw his cane first, then his shoes. I heard his sharp intake of breath, and tried to roll my gaze up to see him. It was too hard, though. My head throbbed. I was getting tired.

"Maxine." Grant knelt, and the fear in his eyes was almost enough to kill me right there. He began to touch me, then stopped. A tremor rolled through him.

I'm fine, I tried to tell him, staring into his eyes. But instead of words, tears burned, and spilled.

My boys. My boys are gone. I felt empty, and too light. *My boys.*

"Someone's coming," Rex hissed. "Must have heard the screams."

"Sweetheart," murmured Grant. "You need a hospital."

"No." Zee touched my right hand, digging his claws into the armor. With his other, he grabbed Grant. All the boys crowded close, Raw dragging Aaz by his tail until they rested upon my leg.

"No," said Zee, again—and we slipped into the void.

I floated, lost, soul flying in that endless night. I listened to my heart. I listened to my blood.

I listened to that dark entity stir inside me, restless and heavy with power.

This is just a vessel, whispered a sibilant voice. *And you are more than flesh.*

More than flesh. I did not know what I was at all. Not now.

If you can fix me, I began to reply, but the darkness laughed, and a hard, fierce hunger surrounded me, filling the void.

What would you give? Your soul?

We were spat out before I could tell that monster to go to hell.

The sun still blazed. My cheek pressed against hot sand, and the air baked each breath I sucked into my tired lungs.

Zee shielded his eyes, cringing. All the boys whimpered, with pain and shock, and fear. Dek and Mal buried their faces in my neck.

"Where are we?" Grant asked in a sharp, ragged voice. "Zee."

"Help here," replied the demon, staggering away. I couldn't see where he went, but a pained grimace passed over Grant's face, and he fought to stand, leaning hard on his cane.

"Maxine," he growled. "Hold on."

Hold on, I thought. *Nothing to hold on to.*

Not even myself. It was so hard to breathe, and I was tired.

Dek bit my ear and began humming "You're All I Need to Get By." I wanted to tell him that Motown wasn't going to save my life, but I clung to his voice—and when Mal joined in, I thought, *Well, maybe it might.*

My eyes closed again, though. Dek scratched my ear, but the pain wasn't enough to keep me awake. Everything was slowing down, including my heart. It made me afraid, but even fear was no cure. I couldn't feel my body. I tried instead to focus on what I could feel: sand, sunlight, blood in my mouth, the terrible wash of throbbing pain in my nose and head.

But I started to drift. I faded.

I heard a woman say, "Hunter."

I knew that voice, but her name was too far away—and then I didn't want to remember, because I heard Grant, and he sounded angry. "What are you—"

"We must hurry," interrupted that woman. "Just as I showed you before, Lightbringer."

"It won't work. She's immune to me."

"No." Zee's low rasp, filled with concern. "Not immune now."

I tried to open my eyes, but the darkness was too sweet. Warm, gentle hands touched the top of my head. I knew it was Grant. His touch was familiar, soothing.

Finally, I no longer felt afraid.

"Listen to my voice," he whispered, and pressed his mouth to my ear. I heard thunder in his throat, then a rumble that was primal and rich, and full of power.

He sang, and carried me away, into shadow. Blissful. Silent. Without pain.

I drifted, lost. I drifted, blind.

I dreamed of a man.

He was made of silver, with silver eyes and silver hair, raining silver every time he moved as though he were nothing but stars, falling. I tried to catch with one hand some of those lost lights—and they slipped into my palm and stayed there, shining.

Five stars. Five lights.

You are strong without your armor, said the man. *You need to be strong.*

I closed my hand, so careful to hold those stars, but somehow they slipped through my fingers. I tried to catch them again, a cry rising from deep inside me, but my throat choked on my own desperation, and the grief that filled me as the stars faded into the darkness was so piercing, so overwhelming, I thought it might kill me.

But I didn't die. I woke up. Fast. Hard. Thrown out of my mind into the world again. I didn't know how much time had passed, but it was still day when my eyes opened.

I saw the edge of a white sheet drawn like a canopy above my head—and the sun shone bright against the cotton, reminding me of clotheslines and Texas summers, and the scent of clean laundry. Past its farthest, fluttering edge—an endless wash of blue sky and that piercing promise of light.

No time to enjoy it. Heat and pain sparked inside my skull like a sledgehammer strike. Even though I lay flat, everything spun and heaved, until I could have been hanging upside down or diagonal, or slumped backward off a cliff with the blood rushing to my brain. I wouldn't have been able to tell the difference.

Vertigo, however, was still preferable to pain.

My head continued throbbing, a shuddering, rolling pulse that traveled from the base of my skull to my eyebrows. A deep ache burned within my spine and across my shoulders. I couldn't move to make myself more comfortable. I tried, but my arms were too weak. My legs twitched but nothing more.

I could *feel* them, though—and I hadn't been able to earlier. A coarse blanket rubbed my skin, and my knee itched. Blood dripped from my nose. I tasted it on my lip.

"Maxine," said Grant. "I'm here."

I cracked open my eyes again and saw a blurred shape vaguely like him. I tried to speak but choked on my dry tongue.

Boys.

I managed to turn my head, and glimpsed my shoulder, part of my arm. All I saw was skin . . . skin that hadn't seen the sun in more than six years. So pale, so white. I was made of snow, I was so white. I felt just as cold, in that moment. Cold and feverish, and ill.

I stared, unable to accept, or believe. It wasn't possible. It couldn't be. What had happened was my imagination, and I was hallucinating.

But when I searched my heart, when I strained to feel the boys, nothing was there but an empty, gaping hole—that terrible lightness.

I struggled to sit up, desperately afraid. "Zee."

Grant held down my shoulders. "No, Maxine. You can't."

"Get . . . *off me*." But I collapsed, dizzy and in pain, dimly aware of another set of hands wrapped around my ankles. I couldn't see who was there, but that grip was large and strong.

"Hurry," said a low female voice. "If you are going to do this—"

"In a minute," Grant snapped. Then on my brow, he placed a rag that was so cold and wet, it felt like it had been soaked in ice. The sensation was delicious, and I closed my eyes, sighing. Water trickled into my mouth. I had trouble swallowing at first, but didn't care. It felt so good on my face, soaking my dry mouth and cracked lips.

"Better?" he whispered.

"Yes," I breathed.

"I have to start again." Grant's voice cracked, midsentence, exhaustion in every word. "I'm sorry, Maxine."

I didn't know what he was sorry for until he started singing.

His voice was no stranger. I had listened to him sing for years, watching how his immense, restrained power changed people and demons, and twisted reality. I had stood beside him, as an observer—an outsider, even—because his voice could not touch me. With Grant, I'd never had anything to lose but my heart.

I heard only a hum, at first. Low, quiet, simmering. A

slow burn of sound, filling my ears, flowing over my sensitive skin in a wash of heat. I thought, *Okay, okay, this is what it feels like to be touched by him*, and I was ready, I was fine.

Then his voice changed.

And I started screaming.

CHAPTER 7

NO more dreams of silver men.
　　I woke up again, disoriented, raging with thirst, my tongue stuck to the roof of my mouth.

I had a fever. I was pretty certain that was it. I'd never been sick in my life—injured, maybe—but not sick. I didn't know what a fever should feel like, but the prickling, terrible heat rising from my skin seemed like a close approximation.

I tried opening my eyes, but my lids were stuck together, keeping me blind. That scared me almost as much as the fever and thirst. I whimpered, and was ashamed.

"Maxine," Grant whispered, somewhere beside me. A cold wet cloth pressed against my brow, but it wasn't enough. I shifted a little, and felt plastic around the edges of my body: bags filled with water. Maybe it had all been ice, but not anymore. I felt so hot. Unbearably, as though I were going to catch on fire.

Something sweet and cold touched my lips. A Popsicle. Strawberry-flavored. I sucked on it, greedy, and Grant's familiar, strong hand cupped my cheek.

"Good," he murmured raggedly. "That's good."

The Popsicle was finished too quickly, but by then I could form words again.

"My eyes," I breathed. "Can't open them."

Grant was silent a moment, which scared me. But then he said, "Hold on."

Another cool, wet rag pressed against my eyes. Soaking them. Then his fingers touched my lids, and tugged, very gently. I felt a pulling sensation, as though my lashes had been glued shut. All I needed was a little help. My eyes opened.

I saw the canopy again, but the light had shifted, softening the glare against the white cotton. Grant leaned over me. He looked like hell. Pale, gaunt, sweating. His eyes were hollow. I was afraid for him.

"You . . . okay?" I asked, fumbling for his hand.

He swallowed hard and tangled his fingers around mine. "Fine. Don't worry about me."

I couldn't see much past him. My eyeballs began to hurt, as though the muscles and nerves attached to them were strained. A similar ache filled the rest of my body, especially in my joints, spreading through every inch of me, from my head to the tendons of my feet.

"Zee," I whispered. "Anyone?"

His jaw tightened. "Gone. I don't know where."

It was so difficult to swallow. Tears burned my eyes. The terrible hurt that struck me was almost more than I could bear and made me wonder if my mother had felt what I was suffering, in the split second before her death. Not betrayal, as I'd always thought.

Just grief. A moment spent thinking, *I thought they*

loved me, I thought we were friends . . . but was it just the prison, just the bond, a compulsion and nothing else?

Was it? Because where were they? I didn't give a shit about their protection. All that mattered was that I missed them.

I missed them like they were my own children, ripped out of my arms—and it was a hollow, piercing loss that kept getting stronger, bigger, and harder inside my chest—until the ache was so keen and sharp, I could barely swallow the damn water that Grant kept dribbling down my throat.

I tried pushing him away. My arm worked, barely, but not enough to make him budge. Grant peered at me with bloodshot eyes.

"You need fluids," he said, hoarse. "I've fixed the paralysis, but something else is happening that I can't touch. I don't know why. When I tried, you acted as though I was killing you."

None of that mattered to me. "Need . . . to find them, Grant."

"No."

"They were . . . weak." I stopped, and had to close my eyes. "Have to make sure they're safe."

A strangled, bitter sound escaped him. "More safe than you, baby."

I shook my head, tears leaking past my eyes. "Please. I have to . . . make sure."

"Your fever *has* to come down."

"Grant."

"They can take care of themselves."

I struggled to sit up. Grant held me down.

"No," he said, with a sting in voice like the tip of a whip.

I felt it crack through the air—and suddenly, finding the boys didn't seem so important. In fact, any concern I'd had for them . . . completely disappeared. Which wasn't . . . right. I could remember my urgency from only seconds before, but it was gone. I didn't feel it at all.

My skin prickled, but not just with fever. An oppressive hush seemed to fall around us, like the tension in a horror movie—just before you knew something awful was going to happen.

"God," whispered Grant, with such quiet shock and revulsion, I felt frightened.

That, and he almost never took the Lord's name in vain. Even now, him saying *God* sounded more like a prayer, or a cry for help.

"What?" I croaked, opening my eyes. "What happened?"

He sat back, trembling, something terrible in his eyes. "I didn't mean to. It was an accident."

I suffered a chill, which would have been welcome if it hadn't been full of dread. "Grant."

"I made you feel something against your will," he whispered.

I stared at him, listening to his words, feeling them— and that same deep hush flowed through me, settling heavy around my heart.

My heart, flickering warm and golden with our bond. It had not faded. Not even a little.

I thought for a moment but felt no anger. Just incredible sadness. "I'm not . . . worried about the boys anymore. Is that what you did?"

Grant closed his eyes and shuddered. "I'll fix it."

"No," I said, more sharply than I intended. I tried to soften my voice, but it came out as a hoarse croak, which was almost worse. "No, I'm fine."

But that was a lie, and he knew it. I tried reaching for him. He began to pull away, then stopped—gaunt, hollow with exhaustion. He stared at my hand with haunted eyes, and I wiggled my fingers at him.

"Please," I whispered. "Come back."

He swayed, as though dizzy. But after a breathless moment, his strong hand wrapped around mine, and I pulled him toward me. Or rather, I twitched him in my direction. I was barely strong enough to lift my arm.

I didn't try reassuring him. It wouldn't do any good. I knew Grant too well. But I refused to let go of his hand, even when he tried to free himself. He could have forced my fingers loose, but all he did was sigh and bow his head and press his cool lips against my wrist.

"You need to rest," I rasped. "Rest with me."

Tears glittered in his eyes. "I need to get you better, sweetheart."

My skin was hot enough to cook an egg on, and my head felt strange. My thoughts, verging on muddled. "I'm better."

He gave me a crooked, heartbreaking smile. "If you say so."

I nodded and closed my eyes. I had questions for him, but the thought of talking filled me with terrible, soul-deep weariness. It could wait. Maybe the boys were gone, but Grant was here, and I was alive.

I was going to stay alive, no matter what. No fever was going to kill me.

Over my dead body, I thought, and cracked a smile.

"What's funny?" Grant asked gruffly, and I heard a rattling sound off on my right. Another Popsicle touched my lips. Orange flavor, this time. I sucked on it, and sighed.

"Stupid joke," I told him.

He grunted and squeezed my hand. "Sleep, Maxine. I won't leave you."

"Mmm," I murmured, savoring the cool sweetness of the juice sliding down my aching throat. "I love you."

"Love you," he said, softly. "Love you, forever."

TIME didn't mean much except for the shifting of light. I slept fitfully, waking only when Grant stacked new bags of ice against my body or tried to make me drink. Sometimes I woke to find him holding ice cubes or Popsicles against my lips, letting them melt into my mouth. I worried for him. Once, I imagined blood dotting his nostrils, but my vision was still blurry—and I didn't have the strength to ask.

No strength. Just delirium. Nightmares.

I dreamed about the boys.

I dreamed they twisted through my veins, dark as night, and poured from me in a river of shadows—ghosts and shadows—lapping at moonlight, drinking down the stars in a fever of thirst, a fever of need that ached and swelled, and burned their hearts. Five hearts, five lights shining through the veil of their quiet flesh.

I dreamed of sunlight, then. I dreamed them eating light, and growing—large as lions, large as bears, larger than the bones of creatures millions of years dead—and when they walked, mountains broke—and when they wept, my heart broke—and when they screamed—

—my dream broke.

I floated near consciousness, hot and spinning, and listened to a woman say, "You will kill yourself, Lightbringer. You must take what you need from your bond."

"No," Grant said, in a harsh voice. "She's not strong enough."

"Then find another. Bond with me, if you like. I am strong."

"Get the hell away."

He sounded so angry—but tired, too. Nearly broken. I tried to open my eyes, or speak, but I was still too close to the edge of sleep. So I listened. I listened to the silence that followed his voice, and floated in the darkness of my mind, burning with fever and the lingering memory of the boys, screaming in my dream.

"You must choose soon," said the woman finally; but she sounded distant, as though she had, indeed, gotten the hell away. "You used so much of yourself, trying to heal her. You took nothing in return. If you would feel more comfortable bonding with your old assassin—"

"No," Grant said, and there was finality in that word, and in the power of his voice, that made the air shiver.

"No," he said again, softer. "My wife, or no one."

"Then you will die," said the woman, "and perhaps we will all be safer for it."

Hell, no, I wanted to say, but my voice was buried too deep inside my throat, and my throat was sinking, along with the rest of me, even deeper into that lush, dreaming night inside my mind.

I fell asleep again. If I dreamed, I did not remember.

CHAPTER 8

THE next time I opened my eyes, I was in a bed.
With demons, and my husband.

I lay on my back, sunk into a soft pallet beneath the open sky. It was night. I could see stars. I had no idea where I was, but a blanket had been pulled up to my chin and smelled like vanilla and coffee. Dek and Mal snored against my neck.

I wiggled my toes. My fingers twitched. My skin no longer burned. Except for my aching muscles, I felt fine. Weak, but fine.

I exhaled slowly, contemplating that miracle. That wonderful, crazy miracle.

I glanced left, and found the source of that miracle. Grant slept beside me on his side, one hand clutching my blanket, near my shoulder. Even unconscious, he looked exhausted.

Sucking on his claws, Raw slumped across my husband's legs. Aaz rested on my right, spines drooping. Candy wrappers surrounded him, along with a half-chewed baseball bat, *Playboy* magazine, and a cloth tote bag filled with thick knitted socks, some of which covered his feet and the spikes on his head.

My boys. My boys had not abandoned me.

It was stupid, how much that meant. I wanted to sob like a kid and curl on my side while hugging Aaz and his stupid porn magazines. I wanted to wrap all those dangerous, crazy demons in my arms and squeeze them until we all hurt a little less, or a little more, or whatever. Whatever. My boys were here.

But that was followed by an equally powerful wave of horror, and loneliness. I felt so alone.

"Maxine," Zee breathed. I turned my head, and found him sitting beside the pallet, hugging a teddy bear. One of its arms had been torn off, and some stuffing clung to the side of his sharp mouth.

I tried to smile for him, but all it did was make me want to cry. "Hey."

Zee took a deep breath and tucked the teddy bear under the blanket, beside me. Then he crawled in with it, clinging to my side. I lifted my arm as much as I could and hugged him close.

"Are you okay?" I asked him. "Do you hurt?"

He shrugged, small, hesitant. "Pain. Then weakness. Tired now, but better."

"You went away from me." I sounded hurt, and couldn't help it.

Zee drew in a ragged, quiet breath. "Safer for you. Safer for us. Sunlight burns our hearts."

"I didn't know the sun would hurt you."

"Doesn't hurt bodies," he murmured. "Feeds us . . . too much."

I remembered my dream. I remembered, and felt too uneasy to ask. So I held him tighter, closer, and stroked his rough, bony back, running my fingers down soft razor spines that could cut through bones like butter if Zee wished.

"But you saw the sun," I murmured.

"Sun," he whispered, as though the word hurt him. "Many suns we have seen, on many worlds. But this light, sweet."

"Good," I murmured, unsure what else to say. I still felt empty in my heart, like part of it was missing. Lighter, but not in a good way. I touched my chest, fingering the spot that hurt most.

"Feel it, too," Zee rasped. "Cut. Missing bits."

"Missing *you*," I told him. "You've been part of me a long time."

"Part of *you* longer. All, you. Every mother, in her blood." He gave me a mournful look. "Lived on your human body. Lived on your heart. We were one. Now, we are broken. Broken, hearts."

"No," I told him, though my voice was too hoarse to be convincing. "You're free, not broken."

"Free," he echoed, softly. "Free is dangerous."

"I trust you. I've *always* trusted you."

Zee snuggled closer. "Dangerous. We destroyed. Left only bones. Worlds of bones. No mercy. No love. Just war."

My boys. I still could not imagine it. "You're different now."

"No." He placed his small, clawed hand over my heart. "Just . . . some things . . . more important."

Some things more important.

Ten thousand years ago—so I was told—the boys had been so terrifying, so monstrous and powerful, the Aetar had committed themselves to the desperate act of binding their five lives to a mortal prison, calculating that it would diminish them, leave them weakened.

And it had. With unintended side effects.

I covered Zee's hand, tenderness and concern warring inside my heart. This moment seemed so peaceful. Normal, even. Me. Boys. Grant.

But I knew it wouldn't last.

It will not. It cannot, whispered a sibilant voice, rising from deep inside my body, speaking with sly, sleepy desire. *We lived within their souls for a thousand years. We know them. We know their hunger. Perhaps they are diminished now, but the longer they live apart from your heart, the stronger they will become.*

With strength, will come need.

With need, there will be death.

Quiet, I told that presence. *You're not welcome.*

We are one, it replied, though that coiled presence drifted and faded. *Never fear, Hunter. We will not leave you.*

I shut my eyes, not comforted in the slightest.

Zee murmured, "It waits, inside you."

"Yes," I said, reluctant to talk about the dark entity living in my soul: a power, and presence, inherited from the boys. Power they had bargained away their lives, eons ago, to possess . . . and which had consumed their strong hearts, and strong souls . . . and given them everything they needed to fight a war in a place far beyond the edges of the Labyrinth.

Power that had slept inside my bloodline for ten thousand years. Resting dormant, until me.

I had fought its possession for a long time. Only recently had we seemed to reach a stalemate—if only because my defiance was almost as strong as its curiosity.

Zee placed his clawed hand over my heart.

"Good," he replied. "Good, you have protection."

I was ready to tell him that I didn't want the kind of protection that dark presence could offer. Before I could open my mouth, he shook his head, ears flattening against his skull.

"Protection, from *us*," he whispered.

I covered his hand with mine. "Don't."

"Must. Might hurt you."

"You won't."

"Our hearts been guided by *your* heart." Zee hesitated, and his voice softened. "Don't know our hearts now. Might be same. Might change. Warn you now, in case."

I wrapped my arms around him in a tight, hard hug. "If you begin to change, remember someone loves you. Remember that."

Zee shuddered. "Love might change to hate."

"Never," I told him, hoping that was true, feeling vulnerable and lost, and afraid. For the first twenty-one years of my life, I'd had two constants in my life: my mother and the boys.

Then, just the boys. My rocks. My family. My home. I couldn't abandon that because of what might be. Not when we had already achieved so much of the impossible.

Zee's gaze shifted. I found Grant watching us, alert and intent. I tried to smile for him, but it felt crooked, sad.

He unclenched his hand from the blanket to touch my lips. Then, with excruciating gentleness, he leaned over and kissed me. I didn't let him pull away. Grant dislodged Raw as he wrapped himself very carefully around my body, both of us all arms and legs, and heat. I wasn't wearing much.

We didn't talk. We soaked, instead. Listening to heartbeats, and deep breaths, filling up on being close, whole, together. Zee and the boys rested around us, quiet, staring at the stars.

"Today," Grant said finally, slowly, "was as close as I ever want to come to dying."

"Melodramatic," I told him, voice muffled against his shoulder. "You could absolutely live without me."

"No." Grant lifted his head, forcing me to look at him—and what I saw in his eyes chilled me to the bone. "No, Maxine."

I met his gaze without blinking. I dimly remembered hearing his voice, and a woman, speaking about bonds and life, and death . . . and was more than certain that was not a dream.

"You'll live a long time, with or without me," I told him. "That's just the way it's going to be. No matter what happens, you're going to *live*."

His jaw flexed once. His eyes so hard, so dangerous.

"Grant," I whispered.

"Maxine," he said, and then softened his voice. "Shut up, and let me love you the way I love you."

I blinked, and he reached beneath the blanket to pull out my left hand. He kissed my wedding ring—closed his eyes—and lingered there like he was praying. Maybe he was. Former priests did that sort of thing.

"Okay," I said, unsteadily. "But I don't like your attitude."

Grant gave me a crooked smile, and curled even closer around me. "How do you feel?"

"Like I've been given a second chance. I'm not paralyzed, and I'm breathing. You're here. The boys are here. It's all good."

"It was close. I thought that fever would kill you."

"You fixed me."

"I fixed some things. Your spine was broken in two places. Your nose and jaw were partially crushed, and you had a fractured skull. Internal bleeding. That fall did more damage than it should have. I'm not entirely sure it was all to blame for your injuries."

Grant hesitated. "What happened, Maxine?"

Before I could answer, Zee stirred. "Tricked. Trapped. Kissed by a *rose*."

Dek and Mal, who I had thought were sleeping, began humming the song of the same title. I rubbed their heads. "All those things. What did you see when the boys were ripped off my body?"

"It was like . . . watching a star torn apart." Grant drew in a ragged breath. "You and the boys, when they're on your skin . . . you mesh. Your light is part of their shadow, and their shadow is part of you. It's . . . beautiful. But when that *thing* began melting in your hand . . ."

He rubbed his eyes, as though in pain. "Who made it, Maxine? Who would want to hurt you?"

I told him about the message written on the stem of the rose. The more I spoke, the angrier I got. Anger mixed with betrayal—rising inside me, bitter and heavy, until all I wanted to do was lay on destruction with my fists.

What the fuck? Who does this to their own child? Why?

My family. My crazy family. Every secret seemed to be wrapped in another layer of secrets, inside another, and another, with no straight answers, ever—only riddles that were deliberately, maddeningly vague. It had been—and always would be—enough to drive me insane. Even though, in hindsight, I understood all the reasons for being so careful with the truth.

Some truths were too big to tell.

But *this*? Ripping the boys off my body? That didn't have anything to do with the truth. That felt like an act of *war*. A first strike. Completely, indisputably unfriendly.

Grant fell silent after I stopped speaking. Zee sighed. Raw and Aaz cracked open their eyes. Dek and Mal stopped singing. All of them torn between watching him and me—but especially me.

You guys know something, don't you?

"Hey," I said, but Grant thought I was talking to him.

"I'm thinking" he replied. "I don't know where to start."

I could sympathize. I'd been too sick to think about what had happened—just that it had, and I was dealing with the consequences. But now my head was clear, I wasn't dying, and all those memories and questions were rocking back on me, hard.

"My mother mentioned my . . . father . . . in that message on the rose." I watched the boys from the corner of my eye.

"The same man we saw in that vision of your mother, when we were trying to close the prison veil . . ." His voice trailed away.

"Yes," I said in a tight voice. "Him."

"You're sure he's your father?"

I tilted my head to look at Zee. "Well?"

The little demon pulled the covers over his head.

Grant frowned. "Okay. Let's assume, however *weird*, that it's true. But the message . . . *forgive your father* . . . sounds as though he's the one responsible for this."

"Not almost. He must be. He must have told my mother what he was planning. *And* she agreed to it."

I flipped away the blanket and found Zee clutching the teddy bear again. He blinked at me with big eyes.

"Answers," I said. "Is the man who crafted the rose my father?"

"Yes," he muttered, scowling as Dek and Mal slithered off my shoulders to nibble on his bear.

Hearing him confirm the truth made me light-headed.

"Maxine," Grant said, with concern.

I shook my head at him. "Until recently, I imagined that my father was a trucker, or maybe a mechanic. My mom liked cars. Or maybe some mystery man she picked up in a bar, just to get the job done. Pregnant in one night, no strings attached."

"Romantic."

"My sex education consisted of watching dirty movies in hotel rooms. My mother didn't talk about men except to say that I shouldn't hold on to them. What was I supposed to think?" I frowned, staring at the armor on my hand. "I would have preferred that he was human and normal."

Grant cleared his throat. "Severing the boys almost took your life. Why would he do that? Why *now*?"

I poked Zee. "You were there with my mother. What did you see?"

He turned away from me. "Always sleeping in the Labyrinth. Always skin-bound."

"In your dreams, then."

"We remember," he said, voice muffled against the teddy bear. "They fought. We tasted her tears. Saw him craft the rose from his skin but did not know its meaning."

"His skin," Grant said, as I thought the same thing. Was that a metaphor or literal? I had seen enough strange things in my life that I couldn't be certain.

"I have to find him," I said, but Zee started shaking his head before I'd even finished my sentence.

"Insane," he told me. "You, brain-dead."

"I need to understand why this was done," I shot back. "This was not random. This was planned. If you know why, and you're not telling me—"

"No." Zee shook his head. "Was *shocked*. Still shocked."

I believed him. But that didn't make it easier.

"Zee," I said, "I don't know how to react to your being free. I don't know if I should be happy for you or afraid."

He sighed. "Don't know, either."

"Okay," I said, thinking that was horrible. "Okay, fine. What was done . . . may not have had a good intention behind it. I need to find the person responsible. Him."

I couldn't say *my father*. It felt too strange.

"Maxine," Grant said, in a voice that was too gentle. "You can't enter the Labyrinth."

"I have to."

"Cannot," Zee said firmly. "Not now. Not as are. Will die."

"I'm not helpless."

The little demon—and Grant—made growling sounds.

Zee muttered, "We go with you, protect you—this *world* dies."

That got my attention. "What do you mean?"

He threw up his clawed hands, looking at me like I was an idiot. "Our prison falls, the other follows."

Grant stiffened. So did I.

"What," I said, "does *that* mean?"

Zee drew his claws down his chest, over his heart. Sparks danced. I shivered, imagining that I could feel his touch on my own skin.

"Ours, first prison," he murmured. "Power that binds, connected to all the prison walls. We break, all break. Army goes free."

"In other words," Grant said, "apocalypse, again."

"Shit," I said.

On the other side of the pallet, Raw reached into the shadows and brought out a grenade. Without hesitation, he pulled the pin and stuffed the live bomb down his throat. Grant and I tensed, but all Raw did was belch.

Aaz growled at him. Raw rolled his eyes, jammed his arm under the pallet, and lugged out a small missile: five feet long, slender. He handed it off to his brother.

"Er," Grant said. "Let's have this conversation elsewhere."

"Uh-huh," I muttered, as Aaz dragged a jar of Grey Poupon from the shadows, and smashed it against the missile's metal exterior. "They've had a very stressful day. It might be a nuclear warhead next."

"With ketchup?"

"Tabasco sauce. And chips."

"Nice," Grant said. "That's . . . wow. Okay. He shouldn't really be biting that part, should he?"

"It won't kill him."

"I'm more worried about us."

"Watching him is making me hungry," I said. "You want Raw to bring us pizza?"

Grant stared at me. "You're a nutty woman."

"I know," I replied.

And though the familiar knot of fear and concern was lodged in my heart, all I could think was that I desperately wanted to prolong the moment, to love and cherish it as though it was my last, with all of us together.

Just in case it was.

CHAPTER 9

ACCORDING to Grant, we were somewhere in Northern Africa, on the edge of an oasis. I saw date palms and clumped grass and smelled water. A short distance away, past the outskirts of where we rested, sand dunes rose and fell like the frozen waves of a dark ocean.

Behind us, I found a structure that looked very much like a Bedouin tent, open in the front and filled with a few small pieces of furniture: a low table that required floor-seating to use, and two more soft pallets that lay on top of woven rugs.

"The desert reminds the Messenger of her home world," Grant said. "Zee brought us to her, so that she could help me heal your wounds."

I closed my eyes, not entirely comforted. The Messenger had no other name. As a genetically engineered slave of the Aetar and descendent of the Lightbringers, she had all of Grant's powers—but unlike my husband, she had been trained from birth to use them. To kill.

She and I did not get along.

"I'm surprised she didn't try to murder me instead."

He grunted. "Who says she didn't?"

I smiled. "And the ice and Popsicles?"

"Her doing, slipping in and out of space. I don't know where she got it all or who she terrified when she did."

"I owe her."

"Don't tell her that," he replied, watching as I changed into a clean set of clothing. Aaz had gone shopping for me—in Paris, by the look of the tags—returning with sleek designer jeans and an off-the-shoulder black silk blouse with fluttery sleeves.

Dressing exhausted me. My muscles were weak, and I had trouble standing. Lying down, I'd been fine, but the fever had stolen all my strength. My spine also ached. So did my head and nose. Dread and fear fluttered in my stomach, but I pushed it away.

I was not paralyzed. I was alive. Everything else could be handled. Even the boys.

I had to finish dressing while sitting down. Twisting around to get jeans on made me breathless. Grant clasped my ankle and helped me put on my boots. "Easy, there."

"You take it easy," I muttered. "You look like hell, man."

"I feel like hell."

"You didn't draw on our bond when you healed me." I looked him straight in the eyes. "Are you now?"

His mouth tightened. "Some."

"Screw that," I replied. "Take what you need."

"I am."

"I don't mean a sip." I grabbed his hand, and squeezed. "I can't lose you, Grant. I need you healthy."

I didn't mean for my voice to sound so hoarse when I spoke, but it came out squeaky and breathless. I wasn't embarrassed because it was Grant, but it did make me worried for myself. Losing the boys didn't mean I could afford to lose my nerve. I had to be stronger than I ever had been before. Anything less might get me killed. And if I died, leaving Grant behind . . .

I didn't want to think about that. It made me angry at him—furious—but when I thought about losing Grant, I wasn't sure I could say that I felt so different than he did. Spending the rest of my life without him . . . filled me with quiet, aching horror. Much like what I felt when I contemplated the next few days—or decades—of my life without Zee and the boys.

"Grant," I said, because he was too quiet, watching me with eyes that never saw less than my entire soul.

"Okay," he replied, and deep within that golden thread of light flared—with heat, and a pulsing thrum that made me feel as though a tiny ghost cat was purring inside my chest. Or maybe that was Dek, with his head draped off my shoulder, humming between my breasts.

"Better?" I said to Grant.

"I'm worried about you," he replied.

Beneath my heart, that coiled presence stirred and grazed our shared light. Power slithered through both of us, and it felt like an injection of adrenaline—or waking up clear-eyed after an especially good night's sleep.

Grant shivered, closing his eyes. "No."

Before the word was even out of his mouth, I shoved that dark entity away from our bond. It was like pushing wet sand, or cement, and its presence held on for a moment too long before fading.

Grant rubbed his chest. "I thought we were done with that thing."

"Not as long as I'm alive," I told him, feeling ill. "I'm sorry. The only way you'll be safe—"

"No," he interrupted, fiercely. "No, we're in this together."

Mal began humming Captain & Tennille's "Love Will Keep Us Together." Dek joined in, making a drumming sound with the clicking of his tongue. I patted their heads, watching Raw and Aaz eat their small arsenal of missiles, grenades, and potato chips.

Zee, though, ignored us all—sitting very straight and staring into the darkness. His claws plucked fitfully at his teddy bear, stuffing falling all around him.

Suddenly, he stiffened.

Raw and Aaz stopped eating. Dek clung to my neck, while Mal slithered to Grant's shoulder, draping over him with a protective hiss.

I was no more vulnerable than on any other night, but I felt worse: exposed, naked, a target. My right hand tightened into a fist, armor glinting. I tried to stand.

"You should stay here." Grant also tried to stand—with difficulty, too. He took my outstretched hand, and I pulled him to his feet. Both of us grunting and wincing and swaying, like we were one hundred years old.

"I'm too tired for sarcasm," I muttered. "So let's just stick with, 'uh, *no.*'"

He leaned hard on his cane, studying the darkness. "On the ridge. I see something."

Zee dragged his claws through the dirt. "Cutters, Maxine." *Demons.*

I took a steadying breath. I had the armor. I had resolve. I was lighter, in spirit and flesh, but still me.

Grant and I limped across the dark oasis, guided only by the glint of red eyes, and starlight sliding off sleek, rippling muscles. Zee, Raw, and Aaz flowed through the night, slipping into shadows, reappearing ahead of us and behind, stabbing the earth with raking claws that hissed as softly as their breath. Dancers, wolves, lost in the night, lost with me, all of us—together.

Dek hummed in my ear. Mal was silent on Grant's shoulders though he made a small sound of pleasure when my husband pulled his golden Muramatsu flute from the case slung over his shoulder.

"Big guns," I said, breathless, tired again.

Grant was also breathing hard. "I want to save my voice. I'm a delicate flower."

"Har, har," I said, as Zee led us up a sand dune. I grabbed Grant's hand, pulling him along. His cane kept sliding, and more than once, his bad leg almost collapsed on him. Dek and Mal sang a military march.

"Go without me," he muttered. "I'm slowing you down."

"What, we're racing to the demons now?" I kissed his hand, and squeezed it. "Chill, dude."

Zee slowed, holding up a clawed fist. Raw and Aaz split off in different directions, flickering in and out of sight across the sand. Ahead of us, I saw a figure outlined against the ridge of the dune. A woman, pale in starlight.

I tensed. Grant made a humming sound. "It's only the Messenger."

I still didn't relax.

The Messenger had her back to us, staring into the dark horizon. Her clothing was loose-fitting, her bone structure raw, angular. A crystalline filament looped around her waist: a whip that she used with deadly accuracy. She wore an iron collar, a brand from her makers.

The Messenger did not turn to look at us.

"Hunter Kiss," she said, voice echoing with power: a skimming current against my skin, starting in my eardrum and traveling down my spine. An uncomfortable, unsteadying sensation.

She had tried to kill me once, with her voice. Failed, because I was immune. Circumstances were different now, and I didn't trust her. Despite our alliance, her motives for remaining on earth, on our side, were still unclear. She had no qualms about taking human lives. Humans were mules to her, beasts of burden who existed only to supply her with the same kind of power that Grant drew from me: a life force, energy to fuel her own strength.

Zee growled. So did Raw and Aaz, circling from behind the woman. Dek clung to my ear with a possessive little claw.

She might try. If the boys don't kill her first. A thought chased by a painful realization: I couldn't take their protection for granted. Not anymore.

"Stop," Grant said to her, with hard warning in his voice. "Tone it down."

The Messenger glanced at us over her shoulder. "I told him he should let you die. You are weak now. That cannot be tolerated."

"And yet," I said.

"And yet," she replied. "You are bondmates. He will not trade you for another."

"As if you would give up the bond to your Mahati warrior," Grant replied.

I was surprised to see a faint smile touch her mouth. It made her seem almost . . . normal.

"He is strong," she said, simply. "Demons are better mules than humans."

The Messenger pointed, and I saw a tall, angular figure standing on another ridge. I couldn't make out much of him—spiked hair, long limbs. He was missing an arm. Most Mahati adults from the prison veil lacked body parts. They had been forced to cannibalize themselves in order to survive their imprisonment.

He was not looking at us, either. His focus was also on the horizon.

I stared, straining my senses, trying to discern what seemed clear to everyone but me. I had expected to see demons, but the sands were empty, and still.

What I noticed instead was the storm.

Flicks of lightning, illuminating a cloud that blocked out the stars and stretched across the lower lip of the sky like a veil. No thunder, but it was thunderous in sight, a wild darkness blacker than night, so deep it made the rest of the world, in comparison, seem full of light.

Zee crouched beside me, and when I touched his shoulder, I was surprised to find him vibrating with tension.

"Like before," he whispered, in a haunted voice. "Gathered from rock and sand, and womb."

I glanced down at him, and found Raw and Aaz watching that cloud with rapt, chilling hunger. Dek was very still on my shoulder. Breathless.

"Maxine," Grant said, quietly.

I looked again at the cloud, and something clicked in-side me.

That was not a storm.

Those were demons.

CHAPTER 10

UNTIL recently, the demons I had typically encountered were little more than wisps of focused, hungry energy—conscious, intelligent, and parasitic. Gutter rats, the lowest of the low of the demon army, imprisoned in the weakest part of the veil. Which meant they had been the first to escape over the last ten thousand years.

Those demons survived and fed themselves by possessing humans who had a weakness in their souls, a crack in the spiritual door. And, once those gutter rats got their hooks in, the misery began.

Demons fed on pain. The more pain, the better.

Humans, of course, were just as talented at hurting each other. The most heinous crimes I had ever investigated had nothing to do with a demonic influence—but there *was* a particular energy associated with violence that demons found sweet. Possessed humans might murder, rape, molest—or just mentally abuse—but the end result was always the same. Someone was going to get hurt. Including the innocent host.

But I had never seen so many parasites in one spot. Not like this.

We stood on the ridge of the sand dune, watching the demons in their approaching storm, churning with sparks of lightning and the roiling smoke of their bodies. So many. Thousands.

"They're being drawn here against their will," Grant muttered, watching the cloud. "So much agitation and fear."

"Do we kill them?" asked the Messenger, as if it would be nothing to strike them down.

"Zee," I said. "What's going on?"

"They know," he whispered, and shared a long look with Raw and Aaz. "They know we free."

"What does that mean for us, right now?"

The boys continued to stare at each other with uncertain, hungry eyes. Even Dek and Mal had gone quiet, leaning off our shoulders as though listening to their brothers speak in silence.

"If not a whore, then a warrior," Zee rasped, as Raw and Aaz closed their eyes and turned their faces to the sky. "If not a warrior, then a queen . . . but there is nothing else between within the army . . . of the demon lords and Kings."

I stared. I had heard that rhyme before, from the mouth of an Aetar, but the meaning had been lost on me. Now, I found it disturbing.

"Zee," I said, and he finally looked at me.

"Means we must be Kings," he whispered.

A chill fell down my spine. Grant and I shared a long look. I couldn't tell what he was thinking as easily as he could read me, but there was no mistaking the glint of unease in his eyes. My right hand formed a fist, and the armor pulsed, softly, as though embedded with small, beating hearts. Reminded me of the boys, sleeping on my skin.

The demonic storm hissed through the air, cracking tendrils of shadows like whips across the sky. I thought of my mother as I waited for it to arrive. I imagined her, standing with me, deadly and strong, with that dry smile, and her sharp eyes. What would she make of my life?

What would I make of *hers*? Because, clearly, I hadn't been told the whole story. My mother had lived a mystery of a lifetime before having me, a life I would never truly understand, or know . . . but I supposed I was doing the exact same thing. Living a crazy, wild, monstrous life that no one but me would ever truly comprehend.

My heart, my mind, my universe. And one day, if I lived long enough, I'd have a daughter . . . and I'd be the mystery. I'd be the wall at her back, as my mother had been my wall. And that kid would never guess, never have a clue.

I wasn't sure how I felt about that.

"Here we go," Grant murmured.

Sand kicked up, carried on the edge of a mighty wind that smelled like the back end of a garbage dump I'd visited in Mexico when I was sixteen. I'd gone there with my mother, who was investigating a kidnapping. We'd found a body, two days dead and mostly bone. The rats and stray dogs had gotten to her.

I kept thinking about that dead girl. Wondering if that would be humanity's fate if the army imprisoned behind the veil could not be controlled. Parasites were one thing— but the Mahati and the other demon clans would make all the worst genocides of the twentieth century look like puppy day at the playground.

If *these* demons knew Zee and the boys were free, then

what about the others? What if Zee was right about the prison veil? Had the walls already fallen?

The storm gathered above us, blocking out the sky. Red lightning flickered, and shadows oozed downward in a spiraling, heaving mass that looked more like wet flesh than smoke. Voices hissed and rattled, discordant screeches ripping through the air, and there were squeals that coiled like pigs' tails, and wiggled in my ears.

I steadied my breathing. I told myself nothing was different, that I was not different. Boys, here. Grant, here. My heart, here.

The storm of parasites gathered in a funnel that hit the dune in a thunderous impact and blasted sand against our bodies. I blinked hard, watching as the base of the funnel formed the loose figure of a woman, with red lightning for eyes and tendrils of smoke that waved about her head like snakes.

I knew who stood before us, though I'd only ever seen her in the body of a stolen human being.

Blood Mama. Queen and mother of the demonic parasites.

She had ordered my mother's murder.

She ordered every death of every unprotected Hunter— part of a strange bargain she had struck with one of my ancestors, who I could only imagine had been incredibly desperate or appallingly stupid.

Over the years, I had been forced to deal with Blood Mama, and though I would have wiped her off the face of this world if I could have, she had made another deal, long ago, to keep herself safe from Zee and the boys—who had been forced by their Hunter to promise that they would not kill her.

Demons always kept their word.

"Blood Mama," I said.

"Hunter Kiss," she murmured, and her voice was dull and strange. Throughout all our encounters, she had been a sly creature, confident and full of power. Flashing smugness and cruel humor.

But I recalled, too, that she had always feared the falling of the prison walls. On earth, she had power. Amongst the other demon clans, she was nothing. Her children, food. Her children, whores amongst the warriors.

I expected her to say more; instead, all the shadows that formed her body poured forward in a thick funnel of smoke— and collapsed at Zee's feet, spreading outward like a stain until the very edges touched the tips of Raw's and Aaz's claws.

Dek licked my ear and slithered off my shoulder, dropping to the sand. Mal did the same, and the boys crawled to the writhing stain, dipping their heads to taste it with their long, black tongues.

All those screams quieted. Cries, falling into a hush.

"My Kings," said Blood Mama, her voice rising from that pool of darkness. "I have come first, of all the clans, to proclaim my loyalty."

Zee's eyes narrowed. "Ten thousand years. Ten thousand revolutions. Never heard you say that word. *Loyalty.*"

Lightning flashed within the churning stain. "None would have. You know the hunger of the demon lords. Had it been them, and not me, ten thousand years would have been reduced to one. They would have killed you to be Kings."

Raw and Aaz snarled at her, and all that smoke flinched.

Zee's lip curled. "Not *all* the demon lords. But, truth, for some."

Blood Mama rippled across the sand. "We have a bargain. You cannot kill me."

"Not kill. But hurt."

"If you must," she said, very quietly. "But I would beg for mercy."

"Mercy," Zee whispered. "Mercy is, as mercy does. You and your *mercy*, upon our old mothers, and our young Queen."

"Those women were your prison. You expected me to show them kindness?"

Raw hissed, raking his claws through the shadowed stain. Blood Mama cried out, high and sharp, while the bodies of her gathered children shuddered—and wailed.

"Played with *arrogance*," Zee told her, a quality to his voice I had never heard—superiority, edged with violence. "Arrogance, because we blood and prison-bound. So you ran free. And you bled *free*."

Aaz stamped his foot upon the stain with such vicious brutality, it was a struggle for me not to flinch—especially when he bared his teeth in pleasure. He did not stop with one blow but continued with increasing speed and violence, throwing back his head and closing his eyes with a shuddering sigh as though he were soaking, drowning . . .

. . . *or feeding.*

I stared, chilled, as Blood Mama grunted with pain, and twisted, and leaked hard bolts of lightning into the sand. Yet she did not try to flee. She stayed, and endured, while Dek and Mal snapped their teeth upon the edges of her shadow—and Raw slashed her yet again, and again, growling with hair-raising, deep-throated fury.

I had no love for Blood Mama. But watching this . . . beating . . . felt wrong. It didn't feel like my boys. Not the boys I loved.

Grant swayed close, watching the abuse with hard, cold eyes. Never had he looked at the boys like that. The Messenger, who stood beside him, also studied the boys—with narrowed, intense thoughtfulness.

I sensed movement on my right: the Mahati warrior, drawing near, graceful as a cat. Silver chiming chains pierced his gaunt body, and his fingers, which were long and shaped like the tines of a pitchfork, rubbed against one another in a steady, coarse rhythm. His gaze met mine, briefly, then he glanced at the boys, staring at them with hunger and fear—and hope.

Zee looked at the Mahati, who immediately bowed his head and held out his remaining arm in what seemed a very specific, ritualized gesture.

"King," he whispered. "If hunger. My flesh, yours."

I had never heard him speak. I had not realized he could. His voice was raspy, quiet, with a particular dignity that reshaped my entire view of him.

The Mahati never received a response, though. He was jerked backward, off balance, as though yanked by strings.

"No," said the Messenger sharply, and the Mahati's eyes flashed with fury and humiliation.

Aaz laughed at him. Dek and Mal raised their heads, and pieces of Blood Mama's shadowed body dribbled from their mouths. They had been eating her. I thought, perhaps, I heard weeping in the air around us—but not from Blood Mama. Her demon children, crying softly with terror.

"Mahati-bound," Zee rasped, and flicked his hand at him, dismissively. "Slave."

Raw spat on the tall demon, and that spit burned like acid upon his pale silver thigh, already pocked with old wounds. The Mahati winced—and looked away at the Messenger, with hate and venom, and despair.

My skin prickled. A cruel smile touched Zee's jagged mouth, but it faded as he looked back down at Blood Mama's flickering stain.

"You," he whispered, crouching with menace. "You, pretender. Walking as queen of warriors. Instead, queen of whores."

"Mercy," murmured Blood Mama. "Please, your forgiveness."

Zee glanced over his shoulder at me, his eyes glinting with terrible, cold light. For a moment, the first moment of my life, he made me uneasy—but when he flicked his claws at me, I went to him. Spine straight, head held high. I realized how important this was. How it was as much a performance as any play. Only the stakes were beyond imagining.

"You are our Queen," Zee said to me.

Dek and Mal coiled around my ankles, and I scooped them up under my left arm. Purrs radiated from their thick chests, and their muscles flexed around me as they slithered to their perches on my shoulders.

"Yes," I said. "I am your Queen."

Raw and Aaz gave me approving looks and stopped smashing Blood Mama with their feet and fists.

"Our Lady of the Kiss," whispered Zee. "Do we forgive?"

I hadn't expected to be asked that question. I remembered my mother's head exploding from a rifle blast. Her blood and brain matter, and fragments of her skull—soaking me, as I stared in stunned horror. The boys, weeping. The boys, digging her grave and singing her funeral song.

I could still taste her blood, spattered on my lips. I could see her wry smile, just before her death.

Forgive *that*?

Rage touched my heart—and with it that darkness stirred, deeper than any shadow, and vaster than the void of *between*. I imagined a soft crack beneath my ribs, like the shell of a breaking egg—and that *presence* oozed free, bearing my soul down, down, into the core, its own heart and coil. An alien entity, separate from me, swelling inside my throat, stretching my mouth into a shuddering, euphoric smile that was not my smile but the darkness growing inside me, tearing my seams.

Will you forgive, Hunter?

I gazed down at Blood Mama's stain upon the sand, and she seemed suddenly small and insignificant: an inkblot, a puddle made for a child's foot, an afterthought. If I stepped on her, she would break. If I touched her, she would burn. That power simmered on the cusp of my heart, on my fingertips, swelling inside me with a whisper.

Once I started . . . I would not be able to stop. Once I said *yes* . . .

I closed my eyes and shuddered.

"We *forgive*," I said, with great difficulty—and the darkness sighed, and retreated.

Zee pressed his face close to Blood Mama's fluttering, obeisant shadow.

"Forgive, for now," he added, rasping those words on a hiss. "Go."

The stain retreated, like water flowing backward, bumping and heaving over the sand and gathering into that churning funnel of smoke. Whispers rose, and soft sobs, but there was also a hush around us that dulled the sounds, until I felt as though I were imagining all that misery floating, falling, through the air.

Then, like an arrow shot, that storm of demons leapt upward into the sky—and scattered.

I watched as the stars reappeared, and felt like a wreck. Knees trembling. Trouble breathing. My heart . . . my heart, pounding . . .

Grant limped close, bearing me up with his shoulder. I leaned on him. Maybe he leaned on me. Neither of us said a word. No need.

Zee stared at the sky. I wanted to hug him—or shake him—but was afraid I wouldn't be able to get back up again. So I kicked sand in his direction.

"What," I said slowly, "just happened?"

He didn't respond immediately though his bony shoulders sagged. And just like that, all his menace faded, leaving him small and lonely. Raw and Aaz flopped down in the sand, reaching into the shadows beneath each other for fistfuls of cigars—which they licked like turd-shaped lollipops.

Dek and Mal exhaled noisily and began humming a particularly high-pitched version of Billy Joel's "We Didn't Start the Fire." I scratched their heads, and so did Grant, his hand leaving them to rest warm against my neck. My muscles relaxed, just a little.

"Zee," I said.

He shuddered, raking claws over his arms—and tilted his head just enough to look at me. Grief, in his eyes. Or maybe that was wishful thinking. Grief and fury, I'd found, were sometimes no different at all.

"Told you," he rasped. "Our prison falls, other opens. Cutter Mama knows it."

And if your prison was restored? came the unbidden thought. I didn't know if, even thinking it, I was betraying them or saving us all. Maybe both.

Who sent me the crystal skull? Who knew this was coming? Was it a warning?

"Zee," I said, a million questions in my voice.

"Memories same as resurrection," he whispered, unblinking, then tore his gaze from mine to look at Raw and Aaz, who threw aside their cigars to peer up at the stars.

"Don't want to remember who *we* are," he said.

CHAPTER 11

THERE was nothing left for us at the oasis. The Messenger exerted her bond over the Mahati warrior and dragged him off into the desert for God only knew what—though Grant assured me it was simply a time-out session for unruly demon warriors who defied their assassin handlers.

Whatever. I wanted a bathroom, a cold ginger ale, and a small dark spot where I could rock back and forth and contemplate all the reasons why I might take up thumb-sucking again, after a twenty-three-year absence from that competitive sport.

Unfortunately, it was not to be. The first thing I saw when we slipped from the void into the Seattle loft was a naked old woman sprawled chest first on the floor, with her legs contorted over her head—eating from a plastic bag filled with fresh marijuana leaves.

The crystal skull was in front of her, and she was peering into its eyes.

I stared because there was little else to do in that situation—and heard Grant mutter under his breath. Even the boys stopped in their tracks. Raw and Aaz shielded their eyes. Zee tilted his head, frowning. Dek and Mal buried their faces against my neck.

I might have blamed their reaction on the old woman, but it could have also been the crystal skull. Or, just as likely, the soft light streaming through the large windows. It was overcast outside, but somewhere beyond the clouds the sun was in the sky. Making day.

Even though the boys were standing in front of me—clinging to my neck—I forgot, for a moment, that our bond had been broken. I glanced down at my arms, expecting to see tattoos. When I didn't, I suffered a disorienting moment of shock—which transformed into aching loss. It reminded me of the first year of my mother's death. I'd think of something I wanted to say to her, and look around—right before I remembered.

I rubbed my face. Grant said, "Mary, what are you doing?"

"Shhh," she told him, frowning at the skull. "I'm *listening*."

Zee hunched down, giving the skull an uneasy look. "Nothing to hear."

The old woman poked the skull in the eyes. "Voices remain. Sins whispered. Thirteen crimes, thirteen signs."

I'd learned to stop being surprised at Mary's insights, but nonetheless, I was taken aback. And slightly uncomfortable. The boys had been ripped from my body. This was one of the artifacts used in the original binding. Which, conveniently, had been delivered to me by a *demon*.

Not a coincidence.

Had Blood Mama told the demon to bring me the skull?

Or had someone else? And for what purpose? If my . . . father . . . was responsible for ripping the boys off my body, what was the point? My mother wouldn't have gone along with *anything* that would hurt me . . . unless there was a good reason.

Seeing this skull, however, was a reminder that Zee and the boys *could* be bound again. Imprisoned. I couldn't imagine how that made them feel. I didn't want the boys to think that I would consider it. Because that would be wrong.

Wouldn't it?

Even if that freedom results in my death? When push comes to shove, just how selfish am I? How ruthless?

Mary's two fingers continued to dig into the skull's eye sockets, and she crooned a little melody beneath her breath.

"Voices," she whispered, again. "Voices that bind."

Raw growled at her. A hard, menacing sound that did not belong in this room, in this company. I had only ever heard him make that sound when he was going to kill someone. I stared at him, startled and uneasy. The way he had growled at Mary . . . like she was prey . . .

Zee gave him a sharp look, snapping his claws. The other demon blinked, choking into silence. Raw barely met my gaze. His eyes were haunted. I reached for him, but he shook his head and backed away. Aaz pulled a pint of chocolate ice cream from the shadows beneath the couch. He gave it to his brother with a sympathetic shrug. Raw slumped on the floor like a little lump and stuffed the entire carton down his throat. I wanted to sit beside him and ask to share.

Mary didn't seem to notice what had happened. Her legs

flexed back down, and she pushed herself off the floor. Grant, who had been making a beeline toward her, turned from that full frontal view with a grimace.

I looked down, too, but not before I saw the stone circle embedded in the old woman's breastbone.

I hadn't had many opportunities to see the object grafted into her body. It was a source of curiosity for me, not just for its location but because the sight of it had frightened and angered both the Messenger—and an Aetar, who was now dead. The things they had said about that emblem kept Grant and me up late some nights.

It was a family crest, representing men and women who had been prominent during the war between the Aetar and the Lightbringers. A family, apparently, that had killed *so* many Aetar, they were legend.

Grant's amulet—inherited from his mother—was also a stone disc. It bore the same family crest.

Mary did not have Grant's powers, but she *was* from his world: an assassin assigned to protect his mother during their wartime escape through the Labyrinth. The two women had become separated—and, as time moved in odd ways in that place, Mary had grown old before finding her way to earth.

Old, *and* insane. Some days, a little crazier than others.

Her thick white hair was frizzled and wild, her leathery skin pulled tight over hard, sinewy muscles. Not an ounce of fat on her. Mary looked at the boys—and then studied me, with a frown.

"Yes," I said, wondering if it was just my imagination that I was feeling feverish again. "Something *is* different."

"Your hearts, split," she said. "Hearts of murder. Waking from sleep."

Zee's spiky spines stiffened. I glanced at Grant, who was peering inside Byron's room.

"Not here," he said. "Mary, where's the boy?"

"Left him downstairs stirring meat," she told him, picking up a dress heaped in a pile on the floor. It was embroidered with moons and stars, and flying dogs, and hung on her like a sack. Over it she pulled on a leather belt, an old-fashioned back brace that cinched everything tight. It should have looked ridiculous—and maybe it did to everyone else—but I thought it suited her.

I walked into the bedroom. Zee followed. Raw and Aaz were already under the covers, using them as a tent—peering out with teddy bears hugged close to their chests. The entire room was a demon playpen: more bears on the floor, along with magazines and knives, and a slightly chewed life-sized cardboard cutout of Jon Bon Jovi.

I picked a bag of M&Ms off the floor. Tore it open and took a couple. Dek and Mal chirped at me, and I gave them the rest. Then, because standing suddenly seemed like too much effort, I crawled under the covers with the boys, who continued to huddle out of the light. Zee climbed onto the bed.

"Can't stay here," he whispered. "Sun is dangerous, Maxine."

I was so tired. "You said it feeds you."

"Light makes us strong." Zee glanced uneasily at the window. "Light reveals."

"Reveals what?"

He never answered. Grant appeared in the doorway, leaning on his cane—all kinds of shadows in his eyes. "Does the sun do other things to you?"

Zee hesitated. "Ten thousand years, since walked in light. Ten thousand years, forgetting what was, what could be. Don't know what will happen. Might wake things, better that sleep. Might be . . . dangerous."

I grabbed his bony wrist and suffered a pang of heartache and loss. My skin looked so pale. So . . . wrong. It didn't matter that my boys were here. It was day, and I was lonely for them. I didn't feel whole.

Zee pressed his cheek to my hand, his ears flat against his skull.

"Sweet Maxine," he whispered.

"I don't want to be your prison," I told him, thinking of that crystal skull. "But don't forget that I am your friend. We're family, baby."

"Family," he murmured, closing his eyes. "Family protects family. Family protects the nest."

Raw and Aaz poked their heads from beneath the covers. Dek and Mal made a mournful sound, and so did Grant, as he lay down on the other side of the bed and straightened out his bad leg.

"Back in the desert, with Blood Mama . . . you started to change," he said, forcing Zee to look at him. "I saw it, inside you. What else, Zee? We know what you *were*. Will you become that again?"

"Stop," I said to him. "They're not like that."

Grant gave me a long look. Zee bowed his head, fiddling with his claws.

"Our nest," he murmured. "Our family. Even as Kings, those things we believed." The little demon crept backward off the bed. "But there was also the hunt."

I followed him, or tried. My joints ached, and so did my

muscles. Fever prickled. But I kept going, determined not to let him slip away. Irrational, I told myself. Zee wasn't going anywhere. The boys weren't going to leave me.

Of course, they will, came the unbidden thought. *They are free.*

"Zee," I said, and my voice sounded strange in my ears, so rough and broken, it made me stop and listen to my heart and hunger.

I pressed my hands against my stomach, holding them there. Grant touched my thigh. Just with the tips of his fingers, but it helped ease the gaping hole in my chest.

Zee and I stared at each other.

"If the sun is dangerous to you," I said, hoarsely, "then maybe you and the boys should go."

He looked around the bedroom, with odd sadness. "The world is dangerous to *you.*"

"I'll protect her," Grant said.

The demon flexed his claws. "Not like us."

I took a breath, and straightened. "I'm getting dressed and going for a walk. I'll be fine. Zee, you and the boys do what you have to. I'll be here if you . . . need me." I forced a smile and slipped off the bed, reaching into a pile of clean clothes for some jeans and a sweater. I bundled them up and went to the bathroom.

I was afraid to look at my reflection. Mirrors and I didn't mix. I'd had a nightmare once, as a kid. Dreamed I looked into a mirror, only to find . . . something else staring back. Not me. Not a person. Just . . . a thing. A vague shadow, burning with incredible violence. Reaching for me, through the glass.

Sometimes, at night, when I had to the use the bathroom, I refused to look at my reflection. Afraid I'd see that shadow. Afraid something would be there, waiting for me.

I wondered, occasionally, if I hadn't already caught a glimpse of that shadow in my eyes.

I braced my hands on the sink, looking at myself. Nothing different. Not really. I could tell myself that all day long until I believed it. Until the shadows and the hard glint of my bleeding heart just . . . faded away.

I'd never realized just how pale I was.

Hot water felt good. I took a quick shower, washing away sand and sweat. My muscles ached less. I tried not to think too hard, but at some point I thought about the rose and that message engraved on the stem—and I remembered the sensation of the metal melting, and the sound of the boys, screaming.

And the fall. All of us, falling.

When I left the bathroom, the boys were gone. I hadn't really expected them to be. I stood a moment, looking around, thinking I'd see a craggy little face peering at me, or a goofy smile, or hear a chorus of high, sweet voices singing rock and roll. But none of that happened.

It hurt more than I could say. It wounded me, and it was childish, stupid. Selfish, even. My boys were free. Why couldn't I accept that and let them go?

Why can't you accept that they're the Reaper Kings and that maybe it's not such a good idea to let them go?

I didn't like that thought. At all.

Grant sat on the edge of the bed, cane resting across his thighs.

"I'm sorry," he said quietly. "I know you'd like for them to be here. I believe . . . I believe Zee genuinely thinks that it's dangerous for them to remain in a place where there's sunlight."

"Okay."

"Maxine."

"I need to be alone," I said to him.

He raised his brow at me. "That's the last thing you want. But you're hurting so bad, you can't lick your wounds with anyone watching."

My breath caught. Grant held my gaze, and I knew it was all just one naked parade of my thoughts and emotions. Everything I was, all my bits and pieces, laid bare in whatever light surrounded me. Grant could read it like a book, just as he read everyone. And, like the priest he'd been, he treated all that light like a confession.

So I confessed.

"I feel like part of me died," I told him. "I never imagined, in my wildest dreams, that I'd lose them. Not like this."

Grant looked down, jaw tight. I half expected him to reassure me that they weren't really gone, that everything would be all right . . . but his silence was long, and heavy. I settled back against the wall. Unable to cross the distance between us.

"Nothing of you died," he said. "Wounded, maybe. Ripped. I can see parts of your soul, bleeding. Zee and the boys . . . they're bleeding, too. All of you, in the same spots." His hands flexed around his cane, so tight, with such strain, I thought he might break it in half. "I could heal that part of you. But I won't."

"I didn't expect you to." I pushed away from the wall to go to him and sat as close as I could, slipping my arm around his, resting my forehead on his shoulder. "I under-stand."

He cleared his throat. "I know you're not afraid of me for what I did to you today . . . the way I took your concern for the boys, and erased it. But *I'm* afraid. I slipped, and all it took was a second. I'm not . . . used to controlling my voice around you. I'm sorry."

I smiled against his arm. "You're not breaking up with me, are you?"

He flinched, giving me a stunned look—which relaxed, only a fraction, when he saw that I was teasing him.

"Not funny," he said.

"I love that you reacted with horror."

Grant made a grumbling sound. "You're going to be fine, Maxine. Wounds heal. I'm here. We have this." He placed his hand over my heart. "And you're too stubborn to give up."

"I notice you don't include the boys in that statement."

"You saw what happened with Blood Mama. And Mary."

Again, I thought about the crystal skull. "And you saw what happened inside me."

"That . . . thing," he murmured. "Yes, I saw. I felt its hunger."

"I'm sorry."

"Don't be." Grant took my right hand, twining our fingers: metal, against his flesh. "But you need to be careful of the boys, Maxine. You need to listen to Zee when he tells you that they might change. Because I saw it, out in the desert. They fed on Blood Mama's pain. They've never done that before."

I looked away and closed my eyes. "I have to believe in them."

"Well," he said, softly. "If it helps, they believe in you. And so do I."

Mary appeared in the doorway of the bedroom, holding the crystal skull under her arm. I didn't look too hard at that carved face, with its sharp teeth and huge eye sockets. In fact, I didn't like looking at the skull, period. It gave me the same strange feeling as a mirror: I wasn't certain what was looking back.

"Know who this is," she said, with a hint of pride. "Finally recognized the face."

Grant and I stared at her.

"Er," I said, wondering just how far in the past Mary had lived, before the Labyrinth had spat her out into modern-day earth. "Who is it?"

Mary lifted her chin, and a cold smile touched her lips. "Old Wolf," she said.

CHAPTER 12

I once asked my grandfather why those who knew him—knew him, really, for what he was—called him *Old Wolf*. He was, after all, immortal. And it seemed to me that when you lived as long as he had, the names that stuck probably had more than passing significance.

"There are many different *kinds* of wolves," he told me, sipping tea and nudging my foot with his. "On every world, in every variation. It has nothing to do with the actual creature, my dear. More like, the *spirit* of the thing. Its *heart*."

I leaned against all his books and crates, careful not to tip over the rare porcelain statues, and rocks, and some odd little bird bones gathered in a silver nest. "And what is the heart of the universal wolf?"

My grandfather gave me a mysterious smile.

"Look into your own heart for that answer," he said, bending forward to pour more tea into my cup. "For we are a *family* of wolves."

APPARENTLY, walls really could talk, because five minutes later the phone started ringing. It was one of the
women who ran the shelter, who'd heard that Grant was
back and *needed* to see him regarding a month's worth of
urgent matters that she'd put aside *just* for his inevitable
return.

"They're going to freak out when you announce you're
married," I said. "When you tell them you're married to the
'violent tattooed woman,' I think kittens may actually drop."

"That's an evil smile you've got on your face," Grant
replied, "and we could use some cats."

I said I needed rest. He gave me a warning look, knowing perfectly well that I was lying—and then took Mary
with him. She'd been out in the living room, fingering her
belt and staring at the skull like she was thinking of getting
naked again.

I placed the skull on top of the grand piano and made it
face the wall, so that I didn't have to see its eyes.

"Jack," I muttered, thinking about my grandfather. "You
got some explaining to do."

I wondered if *he* had felt the prison break. If so, then
what about the other Aetar, far away from this world? They
could feel when one of their own died. What about a
spell—a work of reality-twisting—gone broken?

Too many problems. Focus on one at a time.

Like, why? Why this? Why break the bond between the
boys and me?

I went to my mother's chest, tucked in the corner beside
Grant's worktable. I cracked the lock and began burrowing
through everything that had been important to her—and
me. Photos, papers, dolls. I didn't touch her guns. I refused

to use any weapon that required a bullet. Seeing my mother shot to death had pretty much ruined me on guns.

I pulled out her journals and set them aside. Almost every woman in my bloodline kept some kind of diary—a lesson book to pass down to daughters, a way to keep hearts alive. My mother had written a lot. My grandmother, only one slim volume. I was probably going to be like her. I hadn't written anything yet. Not enough to matter, anyway.

I'd read my mother's diaries backward and forward over the years, and never found one hint of anything regarding my father—or Labyrinths, wars, Aetar—everything I *now* knew she'd been perfectly aware existed. For some reason, she had deliberately left those parts out.

There were, however, several pages that had been torn away. I'd always been curious as to why—but now I was burning up, wondering if my mother had written something she was afraid for me to see.

I set aside the journals and pulled one more object from the trunk. A round stone disc, wrapped in purple silk. I hesitated before picking it up—and then, only handled it with my left hand, *after* putting on a pair of leather gloves. I always wore gloves during the day, in public, to hide my tattoos. That wasn't a problem now.

"Damn it," I muttered, for no good reason other than I still hurt on the inside, and the boys weren't here.

Not here. Not even a hint of them. Gone, as if they had never existed.

That, alone, made me feel insecure—physically *and* emotionally. It was stupid, too. I'd *known* the boys were imprisoned on my body. How had I ever thought that they *wouldn't* leave me if they were free?

It didn't even matter that they had a good reason for being elsewhere—I shouldn't have needed an explanation at all. It was *their* lives now. Not ours. Not ours, bound. Just theirs, on their own. Free.

Free from me. Free from sunrise and sunset. Free to do whatever the hell they wanted.

What *I* wanted was for them to be here—if only to reassure me that we were family, that we had *always* been family. I didn't want that to be a lie. I didn't want that to be a lie that I'd believed in because it was easier than the truth. Which was that five of my best friends in the world, five little hearts that were more than just friends, didn't need me at all. And not only did they not need me, I was nothing but a reminder that for ten thousand years they had been imprisoned and controlled against their wills.

I never questioned their loyalty or friendship. I took it for granted. I treated them as though they were free, but they never were.

I blinked away tears, trying to refocus on the disc in my hand. Answers. I needed answers.

The pale stone disc was the size of my palm, engraved with a series of circular lines—a labyrinth. Similar symbols could be found everywhere in the world, from prehistoric wall paintings to the floor of Chartres Cathedral in France. Cross-cultural meanings that ranged from sacred paths to sacred ancestors to symbolic forms of pilgrimage. Not a coincidence. Maybe no one knew about the real Labyrinth, but the memory was there, in blood, in the unconscious, flowing through humanity.

The disc was called a seed ring and was filled with one year of my mother's memories.

I had only been able to access a few of those memories because odd things tended to happen when handling the seed ring. The armor on my right hand, made of a similar substance, sometimes reacted in extreme ways to its presence—up to, and including, time travel. Which sometimes happened anyway. The armor occasionally had a mind of its own.

I hesitated and placed my left hand on top of the seed ring.

Nothing happened. Frowning, holding my breath, I traced the labyrinth lines engraved in the stone and closed my eyes, concentrating on my memory of the silver rose, the message on the stem, as well as the details of a previous seed-ring vision: my mother, in a soft bed, speaking to a man . . .

I had to see that man, and remember . . .

The armor tingled. So did my entire left arm, starting from my fingertips. Pins and needles, pricking me. I felt dizzy, muddled, as though my thoughts were draining down a dark hole. For a moment, I couldn't remember who I was. Just a shell housing a hammering heart and a whole lot of nothing.

A whole lot of nothing suddenly filled with stars.

I was dimly aware of my body still seated on the apartment floor, but my mind was so very far away that flesh was nothing but an afterthought. I stared into a darkness seeded with small distant fires, burning in the vastness of time, endless space. Hundreds of billions of stars in just one galaxy, and hundreds of billions of galaxies flung across the universe, with more being born, more shedding light, more and more life somewhere, elsewhere, forever.

We are small, said a gentle male voice. *We are small, but precious.*

We are nothing, I said. *All this, all these wars, all this grief and pain . . . means nothing.*

It means something, he whispered. *It means everything. We are all the light, and we are all the thunder, and we are all part of the old song that sprang from one note, one moment, one possibility.*

All I felt was despair. *And what was that possibility?*

Hope, he said, softly, and the stars began streaming toward me—or maybe it was me, streaming toward them. *The same hope I felt when I loved your mother.*

The stars winked out, and suddenly I was back in the apartment, full in my flesh, feeling heavy and turgid, and trapped on the ground. I could still sense forward movement, and when I closed my eyes for just a moment, I was moving, flying, racing across space toward that field of light. Listening to that voice.

My heart ached.

I pushed the seed ring away. Dizziness eased, but I had to slump down, breathing hard, trying not to vomit. Pain trickled up the back of my skull, sinking so deep into my brain I wanted to stick my entire head in ice.

I looked at the back of the crystal skull, which seemed like nothing more than a glorified paperweight

I needed to talk with that demon in the red truck.

IT was still hot in Texas. Hotter than usual. I felt the sun baking through me when I stepped from the void onto a dusty street where the lawns were brown and the fences had once been white picket—and now were just gray, toothy, and broken. Dogs barked, but otherwise, it was a workday, and the neighborhood was quiet.

I saw the red pickup truck parked several houses away.

I stood for a moment, staring. I could see a dent in the front bumper from where the truck had hit my knee. But that had been before, and the boys were no longer bonded to me. I was stupid to be here on my own. Bullets would kill. So would knives, fists, a good slam of my head against the corner of a table. I'd seen every way a person could die, but I'd never thought much about any of those things happening to me. Not for another twenty years, or so.

I had the armor, though. I had resolve. I couldn't hide forever.

The demon's home was a white ranch with broken plastic siding and a gutter that dangled at a forty-five-degree angle. An entire army of plastic gnomes littered the lawn, all of them turned so that their backs were to the street—and their painted eyes glued to the front door. I found that immensely creepy, and I'd seen some sick shit in my life.

I rang the doorbell, the back of my neck prickling from all those staring gnomes. When no one answered, and I didn't hear movement on the other side, I walked around the house.

Thick curtains covered the windows. I didn't see any security-alarm stickers. No gnomes in the backyard, but there were lawn chairs that had seen better days and a birdbath with no water and several dead birds lying beside it.

I glanced around. No neighbors gawking at me. No one at all.

I walked to the back door and knocked again. Listened.

More silence. I took that as an invitation and pulled some picklocks from my wallet. If this had been night, one of the boys would have slipped through the shadows to open the door from the inside. I'd relied on them too much, though. It took me a minute to get back into my groove.

Before I'd met Grant, I'd lived on the road, traveling from city to city—investigating crimes, stalking demonically possessed humans. Sometimes I couldn't wait for night. I just had to get in—to homes, offices, cars. My mother had taught me all the tricks, then she'd taken me to professional criminals for extra training. All those guys had loved her. She put the "Bad" in "Big Bad Momma."

God, I missed her.

God, I was furious at her.

The lock turned. I opened the door, slowly. First thing I saw was a kitchen. It was messy, but not dirty. Newspapers on the table, a dish that hadn't been cleared. I smelled roast chicken.

I shut the door behind me and kept moving, listening hard for creaks, the rub of cloth, or breathing. All I heard was me. I was beginning to think I was alone until I reached the living room.

The possessed woman who had brought me the crystal skull slumped on the couch. I was pretty sure it was her, anyway. Same clothing, same size.

Most of her head had been blown off. Blood and brain matter covered the white wall behind her. I had to turn away, sickened. Reminded me too much of my mother.

When I could breathe again, and I didn't think I would vomit—much—I turned back, tentatively, to examine the area around the dead woman. I didn't see much. A handgun beside her, a box of bullets. A couple well-thumbed issues of *National Geographic* on the coffee table, along with a box of medication. She looked as though she'd spent a lot of time on that couch. There were blankets, a pillow.

I didn't think she'd been dead long. The air didn't smell that bad.

Suicide, I thought. The television was on, but the sound had been turned down. I saw images of toppled buildings, broken roads—and a rolling headline bracketed in bright red. There had been a massive earthquake in Memphis, Tennessee. Over seven on the Richter scale.

Memphis was at one end of the New Madrid fault. I'd read an article about it only recently. Seismologists had been saying the region was overdue for an earthquake, but the timing bothered me.

Nothing to do with you or the boys, I told myself. *Just nature.*

But it would be a perfect feeding ground for parasites. Blood Mama herself was probably there, soaking in the power of that sharp, immediate suffering.

I watched the television a moment longer, concerned for the people in Memphis, then looked back at the dead woman. What a waste.

I walked through the rest of the house—careful, still listening. Did a demon parasite take sustenance from killing its own host? I'd never seen a suicide during a possession. Self-inflicted injuries typically happened *afterward*, when former hosts woke without memories, only to discover they'd murdered people, or molested children, or committed any number of horrible, violent crimes.

The woman's bedroom was clean, plain, and seemed relatively unused. Some clothes had been laid out on the bed, along with a suitcase. No pictures, nothing that was personal.

I found a second bedroom, but that one was totally unused. No sheets on the bed. No clothes in the closet. I didn't know why, but I got the same prickly feeling standing there that I had on the lawn, being stared at by a bunch of plastic gnomes.

I walked through the rest of the house—passed the dead woman—and ended up again in the kitchen. I opened the basement door but hesitated on the threshold, staring into that dark cement hole.

I was scared of the dark. I'd always been, but I'd had the boys. A couple years back, I'd found myself thrown into a real hole—a hole on the edge of the Labyrinth—where there was no light, where I'd lived blind. Buried alive. Only the boys had saved me. Only the boys had kept me sane, and even then, it'd been iffy. I still had nightmares.

The basement reminded me of that place.

I found a switch and flipped it. Light flooded the stairs. I breathed a little easier and forced myself to take that first step—and then another. The wooden stairs creaked. I smelled wet concrete. Something else, too . . . that was floral.

The light covered the stairs but not the rest of the basement. I ran my fingers along the wall but found no other switch. Even though my vision was typically good in the dark, I still had trouble seeing. It made me nervous, and I hated that. I hated that I didn't feel strong enough on my own, without the boys. I'd faced terrible things in my life and done so with my head held high.

But one simple basement had my heart pounding.

Any courage I'd shown before . . . had it ever been real? Or just false bravado because I knew I couldn't get hurt?

I stripped off my right glove and flexed my hand. The armor began glowing. Softly, at first, then brighter. The basement revealed itself—an old metal bed frame, a couple bikes, a weight-lifting apparatus covered in cobwebs.

I also saw a cage.

Inside the cage, a naked woman.

She was curled on her side because the cage wasn't big enough for anything else. Nothing left of her but skin and bones, though the dark hair that draped over her face looked surprisingly clean. I didn't smell feces or urine. In fact, besides mold and rust, the only other scent I could pick up was soap. I saw a hose nearby, attached to a faucet. A drain in the center of the floor.

"Hunter Kiss," whispered the woman, startling me. I'd thought she was dead. In fact, when I looked at her again, she still hadn't moved. I did, however, see a glimmer of her dark aura, barely noticeable in the shadows.

"Hunter," she murmured again. "I thought you'd come here, eventually."

I crouched, checking out the padlock on the cage door. "Are you the same parasite that used to wear the skin upstairs?"

"Yes," she breathed. "Thought it would be better for Delanne to die, rather than wake up and see her sister like this. They were close, before I took over."

"Close," I echoed. "You made your host put her sister in a cage."

"Not at first." The possessed woman's voice was quiet, sullen. "But the pain of betrayal and despair was exquisite."

I stared at those protruding ribs, the gaunt hips, and the

thin towel that was her only protection from the concrete floor. It was impossible to tell what age she was, but I thought . . . young.

I gritted my teeth. "You said you were told, in a dream, to bring me that skull."

The demon groaned, softly. "I didn't know my host possessed it, until that dream. Down here in the basement, at the bottom of a toolbox. I couldn't believe it."

"Tell me about the voice in the dream. Male or female?"

"No voice. Just images. Impressions."

"You were terrified."

"I brought you one of the thirteen keys used to bind the Reaper Kings." A choked laugh escaped her. "I could feel that echo of power. Made me want to jump out of my skin."

"Do you know where the other keys are?"

"No. But what would you do? Use them?" Finally, her head moved, and I saw eyes glitter beneath those long strands of hair. "You're nothing now. Just food, like the rest of us. I wouldn't help you even if I could."

I felt vulnerable. Naked in her gaze. I *was* naked, without the boys. I wondered if she knew that just by looking at me, or if I was still keeping up the mask.

"So why are you here?" I asked. "Dying in a cage?"

"Where else is there?" whispered the demon. "This is home."

I couldn't think of anything to say to that. I turned and walked away. Behind me, that thin, reedy voice called out.

"It was an act of mercy, forcing Delanne to kill herself."

"You told me."

"Not just that," whispered the demon. "A quick death is better than what's coming."

CHAPTER 13

I used the phone in the kitchen and called 911. Explained what I'd found, and hung up. It was a risk—the demon might jump to one of the first responders—but I couldn't let her host stay in that cage and die. Nor could I exorcise the demon without the boys to make it permanent.

I could smell the blood now, maybe because I knew it was there. Made me queasy, and claustrophobic. I didn't leave, though. I stared at my right hand, almost entirely covered in silver metal—bonded as close as my own skin. I could see the knobs of my knuckles beneath, and the indents of my fingernails. No prints. No lines in my palm. Just a flawless surface that would only keep spreading— unless I stopped using the armor's power. Once, maybe, I could have. Not anymore. I was going to lose more than just my hand one day.

Not so long ago, I would have dreaded the idea. Now I hoped I lived long enough to see it.

I ran my fingertips over the armor, thinking about the crystal skull. *Not from earth,* Grant had told me. Radiating a similar energy marker as the seed ring, this armor—and, probably, the rose. All made from parts of the Labyrinth: stone, metal, gemstone. All capable of incredible power.

Power that rested in *potential*.

Potential that could only be manifested through *focus*.

The Aetar had plenty of focus. Had they commissioned these skulls as a means of giving themselves the power necessary to imprison the Reaper Kings? If so, who was the maker? Who had made the armor, the seed ring . . . the rose? Just one person? More than one?

My father, I thought, feeling numb on the inside, and unsure of myself. *Is that possible?*

I closed my hand into a fist. If I entered the Labyrinth . . .

You might never see this world again.

I wanted to think that I was tougher than that, cannier . . . but right now, I didn't trust that I was. I couldn't take the risk. I had to play it safe.

I slipped into the void and returned home to Seattle.

As the demon had said . . . where else was there to go?

I didn't know what time it was until I walked down into the homeless shelter and found the volunteers cooking lunch.

Donna Summers blared over the stereo system, and a clash of pans and loud voices filled the lasagna-scented air. Guys with deliveries from local grocery stores wheeled trolleys around us, and in the kitchen, I glimpsed an army of long-haired men and short-haired women wearing Birkenstocks and fuzzy socks, and white aprons covered in bright-colored pins and logos from local sponsors. Clocks shaped like cats covered the butter yellow walls, along with a half-painted mural that was new to me: a city scene filled with superheroes battling a Godzilla that had tiny angel wings growing from its scaly back. I liked it.

I saw Byron in the mix though he didn't notice me. He had a book and was sitting in the corner out of the way.

The Coop, as it was called, took up an entire block—a collection of warehouses renovated and linked, forming a homeless shelter and community center that provided temporary housing, meals, and other services. Donations funded some of the Coop's activities, but Grant, whose father had left him a fortune, paid most of the bills.

I had my own money. One of my ancestors had started thinking ahead and acted to secure the finances of her descendents with caches of gold and other treasures, including priceless works of art. I owned homes and land all over the world—places in Italy and France, maybe an actual castle in Wales. I'd never visited any of them, but my name was on the paperwork. Every now and then, I received updates from my mother's lawyers.

I'd thought about visiting those places with Grant and the boys.

I rubbed my arms. My sweater had long sleeves, but I felt as naked as I had with that demon parasite in the basement. It was daylight hours, and the boys should have been sleeping on my skin—beneath my hair, between my toes—covering every inch of me with their beating hearts and heavy tattoos. I should have been able to pull back my sleeve and see a wink of a dark scale, a glimmer of a red eye.

I got hit with a wave of loneliness so profound I wanted to run. I was human. Mortal. Vulnerable. Feeling sorry for myself.

A strong, warm hand touched my shoulder. I flinched, before realizing it was Grant. I hadn't even heard his cane.

"Hey," he said, looking at me with such compassion, and concern.

Suddenly, there was nothing more important than wrapping my arms around his waist in a long, hard hug. Kitchen noises dimmed. So did voices. I knew people were watching us—probably because they'd never seen us engage in this much public affection.

I didn't care. And, given the way Grant held me, neither did he.

"It's okay," he murmured against my hair. "I'm here."

Doreen, one of the volunteers, walked in—car keys swinging in her hand, wiping rain from her face and hair. She was a tall blonde with an athletic build and a typical Seattleite personality: earthy, and a little pretentious.

When Doreen saw Grant, she gave him a huge, beaming smile—which faltered considerably when she saw me. I wasn't surprised, but after the day I'd had, I didn't feel like dealing with the usual undercurrents of disapproval.

I had never gotten used to the crowds at the Coop—and, to be fair, some of the people here weren't used to *me*. To them, I was a strange, quiet woman, rough around the edges: a fighter, who kept the peace with her fists. Grant was a handsome, elegant, filthy rich, former priest. Some thought I was with him for his money. Some thought he was with *me* because I was good in bed.

Not that I was going to argue with *that*. Nor was there any way to explain that Grant and I were more alike than any of them would ever be able to comprehend.

"You're back," said Doreen, throwing herself against

him in an overly friendly hug. "We missed you. I can't imagine why you were gone so long. I'm surprised we lasted a week."

"Uh-huh." Grant took a careful step back and slid his arm around my waist. "Maybe you haven't heard. Maxine and I were on our honeymoon."

Doreen stared. I held up my left hand, with its golden ring.

"Yes, it's true," I said. "We're married. And we want *lots* of kids."

I might as well have had a demon perched on my head for the way she looked at me. I almost started to laugh.

Grant cleared his throat. "Doreen, I've got to check on some things in the office. I'll come by the kitchen later."

"Er," she said, but we were already walking away—and Mary was suddenly right behind us, nearly knocking Doreen into the wall with her shoulder.

"Burn your lust," Mary muttered, giving the other woman a dirty look. "Only warriors bond to bringers of the light."

It was Grant's turn to bite back a smile. I shook my head at him.

We were stopped several more times in the hall by volunteers and some of the homeless who regularly haunted the Coop. I stood off to the side as Mary fidgeted, letting Grant do his thing—with his voice, with just the right word.

I saw two possessed men at the end of the hall, posting flyers on the wall. Big guys, dressed in jeans and flannel, with pitch-black auras that flickered close to the crowns of their scruffy heads. I recognized their hosts but didn't know their names.

More than a few haunted the shelter of their own free

will, treating Grant like some kind of messiah figure who could transform them—into creatures who did not need to feed on pain to survive. Which he had been doing for years before our first encounter.

As far as I could tell, those demonic parasites Grant altered *were* different: cut off from their bond to Blood Mama, capable of surviving without the particular energy that streamed from violence and abuse.

Although they still *enjoyed* those bad vibes. Like a warm chocolate dessert.

Both of the possessed men stopped working when they saw me. I was used to that.

What surprised me was that they did not lower their gazes. Instead, the demons smiled at me: creepy, soft smiles, filled with promise and smugness.

I didn't look away from them. I did not blink. I poured every hard, violent moment of my life into my gaze and held it there. Doing less would be the same as signing my death warrant.

If it hadn't already been signed.

It didn't matter that Blood Mama had promised obedience and submission to Zee and the boys. She had a prior bargain with my ancestors—to kill us women when we lost our protection. Which I had, without even a daughter to show for it.

I was fair game. Zee had to know that. All the boys did. Unless they *really* thought Blood Mama would behave.

Unless some risks outweighed my possible murder.

The men continued trying to stare me down. I flexed my right hand. Grant was a short distance behind me, still waylaid. I didn't check to see if he'd noticed them—his so-called reformed demons—looking at me.

Mary brushed my shoulder, also watching them.

"When the cat's away, mice will prey," she murmured, and glanced at Grant, as he finally joined us, frowning at the possessed men—who finally dropped their gazes and shuffled backward, away from us.

Grant followed, leaning hard on his cane. "Stop."

One word, spoken in a calm voice—but I felt the tingle of his power touch my skin, far deeper than it ever had before. It did not affect me because he hadn't intended it to, but he could have made me stand forever in one spot with that same word. It didn't make me uneasy, but it made me wonder if I would have gotten so close to him in the first place had I been vulnerable to his gift.

Would I have let myself trust him? Would I have always been second-guessing whether or not my feelings were real or products of manipulation?

Yes, I thought. *I trusted no one, back then.*

In some ways, I'd been more alone than I was now. I just hadn't realized it.

I stayed close to Grant's side, my right hand loose, ready. Not that I needed to worry. The demons weren't going anywhere. Even their auras, which should have been churning, had gone perfectly still. Frozen.

We reached them. Instead of stopping, Grant limped past, and said, "Follow me."

Like puppets, they did: down the hall, into his office, where the desk was piled with packages and paperwork, all the detritus of a month's vacation. A picture of us on the beach was the only decoration. The rest of the room was austere, and nearly empty.

Mary hummed to herself, leaning against the wall. I

locked the door and stood in front of it, watching the possessed men sweat.

"You're different," Grant said to them, in a voice that was a little too quiet. "You've reengaged your bond to Blood Mama. You're feeding on pain again."

The demons said nothing.

Grant leaned in. "Also, I didn't like the way you looked at my wife."

Someone knocked on the door. I would have ignored it, except a pounding thump followed that knock, and a muffled voice said, "Open up, it's Rex."

I opened the door. Rex, sweating, gave me a hard, uncertain stare—and then peered around me at the demons, and Grant.

"One of us stole a baby," he said. "There's going to be blood."

CHAPTER 14

T HE baby's name was Andrew, and he was six months old. His mother was a short woman with a soft face and curly hair, but less than five minutes after I met her, I couldn't remember what she looked like because all I could recall was her profound, terrible grief.

She was hysterical when we found her, slumped on the floor of the shelter's day care, clutching a soft blue blanket to her face. Sobs dragged away each breath, making her choke.

Andrew had been left at the shelter's day care for two hours while his mother went to a job interview. The twenty-something girl in charge of looking after him had walked away for five minutes to go to the bathroom—a fact corroborated by the elderly former schoolteacher in charge of the day care, who had taken responsibility for the baby.

And then turned her back for just a moment to clean up some vomit.

Andrew was gone when she turned around.

Infants were kept away from the older children, who had reported seeing a man—but little else. Fortunately, there were security cameras everywhere. Rex already had the kidnapping isolated.

I recognized that face. We all did. A possessed man named Horace, who had been at the shelter off and on for a year. His host was a slender white man who always dressed in worn khakis and a navy Windbreaker. I couldn't see his demonic aura in the security tape, but I watched him pick up Andrew, and walk out.

"I fixed Horace," Grant said, sounding sick.

"Free will." Rex glanced at me. "With the Reaper Kings loose, all the rules have changed. No one will want to be without a clan, and those who were loyal to Grant will have to prove themselves to Blood Mama."

"Those demons in Grant's office . . . will they know where Horace went?"

"You think he'd share?"

I hated that we were talking about that baby like he was a meat loaf. I heard Andrew's mother sobbing all the way down the hall, and the low quiet tones of the police trying to speak with her. "What do *you* think, Rex?"

He blew out his breath. "Someplace isolated and close."

We were in the warehouse district. Lots of places to choose from. I grabbed Grant's arm and squeezed. "I'll find him."

"Maxine," he said, then lowered his voice. "You don't have the boys."

"Who says I need them?" My voice only wavered a little. I reached into his back pocket and, before he could stop me, lifted out his cell phone.

I retreated. "No one can protect me forever, Grant. I either learn to live, or I don't live at all."

"I'll go with you."

"Grant," I said, with gentle strain because my heart was pounding, and I knew he could see I was afraid. "I will never be safe."

He reached for me with too much desperation. I clenched my right hand into a fist, thought very hard about baby Andrew—and slipped into the void.

I seemed to remain in that place longer than usual, adrift and lost. The boys had always been with me before, but now I was completely alone.

I focused on the baby. Nothing but him. My thoughts flashed on the image of Horace holding Andrew—

—and I fell back into the world, teetering on the edge of a broken sidewalk. Rain hit my face, and so did the wind. Cold day. I wondered where in the night the boys were hiding, and what they were doing. Hopefully, nothing.

I stood facing downtown Seattle. There was a chain-link fence at my back. I spun in a slow circle and found open lots, along with several buildings across the street. Too many choices. If the boys had been here, they would have guided me in the right direction by tugging on my skin.

I recognized the area, though. I drove through it sometimes. The Coop was only five or six blocks away. I tried to imagine what would look attractive to a demon carrying a baby.

Close and isolated.

The buildings on my right appeared well maintained, with two good strong doors that were in plain sight of the intersection. The lot was clean, without the usual broken glass. No graffiti on the exterior.

Different story across the street. Rough-and-tumble,

with broken windows and boarded-up garage doors that had a few planks loose. Grass grew in the lot, and *fuck*, *suck*, and *ass* had been spray painted in unique, colorful combinations. It was clearly abandoned.

I crossed the street, watching all those windows, trying to catch any sign of movement. I wanted to pretend I was brave, but my heart pounded. Punches would hurt, and I'd never been much of a fighter. Not like my mother and grandmother.

Seconds after I stepped onto the abandoned building's lot, I heard a baby start to cry.

I froze, that sound cutting through me like a cold knife. It was coming from inside the building, drifting through broken windows. I started running, trying to keep my foot-steps silent, light, as I searched for a way in. I pulled out the cell phone, and dialed Rex. He answered on the first ring.

I gave him the cross street, and told him what the building looked like. Grant's terse voice rose in the back-ground, but I hung up before he could take the phone from Rex. I powered off the cell and stuck it back in my pocket.

I heard other voices, then, from the other side of those broken windows. Two men. one stranger, one familiar.

"Whoa," said the stranger, as the baby continued to cry. "Jesus. What are you doing with that kid?"

I recognized Horace's rasping voice, each word deepen-ing, growing harder, as he replied, "Fucking mind your own business, shitface."

I discovered a spot where old plywood had been smashed, revealing a dark hole that was big enough for me to crawl through. I moved fast, breathing through my mouth. It was hard to hear anything but the baby and my pounding heart.

Keep crying, I thought, sweating. *You're still alive if you're crying.*

I found myself in a dark hall stacked with dusty boxes. The air smelled like metal and urine. Footsteps scuffed an old layer of grime on the floor, and I followed the trail into a large room divided by concrete pillars. There was some light, but it was dim, streaming through dirty broken windows high up near the ceiling, almost thirty feet above us.

Horace was in the corner of the room farthest from me. Back to the wall, facing in my direction, though I didn't think he'd noticed me yet. No way to take him by surprise. Too much floor to cover. His demonic aura was thick and oily, heaving over itself in throbbing waves that reached like tentacles for the baby on the floor in front of him.

Andrew was wrapped in a blanket, tiny fists waving as he cried. I couldn't see him well, but he seemed unharmed.

Standing a short distance away was another man. I could only see his back, but he was big, husky, with a long, ragged coat and crazy gray hair sticking out from under his hat. His hands were outstretched, his fingers dirty.

"Put down that knife, man. Come on. Put down the knife and step back from the baby. Those two things don't go together."

Horace gave him a weary look and turned his wrist—revealing a long knife in his hand.

"You should have minded your own business," he said, speaking in a voice that was heavy and resigned, and all the more chilling because of it.

"I was," replied the man. "I squat in this building. You made it my business by being a nutjob with a baby. Now walk away, before I hurt you."

"Hurt me?" repeated Horace, brow arched. "I'm going to kill *you*, stranger. I'm going to cut your tendons first, so you can't run. Then I'll cut out your tongue and gag you, so you can't scream. When I'm done with that, I'll cut the rest of you."

He pointed his blade at the man's groin. "I'll save the best for last."

The big guy straightened. "I'm *not* going to let you do anything to that baby."

I walked from the shadows, and the armor on my right hand glimmered as though burned with moonlight. Horace saw me and started to laugh.

The other man turned and stepped sideways, frowning.

"I've called the police," I told him. "I need you to wait outside for them to arrive. I'll take care of this."

The stranger gave me the same look a lot of big men did: like I was small, fragile, and couldn't possibly handle myself.

Which meant he ignored me, and turned back to face Horace, who was all flesh and shadow, and quiet thunder. That knife was still in his hand, pointed down at the baby. I didn't know how fast I could move.

"Hunter," whispered Horace. "Maybe you should just walk away."

"Maybe *you* should," I replied. "Otherwise, you're mine."

"That line won't work anymore." Horace gave me a grim look. "You fucked us all, you know that? What were you thinking, breaking that last wall? Letting *them* loose?"

"I was sabotaged," I told him. "What's your excuse for *this* shit?"

Horace grimaced. "You *are* my excuse. Morals were fine when life was good, but with the Reapers free . . ." A shudder raced through him, and he closed his eyes. "We need to gorge ourselves now before the clans break from the prison. You thought it was bad before, Hunter . . . but every one of us demon parasites will be going hard for the sweet pain, as much as we can, as fast as we can. Before there's nothing left."

The big man lunged toward the baby.

I'd thought he might make a move—and so, apparently, had Horace. He lunged with incredible speed, slashing that knife through the air. The man cried out, clutching his eye. Blood poured between his fingers.

I crossed the room in seconds and grappled for Horace's knife. The armor flared white-hot over my hand, making the possessed man stumble back. Inside me, the darkness stirred, heavy with power.

I shoved it down, ruthless, and kept after the demon— only realizing, moments later, that I also held a dagger in my right hand.

The armor had transformed, giving me a blade: shorter than my forearm, made of the same silver metal, and light as air. A thin, delicate chain hung from the guard, connecting the blade to the armor. I was not as surprised as I should have been. The armor had shifted shape before, attuned to my needs—usually, in battle.

"You still think you can murder my kind?" Horace snapped, eyeing that blade. "You're *nothing* now, Hunter."

You are a Queen, whispered the darkness. *And those beneath you must remember their place.*

I snarled, slashing at Horace. The demon's host barely

124

escaped the blow, but the tip of that blade caught a fragment of his raging aura, scarring it with a trail of light. He screamed, eyes widening in shock, and staggered back against the wall.

"You're nothing but a gutter rat," I whispered. "A parasite. Who the *fuck* do you think *you* are?"

Horace struck me. I couldn't evade him. I'd never had to be fast, just patient.

He gored my shoulder with his knife, the tip of the blade sliding off bone until it hit my breast and sank in. I felt cold metal pierce my body—a distending, sliding sensation of parting flesh—followed by a bright, unexpected pain. The shock of being stabbed took my breath away.

And then my primitive brain took over, and I grabbed Horace's arm, holding him close with all my strength—his hand still gripping his knife. He tried to pull it out of my breast, but I wouldn't let him. I thought I would pass out from the pain, but I gritted my teeth and focused, focused hard. I was staring at his eyes when I hacked my own blade across his aura, staring into eyes that flickered from rage to horror—horror becoming resignation as my weapon cut through the shadow of his life.

Horace choked on a scream, stiffening beneath my hand.

Behind me a gun fired.

No impact. Just sound. I shoved Horace away from me, biting back a scream when his fingers slipped hard off the knife in my breast. I staggered, light-headed, blood rolling hot down my skin. I refused to look down, even when I grabbed the knife and pulled it out of my body in one hard yank. I should have been used to pain, dealing with the boys waking up every night—but dragging a knife out of my breast made me want to scream.

No time, though. Three possessed humans walked in, from the hall where I had entered.

Two men, one woman, with auras black as night and flecked with lightning. All were regulars at the shelter, Grant's pet demons—and willing converts. I didn't know their names.

In each of their hands, a gun. Pointed at me.

I looked for baby Andrew and found him a short distance away, sheltered in the arms of the big homeless man. Blood streamed down his face, but he was standing, trying not to draw attention to himself. Kind of like an elephant, lying low.

I moved away from him and the baby, keeping the demons focused on me. I was sweating and dizzy, still holding Horace's slick bloody knife. "Takes three of you to put a bullet in me? Only took one to kill my mother."

The woman glanced at Horace, who had slumped to the floor, unconscious. Fully human, no longer possessed. The parasite was dead. I had killed it. Whoever Horace had been before, he would wake up without his memories . . . and find himself accused of kidnapping a baby. His life, officially over. Again.

In the distance, police sirens wailed.

"No hard feelings," said the woman, as her demonic aura flickered. "We have to change with the times."

"Horace made a mistake with the baby," said one of the men, tightening his grip on the gun. "He should have gone for you . . . last of the Kiss women. That *means* something."

I didn't bother replying. My entire body throbbed with

awful, gushing pain. Each breath, agony. No place to run. Big, empty room. A baby still crying.

I flexed my right hand around the blade, and slipped into the void. One thought in my head. One focus as I drowned in that endless night.

I fell back into the world—*behind* the three demons.

My sword hit the woman's demonic aura, burning through her shadow with a hiss. She screamed, dropping her gun and clutching her head. I swung at the man next to her—but my wound hurt like hell, slowing me down. He threw himself out of the way.

The last man shot me in the back.

I heard the blast—flinched—but the bullet did not hit.

Instead, long coiled bodies draped around my neck, purring like steam engines. I turned to find Zee standing behind me, holding a bullet in his hand—and staring at the horrified demon with a look of pure snarling death. Raw and Aaz held down the other possessed man.

"No one touches Maxine," Zee hissed, and the rage that rolled off him carried an actual scent: hot as fried pepper, rancid as rotting meat. It seemed to coat the inside of my throat, and I coughed, eyes watering, forced to swallow hard in some vain attempt to ease that coarse sensation. It was hard to breathe.

"Forgive me," begged the demon, dropping the gun and getting down on his knees. "Please."

"No," Zee rasped, and swiped his claws, knocking that possessed man's head clean off his shoulders.

It happened so fast. Blood spurted, gushing across the floor. I stared in shock, watching that demonic parasite flutter loose of its dead host, attempting in vain to escape.

Only it couldn't. It tried, a small dense mass of shadows straining to be free, but unable to break the bonds of its corpse host.

Zee started to laugh: a chilling, unpleasant sound.

"Your Mama bonded to *us* now," he whispered, "and you bonded to *her*. Own you, cutter. Own your soul."

Zee wrapped his claws around that demonic cloud, and the shadow squeezed inward, within his fist.

"Tell others," he rasped. "Tell your mother. Maxine be *ours*. Touch her, like touching us. Hurt her, like hurting *us*."

Dek and Mal, sitting heavy on my shoulders, sighed in pleasure. Small rough tongues licked the backs of my ears, but that was no comfort.

My boys had never killed a host. Not while on my watch. Hosts were innocent. They knew that. But this . . . what I had just seen . . .

I heard a choked sound behind me: the big man, still holding the baby, his one good eye wide with horror. Swaying, tilting, pale. I held out my hands to him, my trembling hands. Dagger gone, absorbed. I didn't know when that had happened, but the armor radiated a rich warmth that sank into my bones.

"Oh, my God," he whispered, staring at the decapitated man. And then he flinched. "God!"

I looked over my shoulder. Raw and Aaz were tearing into the possessed man they had pinned. Crouched over his body like feeding wolves. His head was already gone, and so was one of his arms. Blood sprayed their bodies, spreading across the floor. Aaz raked a long claw down his back, opening up his spine. Raw laughed, reaching deep inside the body. I heard a sucking sound as he pulled out the man's heart.

I spun away, vomiting.

The big man ran, taking the baby.

I staggered after him, following the child's cry. Outside, sirens. I pressed my hand over my breast, trying to staunch the blood and put pressure on the pain. Dek and Mal felt especially heavy.

"Wait!" I croaked, but the man disappeared down a dark hall at the back of the shadowed room. Andrew's wail echoed.

Tears burned my eyes. I tried to run faster, desperate to catch up, but it was hard to breathe. My breast and shoulder felt like they were on fire, and the boys, the boys . . .

The man clattered up a set of stairs. I groaned, following him, leaving streaks of blood on the steel rail as I pulled myself along.

He turned on the landing, and let out a strangled shout.

"No," I gasped, pushing harder.

I was afraid I'd find a corpse when I reached the man, but he was still standing—staring at Zee, Raw, and Aaz—who crouched on the stairs above him, bodies nearly lost in the shadows, their eyes glowing red.

I stepped in front of the man, heart thudding in my throat, so breathless I could barely speak.

"It's okay," I whispered raggedly, trying to get the man to look at me. "Sir, please."

His terror was profound, a quivering horror that seemed to shave years off his life. He still wasn't looking at me, and I shrugged Dek and Mal off my shoulders, their rippling muscles gripping my arms as they dropped to the floor with quiet thuds.

Rasping growls behind me. Deadly, hungry sounds. I

129

forced myself to breathe, and edged closer to the man. Andrew cried, hiccuping on his sobs.

"Hey," I said in a gentle voice. "Hey."

The man finally looked at me, and the devastation in his eyes was almost more than I could bear.

"I'm crazy," he whispered.

"Let me hold the baby," I said.

He stepped back, shuddering. "No. No, no. Behind you."

"I know," I said. "Please, give me the baby."

His face crumpled with terror, and he tried to run back down the stairs. Raw and Aaz slipped from the shadows, blocking his path—and the man teetered, crying out. I grabbed his jacket, trying to steady him, but my touch only made things worse. He flailed in shock and terror, spinning around with his fist raised.

Raw attacked.

I shrieked at him, but it was too late—and he was not listening. The little demon took off the man's left leg at the kneecap, and in the same breath grabbed his stump and yanked down. The man crashed, screaming, and I fought to reach the baby slipping from his arms.

I tumbled on all fours, scrabbling and crawling. Raw reared high over the writhing man, sharp teeth bared in a hideous grin that bubbled with blood and strips of flesh.

I threw myself on top of the man's chest—and the baby—just as Raw's claws raked down. I gasped as something hard hit my shoulder, but felt no pain except for the stab wound in my breast.

Breathless, heart pounding, I peered over my shoulder.

Dek had blocked the blow. Over him, Raw stared at me in horror. I was sure I had a similar look on my face.

Aaz dragged his brother away. Zee took his place, staring down at me with grave, solemn eyes. Silence, between us all. Silence, except for the rasp and moan of the man beneath me and the quiet sob of a baby.

I closed my eyes, swallowing my own sob.

Slowly, carefully, I slid off the man. His chest hitched for air, like a wet hiccup. Blood gushed from his lower leg, flowing down the stairs. It was a terrible wound, accompanied by bone-deep lacerations across his thigh from where Raw had grabbed him.

I eased the crying baby from his arms. Except for my blood on his blanket, he seemed fine. It was a miracle. I bowed over him with a trembling sigh. At the bottom of the stairs, just out of sight, I heard police radios crackle and the pound of feet. I hesitated, torn, and laid Andrew on the floor beside the man who had tried to save him.

I tucked the blanket higher around the baby's face, then peered down the stairwell.

"Hey!" I cried, hoarse. "Help! There's a baby up here!"

Shouts. A flashlight beam pierced the shadows. I leaned against the wall, and pressed my armored fist against my brow. Around me, the boys gathered—quiet, and solemn. I heard the police running up the stairs.

"You're safe," I whispered to the baby, but I was looking at the dying man beside him, whose eyes were mere slits as he stared at my face.

I grabbed his jacket, and we slipped into the void.

CHAPTER 15

I left the man just inside an emergency room, listening to startled screams as I pushed him from the void onto the cold tile floor. I had never done that to another person, but it was instinctive, a moment when I hovered between this world and another—lost and found, half darkness and half light.

Maybe people saw disembodied hands. Maybe they saw my face, peering from a window of darkness—maybe all that anyone noticed was the blood-soaked, dying man who fell into the hospital, out of thin air.

Only a week ago, a day, I would never have done anything so public. So flamboyant. But the demons had been right. The rules were different now. Times were changing.

Starting now.

I left the man and closed the void.

Next time, I stepped into the apartment. I staggered, clutching my breast, blood running slick over my fingers. I started to fall, and strong hands caught me.

"Maxine," murmured Zee.

"Hey," I whispered, hurting from more than a stab

wound. Raw crawled on his belly toward us, claws curled under his hands, out of sight. Aaz was close behind, gaze torn between him and me, eyes big with worry. Dek and Mal slithered near, rough tongues scraping blood off my fingers.

I sat down, exhausted. Now the boys seemed calm. *Now*, here. It was surreal. I felt as though I was losing my mind. I had seen the boys wild before, seen them kill in hideous ways. Not once had it bothered me.

But *this* time had been different. Not just for what they'd done, but *how*.

"You killed hosts," I told them, hoarse. "Innocent hosts. You may have murdered a man who was trying to protect a *baby*. You know better. I know you do."

Raw looked away. Zee murmured, "Knowing not instinct. Instinct is hunger. Instinct is blood."

"No. If I hadn't put myself between Raw and that baby . . ."

I was unable to finish the sentence. It was too horrible to contemplate.

Raw gave me such a mournful look my heart broke again. I had to breathe through gritted teeth, trying to control the terrible, awful pain radiating from my breast. It filled and consumed my entire body. My aching heart felt worse.

I fumbled for the cell phone in my pocket, but moving my arm made my wound rage. I had to stop, holding my breath. I told myself this was no worse than having the boys wake up off my body—and went again for my phone.

Aaz beat me to it, reaching under me and slipping his claws into my back pocket. He put the phone into my hand. Raw placed a cool wet rag on my brow. I didn't know where he'd gotten it, but Zee nudged him out of the way and lifted my head just enough to push a straw in my mouth. Ice-cold ginger ale fizzled and burned down my throat with perfect sweetness.

"Little nurses," I muttered at them, and dialed the phone.

This time Grant answered, voice strained, tense.

"Upstairs," I told him.

"They found the baby. But Maxine—"

"I was stabbed," I interrupted, and lay flat on the floor, wincing. "In a not-so-great place."

I heard the sharp intake of his breath. "I'll be right there."

"Bring Rex," I said, and hung up. Dek pushed his snout beneath my head, slithering beneath my neck until he became my purring pillow. Mal crawled under my knees, propping them up. Aaz threw a blanket over me, curling against my side—and moments later, Raw joined him, still watching me as though he expected anger, a cutting word.

I had no anger. No cuts. Just concern.

I had been told all my life that if the prison veil broke, and the demon army was set loose, it would mean the end of the world. I'd had a taste of that. The veil *had* broken, and some of the army had escaped: the Mahati, a warrior clan, imprisoned on the second ring. Fierce, starving, ready to kill.

But still loyal to Zee and the boys, who had been their Kings.

Kings, who were loyal to me.

Learning that the boys were the Reapers, the most dangerous of the demons, had been horrific . . . but we had gotten through it because the boys had changed. Zee and his brothers were not the vicious, ruthless creatures they had been ten thousand years ago.

I believed that, with all my heart. I had faith in them.

Unless it was the bond keeping them that way, I wondered now. *The boys have always been guided by the spirit of a Hunter's intent and desire. Led by the strength of the Hunter's heart. What she is, they become.*

And now? How strong were *their* hearts?

Zee had warned me they might change, but I hadn't wanted to think about what that meant. Now, though, I'd had the barest, faintest glimpse.

I only wished my grandfather were here. Jack. Old Wolf. He would have some answers, assuming I could pry them out of him.

If he knew the boys were free . . .

He will freak the hell out.

"How did you know I was in trouble?" I asked Zee, who sat close, rubbing his claws and watching his brothers with particular sadness.

"Felt it," he murmured. "Like thunder in the heart. Like the edge of a howl, on dying."

I extended my hand to him, and he laid his rough cheek upon my palm.

"Thank you for coming," I said.

"Maxine," he rasped, with a sigh. "We change."

I could still see Raw digging out that possessed man's heart. "I know."

"No." Zee shook his head, spiked hair swaying. "Only strong survive. So we must be strong. Strongest. Make others fear. Fear, and obey."

"You have to be the baddest bad?" I stared at the window, thinking of what I had seen inside the prison veil: another world, another dimension with cities and totems, and demon children playing—and starving. "So what if you *are*? You rule the army, then what? You know what they'll want—what they'll *need*—once they're free."

"Humans," he whispered, softly. "To feed."

I closed my eyes. "By the time you're . . . bad enough . . . to lead them, will you want the same thing?"

He fell silent. Dek and Mal stopped purring.

"Do not know," he whispered. "Do not know our hearts. Not like you, an arrow straight. We, our hearts, curve and twist, full of night."

"Night is sweet. Night has stars."

"We have seen the other side of light," he whispered, chilling me. "But light will not lead the Lords of Bone."

The apartment door banged open. Grant limped inside, so grim, pale. Not a word when he saw the blood covering me—just a glint in his eyes that was hard and resolved.

I tried to sit up. He snapped, "Don't even think about it."

"Eh," I muttered, wincing. "Be gentle."

Grant growled, lowering himself to the floor and giving Zee and the boys a critical look. "Where were the five of you when she got hurt?"

Dek and Mal began singing a vigorous rendition of "Night on Bald Mountain," which, after a few strains, was surprisingly creepy.

Grant grunted at them. "Zee. Cut away her sweater."

The little demon extended his claw and cut through cashmere like it was nothing but air. I dug my fingers into my palms, gritting my teeth as the soaked sweater was peeled slowly off the wounds in my shoulder and breast. The scent of blood was overwhelming.

All the boys hissed. So did Grant.

"She takes a lickin', but keeps on tickin'," I murmured.

He placed his large, warm hand on my brow. "This will take a couple minutes, sweetheart. It might feel uncomfortable."

It was more than uncomfortable. Grant began humming, and almost instantly the inside of my breast, around the wound, felt as if it was crawling with ants. A lot of ants. Big ants. Ants that were biting me.

"Whoa," I muttered. *"Whoa."*

Zee caught my hand. Raw took my other, holding me so gently. I tried pulling free, but their grips tightened, making me squirm as the biting sensation intensified. Skin hot, skin twitching, skin growing beneath Grant's voice, which rumbled from his throat in a deep, multitonal bass. Primal. Sinking through me, twisting through my body like lightning in my veins. All he was doing was healing me, but my soul felt as though it rode the crest of a tsunami: out of control, hurtling toward a fall.

And I fell, and fell—control lost— helpless to do anything but endure as Grant forced my body to heal. My flesh protested. I wanted to protest, too, but I kept my mouth shut because I needed this, fast.

Made me uneasy, though. I couldn't help it.

Grant's voice faltered, and fell silent. My breast ached and burned, skin twitching like an electrical current was running through me. I looked down, and saw a pink line of mostly healed flesh beneath all that drying blood.

"If you're careful, there won't be a scar." Grant spoke so quietly. I searched his eyes, and found them grim, and resigned. This was his worst nightmare: me, uneasy with him. Me, unable to trust him. We had talked about it, late at night when neither of us could sleep. Poured out our worst fears, our smallest hurts. Blankets and legs tangled, staring into the shadows, listening to hearts beat, and rain pound, and our voices mingle. Taking reassurance in each other and small truths that we thought we could depend on.

That we loved each other. That the boys would never leave me. That I would always be immune to his power.

Small comforts against terrible odds.

"I'm sorry," he murmured. "I'm sorry that you feel . . ."

He could not finish. I tugged my hand free of Raw's grip and brushed my fingertips against Grant's chin. In my heart, I poured my love. My love. Melting down, pretending it spread through, and around me.

"See what else I feel," I said to him. "That will never change."

The corner of his mouth tugged into a sad smile, and he kissed my palm. "I used to be a stronger man, you know. No one ever tore me up like you do."

"Whiner."

His smile twitched with warmth. Zee sighed and leaned back on his haunches. "Our fault you hurt."

"Horace, not you," I told him. "The demon's dead, by the way. Grant, *all* your demons . . . your converts . . ."

"I know," he said in a heavy voice. "I know. Rex is the only one who's left. Everyone else made their choice."

"Should have killed them," Zee rasped.

Grant gave him a dirty look. "Easy for you, right? I talked to the police. They said it was a massacre in the warehouse where Andrew was found."

"Cutters going to blast Maxine. Punishment fit crime."

"No, it did *not*," I told him—at the same time Grant said, "What?"

I sighed, weary. "Some of your demons came with guns to kill me. I don't know their names."

Grant sat back, staring with anger and betrayal in his eyes. I shared that sting, more so than I would have imagined possible. I should have known better. Both of us should have. I had warned him this might happen—that one of the demonic converts would turn as Horace had, and try to hurt someone.

But I'd also begun to buy into Grant's optimism. I believed now in shades of gray. I believed in the possibility of redemption.

"Cannot rule by free will," Zee rasped, with a hint of anger. "Hunt is made of iron. So must be the fist."

Grant closed his eyes. "Controlling others against their will? Playing God? Committing murder? I'd be no better than the Aetar if I did that."

"Maybe *need* to be no better. Maybe, to survive, need to cleave your heart with night."

"Zee—" Grant began, but stopped as behind him, the apartment door opened.

Rex walked in, demonic aura yo-yoing around him like tethered fireworks. When he saw the boys, I thought the demon might explode out of his stolen body. His face was hollow, sunken, a gray undertone beneath his dark skin.

Rex kept his gaze down. "My . . . Kings."

Zee stared with narrowed eyes. Grant tugged the blanket over my naked breasts, put the bottle of ginger ale in my hands, and then tried to stand. Rex began to help him. Raw and Aaz stepped in his path.

The possessed man exhaled, lowering his head. His aura trembled. So did the rest of him.

"Boys," I said. "Don't hurt him."

"If loyal, no need," Zee replied, in a dangerous voice. "You loyal, cutter?"

Rex hesitated. "Yes."

Raw hissed. Aaz snarled. Concerned, I struggled to sit up. Grant was doing the same. Mal pushed his head under his hand, helping him. Dek coiled around my wrist.

"What is it?" I asked them sharply.

"He lies." Zee dragged a claw through the air in a menacing gesture. "Not loyal."

Rex's head shot up, and finally he looked at them. Bold, unblinking, full of defiance—and fear.

"You're right," he said in a hard voice. "You little fuckers. You're *damn* right. I'm *not* loyal to you. I'm loyal to *him*." He pointed at Grant, then me. "And I'm loyal to *her*."

Each word was clipped, fast, snapped out like rocks and bullets. I felt hit with his words. I wasn't even certain I'd heard him right. Rex and I had been at odds since we'd first met—coming to blows, treating each other like shit. We said "fuck you" to each other more often than we said "hello." Maybe that *was* our hello.

I stared, numb, as Rex stepped closer to Zee—trembling, but holding the little demon's gaze with the same defiance and disdain he'd always shown me.

"Reaper Kings," he whispered. "I was born after your imprisonment, but I know the stories. All you created was war and suffering. All you built with your power was an army that devoured and tortured everything in its path. And *my* kind? We were nothing but *slaves*. Whores for the warriors, used to feed them *pain*."

None of the boys moved a muscle or made a sound. Silence because they were listening—or silence before a kill. I could not tell which, but it made me nervous. Grant was equally tense, watching them so carefully—one hand edging toward mine. Not for comfort, I thought—but to pull me out of the way. Just in case.

Rex took a breath, but it was shaky, and his defiance was suddenly mixed with fear.

"Now you're loose," he said quietly, "and it'll start again. First, this world . . . then when you're done, back into the Labyrinth, hunting, hunting for more bodies, more ways to destroy. So no . . . let me repeat . . . I'm *not* loyal to you, or any demon. I'm loyal to them. The *people*. At least they create something. At least they know what compassion is."

Perfect, horrible silence fell. I held my breath. So did Grant.

Zee, however, relaxed. All the boys did, though if I hadn't known them so well, I might not have noticed the easing of tension in their spikes—and the shift of light in their eyes.

"Good," whispered Zee. "That was truth."

Rex stared at him. Then, he swallowed hard and looked at Grant. It took Rex a moment to speak, and he wet his lips, "The police are still here. They want to speak with you. If you don't go to them, they'll come to you."

"Okay," said my husband, knuckles white around his cane. "But you and I need to talk first."

"We all need to talk," I muttered, holding the blanket closer to my breasts.

Without a word, Rex strode toward the stairs that led to the rooftop garden. His aura strained from his flesh like smoke contained in a man-sized jar. Dull, red daggers of lightning pierced the shadows.

Grant gave me a brief glance and followed. Mal rode on his shoulders. Zee, still watching Rex, hissed to himself and scratched his belly. Behind him, Raw and Aaz picked their teeth with long claws. Strands of meat came free, which they licked back into their mouths.

I took a slow, steadying breath. Dek chirped at me, and I scooped him up to my shoulder.

"Toothpaste," I said, as the little demon coiled around my throat. "Go, eat some. Along with bleach."

Raw and Aaz gave me confused looks and continued picking their teeth.

I shook my head at them and followed Grant, who was already limping up the stairs. I stayed behind him, hooking my fingers into the back pockets of his jeans. His shoulders relaxed, and he tilted his head toward me. I gave him a crooked smile.

He stopped on the stairs, pulling me up beside him. No words. Just a hard kiss, long, deep, and warm. His fingers slid through my hair, tightening, holding me close. My heart bathed in his light. My body soaked in his heat. I felt less naked and empty, less vulnerable, with him touching me. Dek and Mal twined together, humming.

Rex appeared at the top of the stairs. "You both make me sick."

"Forget it," Grant replied, voice muffled against my cheek. "We're onto you, now. You *like* us."

"You really, *really*, like us," I added.

Rex made a disgusted sound. "Whatever. Just . . . hurry up, will you?"

I hitched the blanket higher. Grant kissed me again and gestured for me to precede him. This time one of his hands stayed in my back pocket.

The garden hadn't changed. Barrels of roses were scattered around, along with low planters filled with limp flowers and ferns. Everything looked brown, dull, or disinterested. I didn't know if it was the Seattle clouds, or just the fact that no one in this odd little family had a green thumb worth spitting on.

The sky was overcast, but Dek and Mal wriggled in that dim daylight with little sighs. Rex waited for us in the center of the garden. I wondered if it was a deliberate decision not to stand near the roof's edge. He gave the demons on our shoulders unhappy looks.

"I was hoping this would be private," he said.

"Someone tried to shoot Maxine," Grant replied. "Forget it."

Rex grunted, still eyeing Dek—who began humming Eric Carmen's "Hungry Eyes."

I scratched his head. "Can I expect every demon to start trying to kill me?"

Once upon a time, Rex would have answered that question with bitterness, sarcasm—and heaps of insults. He would have cursed at me, accused me of every imaginable crime against his kind—and *only* then, said what I already knew: that, yes, every demon would try to kill me. Because I was fair game. Because it was just plain fair, after all the demon lives I'd taken.

But instead of the reaction I expected, he went quiet, thoughtful.

MARJORIE M. LIU

"Only the stupid ones," he said, surprising me. "Before, you would have been dead by now. But the rules have changed with the Reaper Kings' freedom. If you're under their protection, word will travel fast. You may be safe."

"May," Grant said.

Rex finally looked at us like we were idiots. "The Reaper Kings ruled the demon army because they were strong—the very strongest, possessed with power that no other demon lord could match. They had no weakness. None." He hesitated, meeting my gaze. "Until you."

Dek and Mal twitched.

"They care about you," Rex went on, watching them. "They call you their Queen. If you were like them, *strong* as them, that wouldn't be a problem. But you're *human*. Weak." He waved a dismissive hand at the armor on my hand. "Even *that* won't keep you safe."

"You wanna bet?" The words slipped out before I could stop them. I should have felt like an idiot, but instead, hearing my challenge made me feel better. I sounded more like myself. I sounded as though I believed I had a chance.

Rex did not mock me. Instead, he gave me a peculiar, assessing look.

"Hunter," he said quietly, "they'll have to choose between you and power. Trust me . . . they'll choose power. Because it'll mean their survival."

Mal hissed at him. Dek gripped my ear and growled. Rex took one step back, but with defiance still in his eyes.

"And yet, you're still here," I said.

"Where else would I go? I cut my ties to Blood Mama years ago. Maybe *you* don't know what that means, but every other demon will. I have no clan."

Grant leaned forward. "No clan?"

"Why do you think the others abandoned you? Clans are power within the demon army. If you're part of a clan, you have *something*, even if it's shit. But I don't even have that. I'm an individual, now. I left my clan. I gave up my bonds. Which means I have even less protection than my brothers and sisters who are linked to Blood Mama. If I'm caught by any of the warriors in the veil . . ." Rex stopped, as though ill. "It would be better for one of you to kill me soon. In the next day or two, but no later. I doubt the prison veil will stand any longer than that."

Grant and I stared at him, and his aura shrank and shriveled as though his demonic soul was sucking in its breath, and holding it.

"You're that afraid?" I said.

Rex pointed at me. "You were the prison of the Reaper Kings, and that gave you power. Now that your bond is broken, you still *have* power, inside you. Others who don't know you might not be able to taste it, but I can. You're the Vessel of whatever godforsaken entity those Reaper Kings summoned, eons ago. But that means nothing because you won't use that power. You're afraid of it. Which makes you no better than any other human. Food, like the rest of us. All you can hope for is the mercy of a clean death."

The demon possessing the caged woman had spoken almost the same words. True or not, I was getting tired of hearing that doomsday crap. I grabbed his finger, but didn't jam it backward. Just steered his hand away from me.

"I don't want mercy," I said to him. "I don't want a clean death. When I die, it'll be fighting . . . right to the bitter end."

"You're an idiot."

"She doesn't give up," Grant told him. "That doesn't make her an idiot."

"Then what does that make *you*?" Rex closed his eyes, sweating. "You, *Lightbringer*. Blood Mama didn't want to possess you, all those years ago, just to control humans. She wanted you because she thought you'd be a weapon against the Demon lords."

"Zee and the boys are beyond my power. What makes you think I'd be effective against any of the others?"

"Don't play dumb. Even if you don't know exactly what you're capable of doing, you know damn well that you have power. You're a member of a race that could have destroyed the Aetar . . . and the Aetar nearly destroyed us. That's not something you waste here, on a bunch of drug addicts and assholes like me." Rex leaned in, aura flaring, matching the wildness in his eyes. "You do something that matters even if you don't have the stomach for it. You *fight*."

Tension leapt across our bond. I slid my hand around Grant's arm and felt the strain in his muscles—which I shared, in my gut, when he glanced down and I saw his eyes.

"You fucking deserve each other," Rex whispered. "Both of you, unafraid of anyone but yourselves. You have power. You have the means. But you won't take it because you think it'll change you. *Of course* it will change you. But is that worse than dying?"

"I don't know," I said, speaking not to Rex, but to Grant—and I could see the same torn conflict in his eyes. We both knew it wasn't a matter of change but of transformation. Losing ourselves. Maybe losing each other. Possibly becoming the very thing we were trying to fight. We'd had a taste of all that tremendous power . . . and it was not sweet.

Dek tilted his head, looking behind us. I tore my gaze from Grant and found Zee, Raw, and Aaz moving slowly from the stairwell to the roof. It was strange, seeing them in the light. Unreal, even. I had to force myself to breathe because looking at them when they should have been part of me made my chest constrict with longing and loneliness. My skin ached. I felt cold.

The sky brightened, just then: clouds thinning, burning silver. Seattle light, diffuse and shy. Moments later, though, the actual sun broke through and flooded the roof, hitting us all.

Zee and the boys hissed, their eyes glinting red. At first, I thought it was with pain, but their spines arched, and so did their backs, and their ears perked in pleasure. All of them, stretching, twisting, like stroked cats. I heard popping sounds, cracks—bone, muscle. Aaz threw back his head, closing his eyes as he rolled his shoulders in the light.

"Sun fed," Zee whispered, as Dek and Mal writhed and twisted over Grant's and my shoulders, exposing their sleek, silver-veined stomachs. I winced as small claws scratched my neck, leaving a trail of fire. It was an accident, but still surprising—the boys had never scratched me, not once, ever.

Something warm and wet trickled down my skin. Blood.

Dek stilled, and his purr died. A slow tremor rolled through him, followed by another sound that chilled me to the bone. I couldn't believe it, at first.

"Maxine," Grant said, staring at him. "Maxine, don't move."

I had already frozen. That low rumble rolling from Dek's throat . . . was hunger.

Zee edged forward, hissing at the little demon. Mal did the same, half-sliding off Grant's shoulders, his scales undulating in the silver sunlight. Dek, however, continued vibrating, and my blood kept flowing, and I felt his tongue rasp across my skin—drinking me in.

The sensation was so strange. It went deeper than physical, as though something drained from me, into him—a momentary spark, there and gone, too fast to be certain it was even real. It didn't scare me, exactly. I trusted Dek.

But it didn't feel right, either.

I never saw Zee move. One moment he was on the ground, and in the next his fist punched Dek off my shoulders, slamming him into Raw's arms. I swayed, lightheaded, and deep inside me—very deep—that dark entity stirred, its sly voice flowing soft through my soul.

Nothing is sacred, it whispered. *What is holy will pass into darkness, and be lost. Gods live and die in memory.*

So does the heart.

Grant caught me. I stared at Dek, who coiled into a ball within Raw's arms, hiding his face and making quiet, desperate clicking sounds. All the boys stared at him—and then me, with startled, stunned expressions. I started to ask them what was wrong, besides the obvious, but my neck throbbed and I was suddenly too sick and sweaty with nausea to even think about opening my mouth.

"I told you," Rex said, his voice low and hard with unease. "Nothing is sweeter than power."

I didn't know what power had to do with my blood. I heard a low, vibrating hum—Grant's voice—and that cut began itching like hell. The pain eased, though. When I touched the cut, I found only smooth skin.

Grant sighed against my ear, his fingers loosening around my arms. "I hate this."

"I know," I murmured to him, then pulled away to kneel before Dek, who shuddered and mewled.

Zee gave him a hard look—far angrier than I would have expected, given that the others had been ripping people apart with their teeth and claws less than an hour before.

"It's okay," I said, though Zee grunted in disagreement, and a flare of irritation filled my bond with Grant.

I ignored them both and brushed Dek's neck with my fingertips. I hummed a little Bon Jovi for him: "Born to Be My Baby."

"Come on, baby," I crooned, taking him from Raw. "Come on, sweetie."

Dek was knotted up so tight, I wasn't sure he'd ever come undone. I couldn't see his face, but he shivered when I cradled him in my arms, stroking his sleek, muscled skin.

"Sun cut," Zee whispered, and then: "Maxine."

I didn't look away from Dek. "Yes?"

Down below, at the bottom of the stairs, I heard the apartment door open and a muffled voice.

"Mr. Cooperon? It's Detective—"

I didn't hear the rest. Grant's low curse drowned out the man's voice. That, and Zee had slid his arm around my shoulders, pulling me close. He laid one claw upon my armor, and all the boys—in a heartbeat—curled around us. Mal landed hard in my lap, licking Dek.

Outrage flickered over Grant's face. "No, you don't."

"Must," Zee said.

"Wait," I argued. "Zee—"

Grant reached for us. "Take me with you."

"You are a warrior," Zee rasped to him, "and consort of the Queen. But you are no King."

And with that, we slipped into the void.

CHAPTER 16

I T was night on the other side of the world, in a desert filled with tumbled ruins broken in the sand and cracked rows of delicate columns that rose like pale fingers toward the stars. I stared, drinking in the stillness of the place and the endlessness of its stone remains, tumbled and fallen. It reminded me of a mass grave. I tried to imagine the city that had been here but could not. All I knew was that this was a burial ground for something that had been beautiful and that time had torn it down.

Even stars die, whispered the darkness inside me. *We have tasted their last fire and burrowed through the veins of their fading hearts. Accept us, and we will do so again. We will hunt the stars for light, and you will be our Vessel.*

Zee shivered and backed away from me. All the boys did, even Dek, unwinding with a hiss and slithering into the sand. My neck tingled. I touched where he had scratched me, but the skin was still smooth. I dropped the blanket, and the cool night air wrapped around my naked upper body.

"You should have warned me," I said to Zee. "Why did you bring me with you?"

"Safer," he rasped, as Raw and Aaz prowled, stone breaking beneath their claws. "For all of us."

I thought about what Rex had told me and picked up the blanket again, throwing it around my shoulders. "And Grant? You should have let him come."

Zee's broad chest rose and fell. "No place for him. Not yet."

I heard strain in his voice and something else that made me uneasy: resignation, perhaps even guilt. A terrible sinking sensation hit my gut.

I straightened, staring at him. "Why are we here, Zee?"

He did not answer. Aaz nudged me. I hadn't felt him draw near. He pushed something soft into my hands: a long-sleeved crew-neck shirt, navy or black in color. I took it gratefully, pulling it over my head.

When I looked for Zee again, he was gone.

I found him a short distance away, bounding over the ruins like a slick shadow. Raw and Aaz joined him, also taking graceful, bounding leaps—skidding, almost dancing, with light, clawed steps over the uneven terrain. My wolves, in the night.

I felt light-headed watching them, a sense of déjà vu. I had never been here, but I felt as though I remembered this, somehow: some vision of them racing through a desert night, in the middle of a fallen city—faster, harder, with deeper purpose.

Dek hugged my ankle, and I scooped him up. I did the same with Mal, placing them on my shoulders as I followed the others across the ruins. I had to take a round-about path, trailing my hands over fallen columns and carved rubble. I had seen similar ruins in books—these were Corinthian, perhaps.

A heavy hush surrounded us. I could have floated in that silence.

I found Zee and the others prowling around a towerlike structure that had four walls, a solid base, and a standing row of pillars in front of it. The stone was pale in the starlight, with no windows, and enough gaps and breaks in the fitted blocks to make the surface look pockmarked.

"Where are we?" I asked him.

"Old city. Been a city, always. Remember it, when." Zee paced in front of the structure, his claws dragging through the sand. Raw and Aaz gave him uneasy looks that he ignored, glancing back at me, his red eyes glinting. "Trust us, Maxine? Trust us, with you?"

"Yes," I said.

Zee looked away, and a growl rumbled from his chest, rolling through the night like thunder. Without warning, he reared back and slammed his fist into the ancient stone wall.

It sounded like an explosion. I stumbled back, stunned, as he tore through the rock. A priceless artifact, thousands of years old, standing against time. I almost screamed at him to stop.

Instead, I swallowed my voice, watching him tear and mangle those carved stone blocks, yanking, clawing through them and burrowing through that immense foundation into the ground itself, moving down, down, digging deep below the structure. Dust kicked up, making my eyes sting, my nostrils burn. I covered my mouth, coughing, watching him disappear into the hole while Raw and Aaz crowded close. Even Dek and Mal leaned off my shoulders, trembling.

Finally, silence. A long minute passed.

Then, a scraping sound—so heavy, immense, the ground vibrated—as though part of a mountain was shifting beneath our feet. I moved closer to the hole, feeling more of those vibrations, listening to a tremendous cracking sound—like the bones of a giant were breaking. Closer, louder. Until it was no longer the ground shuddering, but my eardrums.

Zee finally crawled free. Slow, careful, dragging something behind him. I couldn't see much, but it was massive. The hole was not big enough to let it out, and Raw and Aaz broke away dirt, rock, widening the way. Zee tugged again, and the other boys joined him, digging their claws down into—stone, I realized—pulling hard.

Dek and Mal coiled tense on my shoulders as the object was pulled free from the hole. I found myself staring at a stone block: approximately eleven feet long, five feet wide, almost as tall as me. Smooth surface, but unpolished, as though it had been taken whole from the earth and fashioned in the rough shape of a massive rectangle. No engravings, no markings of any kind.

I searched for seams but found none. It either had no lid or was sealed so tight nothing was visible.

Zee beckoned me closer. I looked where he pointed.

I had been wrong about there being no engravings. I found one, carved into the top of the stone block. It was small, less than the size of my palm.

It looked exactly like the scar on my jaw, just below my ear.

A jagged line, twisting and daggered. Given to me by a creature that was not a demon or anything that could be named—except that he was another kind of hunter, devoted to one of my ancestors, who had shown him trust and friendship when no other would have.

He had become an odd ally and friend—though I still hadn't forgiven him for scarring my face. Marking me with a symbol that I'd seen tattooed on a priest and set inside my grandfather's arm.

A symbol that meant death and rebirth. A symbol that meant either the end of everything—or the beginning of tremendous possibility.

All of which was inside me.

All of which had once been inside the boys.

A chill hit me. Raw and Aaz crept close, all the spikes along their spines flexing with tension. Zee watched my face.

"Why did you ask if I trust you?" I said to him.

He did not answer. A single look passed between him, Raw, and Aaz. Dek and Mal began humming "Ain't No Grave," a Johnny Cash song I'd been listening to a day or a lifetime ago. Back in Texas, on a porch with a ginger ale in my hand. Another world from here.

"Ain't no grave can hold my body down," I recited in my head, and stepped back as Zee and the boys jammed their claws into solid stone and started tearing it apart as though it was little more than a butter block, already soft from the sun. It sounded like silk tearing.

Dek and Mal dropped off my shoulders, winding close with sparks of fire trailing from their nostrils. They attacked the stone with the same ferocious grace as their brothers, chewing it with their teeth.

Less than a minute later they broke the surface—and I

realized that that massive, seamless block of stone was hollow as an egg.

I forced myself to breathe as Dek shot inside, Mal behind him. Zee snarled, ripping out another block of stone, and tossing it aside. Raw and Aaz redoubled their efforts, lips pulled back over their sharp teeth, red eyes narrow and glinting. Faster, harder, claws ripping into that rock with a brutality and desperation that made me profoundly uneasy.

I didn't feel any better when I saw what it held.

"Those are bones," I said, listening to myself speak as if from a distance, *feeling* distant, numb—because it wasn't just bones I was looking at, but scraps of clothing and desiccated flesh attached to bones, and what I should have said was, *those are bodies*, but my mouth wouldn't form that word—that raw, painful, word. *Bones* was easier. *Bones* were cold and dry, and remote. *Bones* weren't bodies stuffed inside a hollow stone and buried beneath the desert. *Bones* weren't bodies that had died in positions of agony, hands still reaching, clawing at the walls of an impossible coffin.

Zee made an odd sound, almost a gasp, and dragged his claws over his eyes. Raw and Aaz leaned on each other, shoulders slumped. I heard a mournful humming from inside the stone slab, deep amongst those remains. It made my heart sink.

I stared at the boys. "What is this?"

Zee let out a slow breath and jammed his claws into his chest as though he were trying to dig out his heart. Again and again he stabbed himself, as if the pain would bring him relief from whatever he was suffering.

And he *was* suffering. I could see it in his eyes.

"No matter now," he finally rasped. "No matter."

Raw and Aaz closed their eyes. I said, "It fucking matters to *you*."

Zee snarled at me, and I flinched. He didn't seem to notice, instead spinning away from me and facing that jumble of dried flesh and bones, tangled together inside the stone block, which had been ripped open until it resembled little more than a cradle. Dek and Mal moved slowly through those remains, caressing them with their bodies.

Zee crouched, and touched one of the dead—a hollow, shrunken face covered in dark dry skin, and bits of black hair. I could not see enough to tell if it was human, though it didn't matter. He was so careful, even reverent. Made me hold my breath, watching him.

"Aetar wanted to punish us," he whispered. "Buried our hearts alive."

An ache spread through my chest, into my gut. "Who are the dead?"

"Our hearts," he echoed again, and looked at Raw and Aaz. "Made us watch them die."

Some of those bodies shifted, stiff and crumbling in the night air. Dek and Mal appeared, pushing them aside, with gentleness and soft melodies strumming from their throats. Zee's shoulders rose and fell, and he leaned forward to reach beneath those remains.

He pulled out a crystal skull.

I stared, startled. The skull was larger than the one the possessed woman had given me, and the face was different. No sharp teeth. A jutting jaw. Only one socket, in the center of the head. Like a Cyclops.

"Um," I said, watching as Raw stepped forward to take

the skull from Zee, who reached in again—deeper, this time—and pulled another crystal skull from beneath the dead. This one was partially wrapped in a threadbare cloth that crumbled when Zee touched it, falling away and revealing a crystalline carving that resembled a horse's skull—except for the long, spiral horn embedded in the brow.

Zee moved deeper into the stone cradle, sifting through the dead until he pulled out three more skulls. Each one was slightly human, and slightly not, with differences that ranged from the shape of the cranium to the numbers of eye sockets. One skull sported bull horns and an overly large forehead that would have looked good on a Neanderthal.

Raw and Aaz lined the skulls in the sand and stepped back, staring at them. Zee crawled free of the dead, also watching the skulls. I had no idea what those artifacts were doing with the bodies, but I was certain they hadn't been meant to see the light of day again.

Thirteen skulls, I'd been told. Thirteen keys to bind the Reaper Kings. And here were five of them.

The armor on my right hand tingled, pins and needles flowing up my arm, over my entire body. A chill. That deepening unease.

"Guys," I said.

"Trust," Zee whispered, looking at me. "Only have one heart now. Won't lose it. Won't lose *you*."

He turned back, raised his fist, and slammed it down on the skull nearest him.

Crystal shattered. I staggered back as shards hit my legs and chest—other, larger, fragments sinking into the sand beneath the force of his blow. I gasped at him, stunned, shielding my face as Raw and Aaz tore into the remaining skulls, breaking them with their fists, raising them over their heads and hurling them down on stone, on their knees, on each other's backs—destroying them with deliberate, relentless, determination.

Loss hit me, all my unease exploding into fear.

I realized that I'd been lying to myself. I *was* scared of the boys no longer being bonded to me. Scared of what they would do. I'd been looking at that *other* crystal skull as a way out. A possible solution in case things got bad.

Clearly, the boys were not going to cooperate. And why would they?

"Fuck," I whispered, as Zee reached back and flung a baseball-sized chunk of crystal into the ruins. I heard it crack against stone, then silence fell, hard and heavy, smothering even the sound of my pounding heart.

"Never again," he whispered, trembling.

CHAPTER 17

THEY burned the bodies. Dek and Mal coughed fire upon the remains, and the sparks turned to flames in seconds, spreading with a heat and ferocity that made me keep my distance. The boys did not retreat. They stood in the fire, holding those bodies as they burned in their arms.

I watched them and wanted Grant. I almost left them to return home, but every time I came close, I stopped myself. I needed to be here. I didn't know why, but my gut said so. Leaving would have felt good but not right.

So I found a tumbled column and sat on it, trying to steady my pulse as I took slow, even breaths, drawing in the cool desert air—closing my eyes, emptying my mind of hard thoughts. I drifted. I sank. My bond with Grant throbbed golden and hot. Beneath that, I suffered the weight of a sleeping giant, coiled beneath my heart.

Zee left the fire first, small body outlined against the flames. He watched me. I watched him.

"I'm sorry," I said to him, quietly. "Whoever they were to you, I'm so sorry you lost them."

"Lost many," he replied, just as softly. "Lost many in the

160

beginning, lost a whole world. Too desperate not to lose any more."

He hesitated, looking back at the fire. "We lost, anyway."

"You loved them."

"Did not know it was love." Zee glanced back at me. "Know better now."

I sighed. "Why did you wait until now to come here? You could have unearthed that tomb at any time since you've been free. You could have asked your old mothers to come here. My mother. My grandmother. Me."

"No point warming cold secrets."

I dug my fingers into the stone beneath me. "Are there other secrets?"

"Always." Zee pressed his small fist over his heart. "Each breath a secret."

Each breath. Each moment. *I* was just a moment, a mortal heartbeat that would last a couple decades, then fade into memory. Our lives together were a secret no one would ever understand. But that was just one life. Each of my ancestors had lived a secret lifetime with the boys. Secret, between them. Remembered *only* by them.

But before that? Before being imprisoned? How many memories could burn over the millennia?

Had my mother known this was going to happen?

Does it matter? Because you're here, and she's not, and this is your game to handle. Your hand to play.

I just didn't know what hand I'd been given yet. The boys were free, yes. But I had no idea what that meant or what they would do with that freedom.

So deal with it. Get your shit together.

I patted the spot beside me. Zee prowled close, graceful and sleek. He did not sit beside me but crouched between my feet, facing the dimming fire. Dek and Mal were singing softly, coiled on top of Raw and Aaz, who continued to kneel in the flames.

I stroked the spines of Zee's hair, burying my fingers behind his ears and massaging his hard skull. I had seen my mother do this, and over the years, I'd taken up the habit.

"This, peace," he whispered. "Peace will not last, Maxine."

"Okay," I said. "You brought me here, we unburied some bodies, you destroyed those skulls. Was that part of a plan or just something you had to do?"

He tensed. "Need to protect. Need to think ahead, not just to army, but Aetar. War comes, Maxine. War comes, but we will be *free*."

"And this world? Will it be free?"

He hesitated. My hands stilled. "Zee."

He pulled away from me. I reached for him, but he slipped out of my grip, dragging his claws through the sand as I stood up. I moved too quickly and swayed, dizzy.

"Maxine." Zee touched my hand, steadying me. "Need to sit."

"What I need are answers," I told him, digging my palm into my eye. "I'm scared. I'm scared of what's coming."

"Scared of us," he whispered.

I swallowed hard. "A little, yes. Is that why you destroyed the skulls?"

"Destroyed so the Aetar could not use them. Destroyed so that you would not die in the belly of a stone." Zee tugged on my hand, forcing me to sit. "Will do what it takes to keep you safe."

"No. There are limits."

"No limits."

"The limit is harm," I told him. "Promise me you will keep this world safe, Zee."

He looked away to Raw and Aaz, who had left the fire and were watching us, with Dek and Mal draped over their arms. I felt something pass between them in that silence. I felt it in my gut and heart.

"No," he said. "Will not promise."

"*Zee.*"

"Many worlds. Worlds, always reborn. Not you." Zee gave me a hard, desperate look. "Not you."

My eyes stung. "I will die, one day. I am not immortal. I am not forever."

Zee pressed his claws over my heart. "Ten thousand years, in your blood. Ten thousand years, sharing hearts of mothers. Good mothers, bad mothers. Our mothers. Our *babies*, becoming mothers. Birth to death. *Birth to death.*" His voice grew rough, hard, and his eyes began to glow. "Now we free . . . but your blood, still ours. Our clan. Our babies. Our mothers. Ours."

He withdrew his claws but leaned in, holding my gaze. "Worlds die, always . . . but if blood lives . . . so does heart."

His words burned through me, sharp and aching. I could not look away from him, but when I tried to speak, nothing worked. I hurt too much. I hurt for him, and myself.

"I love you," I whispered. "But I cannot let you harm this world. Not even for me."

Zee glanced away at the others. "May change mind, Maxine."

"No, I will not."

Dek mewled at us. Raw covered his mouth. Zee gave them a hard look, then met my gaze again. "Need to go. Need you with us."

"We're not done here."

He bared his teeth at me, snarling. I refused to flinch.

"No," he snapped, and grabbed my right hand. Before I could take a proper breath, we slipped into the void.

Seconds passed into eternity. When we stepped free, I gasped for air, stumbling—shielding my eyes against a terrible, harsh blast of sunlight. It was so bright. I glimpsed blue skies, spinning—

Strong hands caught me. Not Zee. The grip was too large, and I glimpsed long fingers, shaped like pitchfork tines.

My heart stilled. I looked up, breathless, and stared into piercing green eyes set in a sharp, angular face. Silver hair fell into long, knotted braids, tied like armor around a broad chest the color of silver, while silver chains of chiming hooks glinted around a muscular waist.

"Young Queen," murmured the demon.

"Lord Ha'an," I said, stunned to see him. The last time had been inside the prison veil. We had come to a truce, of sorts. An alliance, even. I had promised to return to the veil and help him subdue the other demon lords, should they break into his section of the prison and try to conquer his people, the Mahati.

Apparently, those demons clans did not get along. Apparently, they had *never* gotten along. Only the Reaper Kings had kept the peace and managed to unite them under a common cause.

Survival. War. Death.

Grant and I had sealed the breach in the prison veil that had set the Mahati free on earth. If Lord Ha'an was here, though . . .

"Oh, God," I said to him, horrified. "The prison is open."

"Not exactly," he said quietly, and released me with great care. I looked past him, around him—and found that we stood on a vast stone veranda filled with tropical plants, burbling fountains, and a small wading pool where several well-endowed and very naked human women were lounging with drinks in their hands. They gave me a disinterested look—and didn't seem to notice the seven-foot-tall demon standing in their midst.

I stared, blinking. "Where the hell are we?"

"An island on your world." Lord Ha'an touched my shoulder with the tips of his long fingers. "Come. We must talk. Quickly."

His concern was palpable. I glanced around for the boys. No sign of Zee, Raw, or Aaz—but Dek and Mal appeared from the shadows between some potted plants and slithered toward me with an urgency that made my chest tighten even more. I scooped them up to my shoulders, and Lord Ha'an exhaled slowly, bowing his head to them.

"My Kings," he said, and the two little demons crooned at him with a cold, melodic trill. Not for the first time, I had a *what the hell* moment, wondering what it was, exactly, that made a warrior like Lord Ha'an act so deferential to two little demons who weren't much bigger than snakes and whose favorite hobbies were eating M&Ms and teddy bears and singing classic Bon Jovi.

We walked across the veranda toward a stone rail shrouded in thick vines. Exotic blooms swayed in a warm, gentle breeze that washed over my body, carrying a sweet scent like honey and sugar and the sea. I inhaled deeply. I felt nauseous.

When we reached the rail, I looked down and saw a startlingly blue ocean between the craggy slopes of a tropical, lush hillside. I wondered if we were in Hawaii, and found that idea just plain weird.

Ha'an stood at the rail, gazing out at the ocean with a thoughtfulness that seemed both wistful and uneasy.

"You still care for this world," he said. "You still wish to save it."

"Of course," I told him, suddenly afraid to ask the questions burning inside me. "It is a good world, with good people. You love your Mahati. I love my humans."

He grunted. "*Love* is not a word my kind use."

"But you know it."

"I know enough." Ha'an glanced at me, then looked away. "I admire your loyalty . . . but hate it, as well. We must feed or die."

"You have no qualms about murdering a race of people who are just as intelligent, passionate, and . . . *cultured* . . . as you? That gives you no pause, whatsoever?"

Ha'an raised his brow. "You think we are cultured?"

"I know it. I saw it, when I was in the prison veil."

He snorted but not in derision. "What do you wish me to say, young Queen? Yes, it gives me pause. But as I have told you, it is not just flesh that feeds us but the energy of the kill. The pain. The fear."

"You didn't always have humans to hunt."

"No," he said, quietly. "We changed, after the war. Our . . . *needs* . . . changed."

I wondered what that meant. Before I could ask, Ha'an drew in a deep breath and pointed at the ocean. "Where I was born was never like this. It was a desert land, sharp and hard. Beautiful, in its own way. I have found other places on this world that remind me of it, but this . . . this is also comforting."

"Other places? Places you visited a month ago, when the veil broke?"

"No. I had no time, then. Nor has it been a month, inside the prison. Much shorter. Days, perhaps. Time moves differently there."

I stared. "How long have you been free?"

"Two sunrises," he said, looking down at me. "I thought you knew."

Dek and Mal stilled. Cold hit, followed by a streak of heat that blossomed in my chest. I gritted my teeth, and reached up to touch those two little heads buried against my neck. I wanted very much to throttle them.

"No," I said, in a hard voice. "I did not know."

"Ah," said Lord Ha'an, and his long fingers wrapped around the rail. "Then it is very good we talk now, before the others arrive."

"Others?"

"All the demon lords are free," he said in a soft voice, and the stone rail cracked beneath his hands. "We were summoned, and brought here by our Kings."

I tapped my armored fist against my thigh. "You were *summoned*."

"Shall I repeat myself?"

"No need." I glanced across the veranda as Zee finally pushed free of the shadows deep within a tangle of vines. I had felt him there, watching—wondering when he would finally have the courage to show his face.

He gave me an assessing, unapologetic look—and I said, "Two days? Two *fucking* days?"

"You, sick," Zee replied, sparing Lord Ha'an a hard glance. "Not ready."

"So this is what you were doing while you were gone," I snapped. "Bringing demons into this world. For what reason?"

"Control," Ha'an said, and the rail finally crumbled beneath his tight, strained grip. "Preemptive control. Promises kept. We all felt our Kings fall free of their bonds. It was like being struck in the heart with a blade. When that happened, the rings inside the prison, those walls separating the clans . . . began crumbling. It would have been war if our Kings had not come. My people would have been massacred for their flesh."

"Your Mahati are powerful warriors."

"We would have been massacred," he said, again. "We almost were."

"The Shurik are strong," Zee said, glancing over his shoulder as Raw and Aaz loped across the veranda toward us. "The Yorana and the Osul also strong, but not like Shurik."

"Why?" I asked them, as my head began hurting. "You act surprised."

"Not surprised," he muttered. "Disappointed."

Disgust flickered over Lord Ha'an's face. "They ate their children to survive, then kept having more children. To raise as food."

The urge to vomit was so strong, I had to lean on the rail. "What?"

"Survival," Zee muttered, also looking ill. "Adults survive, can always make more babies, when free."

"Free and strong," Ha'an said to him. "Lord Draean is more ruthless now than ever. He will not be easily appeased this time."

"Will kill him," Zee said. "Will shatter his bones."

"There is no one left to replace him. You kill him, you kill *all* the Shurik."

I held up my hands. "I don't understand."

Ha'an stared at me—clearly surprised—and then gave Zee a hard look. "You have been lax with your Queen."

Zee growled at him. "Silence."

"I cannot be silent," he replied. "Punish me. Kill me. But I will speak the truth. She should already know these things."

"What things?" I persisted.

Ha'an shook his head, and even though every bit of him was inhuman, his posture, his eyes, retained some indefinable quality that was emotional, and familiar.

"I derive strength from my people," he said to me. "Every one of them is bonded to me. It is so for every demon lord. We are as strong as those beneath us. But the reverse is also true. What we are defines those with whom we are bonded. And if a demon lord dies without there being one to pass on this responsibility, our people will die. Not immediately, but soon enough. For we are one."

Lord Ha'an looked at Zee. "Every demon lord, in the past, shared a bond with our Reaper Kings. We fed them our strength, and the strength of our people . . . and in turn, they gave *us* strength and defined us with their hearts. It united the clans. It made us . . . invincible. Until the war with the Aetar."

I took a slow breath. "Zee. Did you bring the demon lords here to bond with you and the others?"

"Only way," he muttered. "Must control the army."

"The bond must be freely given, but there is much anger for those years spent in the prison veil." Lord Ha'an hesitated, looking from me to Zee. "And forgive me, but you are no longer the Vessels for the power that united us, before. Your Queen is, and they will *not* follow a human. *You*, my Kings, have nothing to offer them that they cannot take on their own."

"So why haven't they started *taking*?" I asked, deeply uneasy.

"Caution. Curiosity," Zee muttered, as Raw and Aaz gave him grim looks. "Memory is strong. Will test us first."

"I'm surprised they didn't already try."

"Too distracted by the bounty before them," Ha'an said in a cool voice. "They have been feeding these last two days. As have I, young Queen."

I remembered the last time I'd seen the Mahati feed. "You killed people?"

"Only the old and weak," he replied, as though discussing a lame deer in the woods. "It was quick, clean."

Zee grunted. "Moment for peace, Ha'an. Need to speak with our Queen."

The Mahati lord bowed his head and backed away. I stopped him, with a brush of my fingers against his arm. "Who are those women out there, and why aren't they frightened?"

"Lord K'ra'an left them here," he replied, in a voice that was a little too careful. "No one ever fears him. Until it is too late."

Ha'an held my gaze a moment longer, as if making sure I understood. When I nodded, he turned without another word and strode away, long fingers flexing through the air, that silver chain around his waist chiming, delicately. I watched him, then leaned back on the rail, staring at the boys. Zee met my gaze, but Raw and Aaz studied their claws. Dek and Mal were too quiet on my shoulders.

"Will not apologize," Zee muttered.

"I don't want an apology," I shot back. "I want to know how you're planning on controlling a bunch of baby-eating demon lords."

He dragged claws over his round belly. "Will do what it takes, Maxine. Must be cold. Must survive."

"Like Lord Draean survived?"

"No," Zee spat, and held out his hand. I hesitated, and set my left palm flat against his. Human flesh, pressed against demon. Fingers and claws. Though I had held his hand many times before, the differences, in that moment, seemed stark and cold.

"Forgive us," Zee whispered, and his claws closed, biting into my flesh, drawing blood. I grunted, but did not pull away.

Behind him, out of sight on the other side of the veranda, I heard voices. Deep, masculine, slithering through the air and across my spine. Raw and Aaz stiffened and turned to face in that direction.

"Maxine." Zee drew my attention back to him. "Are we of one heart?"

I felt sick to my stomach. "Why are you asking me?"

"Matters. Life or death. Yes or no." He pulled me closer, staring into my eyes with an urgency that frightened me as much as those voices. "One heart, or five?"

"One," I said, confused and uneasy. "It's always been one."

Zee closed his eyes. On my shoulders, Dek and Mal trembled. So did I. I felt very strange, at that moment: light-headed, skin prickling, short of breath. My armor tingled, growing warm.

When Zee leaned in and licked the blood off my hand, I couldn't move. I couldn't move even when Raw and Aaz took his place, their long black tongues rough upon my skin. Mal uncoiled, slithering down my arm, licking the cuts. Finally, Dek . . . though he showed the greatest reluctance.

Deep inside the darkness stirred, a slow swell beneath my soul. When I tried to push it down, my *will* slid over it, slippery as ice. I tried again and again, but it was futile. I could not touch that power, not even to control it.

I heard a sigh inside my mind, a whisper without words.

And then my bond with Grant flickered, and was joined with . . . something else.

A heaviness, like iron weights hanging from the bottoms of my ribs. Not dragging me down, but anchoring me. Rooting my body to the earth, to each heartbeat, as if I were some . . . unmovable giant.

But the anchor disappeared as five pulses surrounded my heart—literal pulses, as though five claws were tapping the inside of my chest, creating five separate rhythms that flooded me, threaded through me, each one harboring a wild roar of emotion that I was utterly unprepared to experience. I lost myself for a moment, swept away, tumbling down a hole made of impossible hunger and concern, and frustration.

I took a deep breath, blinking hard as my vision blurred. "What have you done to me?" I could barely speak, and those words sounded like gibberish on my suddenly thick tongue.

"No time," Zee whispered, pulling me close. "Forgive us."

"You already said that," I muttered, trying to regain my balance. I felt sick, but he was right: There was no time for that because I glimpsed movement at the other end of the veranda.

The demon lords had come.

CHAPTER 18

"LIFE is no better than a game of cards," my mother once said. "The hand you're dealt is fate. The way you play it is free will."

I was sixteen when she spoke those words. It was near sunset, golden light diffuse and warm. We stood on a hill overlooking Roncinha, one of the largest slums in Rio de Janeiro. It resembled a teetering, steaming pile of matchboxes, stacked and glued together, painted with the occasional splash of bright green and blue.

We'd only been in Brazil a week. My mother had never explored much of South America, and had decided, seemingly on a whim, to take us down there—crawling through the jungle, riding motorboats up brown rivers, exploring lost temples, listening to live bands on sweaty nights while eating hot *feijoada*.

"Lots of people will tell you, baby, that you have no choices. Sometimes you'll tell yourself the same thing. Your back will be to the wall, and you won't know what to do." My mother looked me dead in the eyes. "When that happens, stop. Stop and breathe. You *always* have a choice.

Maybe not an easy one, but you can play the cards, baby. It's your hand. No one else will know what you do."

"Some hands can't be won," I remembered saying to her.

"Well, then," she said, smiling, looking away at that last light burning over the mountains. "You take out the other players."

❦

I'D learned, from a young age, to be wary of the little things in life. A tiny spider could kill with a bite. A small knife could cut a throat. A demon the size of a child could punch a hole through a man's body with one blow.

Unfortunately, it wasn't just size—but also the *ordinariness* of a thing that could mask the most danger.

So when I saw that one of the demon lords was no taller than me and looked perfectly human, I pegged him for the one who would be the most trouble. The one who would try to kill me first.

He led the way, with the sort of confidence I usually associated with businessmen at power lunches, swaggering around with cell phones in one hand, and fist-bumping golf buddies with the other. He even wore a suit, gray as a tombstone, and had muddy blond hair, muddy brown eyes, and lips that were a little too red—matching the color of his ruddy cheeks.

He scared me. But he also made me angry. I wanted to kill him. I really did. That sudden, visceral hatred came from five sources, five wild heartbeats, flooding through me like a spilled barrel of boiling water: clean, hot, and overwhelming. I latched onto that anger, though. It was better than fear.

"Lord Draean," Zee rasped.

The demon smiled: all teeth, brilliant and white, and sharp. "How sweet to hear your voice, my King."

Sweet like poison, I thought; his lie so obvious, so condescending, it was the same as a challenge. I felt the challenge, in my bones. In those five heartbeats, strumming against my ribs.

Then, the demon looked at me. Something cold and black slipped into his gaze—so devastating, so filled with raw hunger and loathing, that if I'd been anyone else—lived a gentler life by any degree—I might have fallen on my knees. Instead, my soul braced itself, and inside me the darkness rose, and though I could not touch it in that moment, it felt cleaner and *better* than the rot of the creature staring back at me.

"Sweet," said the demon, drawing out that word with a sucking sound. "But not as sweet as *this* creature. Tell me, Zee'akka . . . is she good enough to fuck?"

Raw and Aaz snarled. I stepped forward, right hand flexing. "You couldn't handle me, you piece of shit."

Lord Draean stared, and again, I felt the power behind those eyes, power hidden in his human flesh: a penetrating strength immense and barely controlled, and burning with madness and fury.

A laugh escaped him, pricking the air as though his voice were made of needles.

"Lord Ha'an squealed a story about a Queen," he murmured. "Grunting a little tale about a human woman with a grip around our Reaper Kings. I did not believe him. I still do not. You are thunder, and nothing else. A woman who will be *fucked*, and nothing else."

Dek and Mal hissed. I smiled. "Then come fuck me. And we'll see, won't we?"

I spoke those words with an unfamiliar viciousness that made me feel too good. I could taste the barely suppressed rage in each syllable and breath, and I craved the cruelty of a fight with this demon. I wanted to make him scream with pain.

I wanted to *feed* from his pain.

Rage flickered through Draean's face, and something moved, something hideous that flowed just beneath his skin.

I saw it, a round object pushing up, distorting his cheek, then making his right eyeball bulge out as it passed upward like a golf ball traveling through the vein on his forehead. Bone cracked. Blood seeped from his nostrils and ears. I had the horrible feeling I might see a man's head explode.

Zee bared his teeth. "Come, Draean. Fight us. Not our Queen."

"No, fight *me*." I curled my right hand into a fist. "Let me humiliate you."

Lord Draean lurched forward, but was grabbed by the demon standing behind him. Tall, lean, humanoid: two arms, two legs, standing upright and clothed in a loose, clinging material that looked like black silk. Triangular gemstones resembling massive rubies had been embedded in his muscular chest; and his skin was the color of cherries, a dark, bleeding red.

The demon's face was both masculine and beautiful. Hauntingly so. I could not say how or why, just that staring at him, once I started—drinking in his presence, once I noticed him—seemed like the only thing worth doing. Except I knew better and kept telling myself that—again and again, until all I felt when I looked at him was cold distance.

"Let go, K'ra'an," rasped Draean.

"Calm yourself," murmured the handsome demon, giving the boys and me an assessing look. "I do not think you want to fight that woman."

"Let them battle," growled the last unfamiliar lord, crouched on all fours with his spiked tail lashing the air. Massive pads of metallic armor rubbed against a long, muscular back, and a helmet covered part of his face, revealing leonine features and ice blue eyes. He resembled a cat, or wolf—maybe a combination of both—and was huge, maybe six feet tall at the shoulder and more than twelve feet long from nose to tail. Tiny hooked claws covered his legs, jutting from beneath his sleek steel gray fur.

"Oanu," murmured Lord Ha'an, bringing up the rear. "Do not goad Draean."

The demon flashed him a toothy grin and settled back on his massive haunches. "I goad him because I think she might win."

Lord Draean gave him a hateful look. "For that, I will go into your territory and steal your Osul to be my slaves."

Oanu spat at him. "We will kill you first."

"Not if we own your bodies."

Zee slammed his fist into the ground, punching through solid stone and making a crater large enough for me to stick my leg into. I felt the impact, not just in my feet but in my chest. An emotional collision: a spike of rage, seething and terrible, and hungry.

Not my rage. Not mine.

My left hand stung. I clenched it into a fist, a different kind of unease filling me—one that had nothing to do with those demon lords.

"Fight us," Zee snapped. "Fight *us*, if must. But not each other. Never survive without each other."

Lord K'ra'an rolled his wrists in a delicate motion, gliding sideways across the veranda. Black silk hissed against his skin, and the gems embedded in his chest gleamed.

"You made this speech before," he said. "I was a child when my father pledged his blood to you . . . and when he died and passed his bond to me, you said those same words. After all these years, I thought perhaps you might have . . . composed something *different*."

"Truth never changes," Zee retorted, digging his claws into the stone. "Truth, then. Truth now. Will prove ourselves, if must. But to you, each other, must be honor. Clans not fight clans. Lost too much already to lose to each other."

Oanu grunted and glanced at Ha'an, who did not seem to notice. He was too busy watching Lord Dracan, whose face was even redder, the golf ball–sized lump moving through his throat into his chest. Blood continued trickling from his nose, and the crotch of his gray slacks was stained red, as well. I didn't want to think about what was happening inside that body to make it bleed from all its orifices.

"Are you proposing peace?" he asked, incredulous, as blood tricked over his lips and ran down his chin. "Or are you asking for the same promise we gave you, all those years ago?"

"Asking for faith," Zee told him, as Raw and Aaz moved sideways, flanking me. "Asking for trust."

Lord K'ra'an shook his head. Lord Draean laughed outright, blood spitting from his mouth, pouring faster from his ears and nose. His face was a mess of blood, and the stain in his pants spread down his leg.

"We pledged ourselves to you because we were at war," he said with disdain. "When the war was over, we could not break our pledge . . . but we hunted, and we conquered, and so our bondage was *tolerable*. Now? Where is the war?"

"There is none," added Lord K'ra'an. "We are free, Zee'akka. We are *free* of *you* and your brothers."

"Free?" Zee bared his teeth in a terrible smile. "Too *stupid* to be free. Will fight, will feed, and then?"

"War and conquer. You taught us that."

"Conquer who? Other clans? War each other? And when Aetar come, who will fight *them*? Will you stand alone?"

"You lost to the Aetar," said K'ra'an, his elegant hands still making those delicate motions. He only had four fingers, each one tipped with hooked claws. "You lost, and we were all imprisoned. You will lose again. Our faith is already gone."

"Not mine," said Lord Ha'an, stepping forward. "I believe."

"You *would*. You and the Lady Whore, wherever she's hiding now." Draean's lip curled, and he gave all the boys a challenging look. "Maybe there *should* be a king again, but not you five. You had your time. We gave you everything, and you lost. You even lost your power. You are no longer the Vessels. I can feel it."

"Can you?" Zee asked in a deadly soft voice.

Draean tugged on his bloodstained suit, his smile pure cold menace. "I'll prove it by taking your human woman for my own. I will fuck her from the inside out and make you watch."

Like hell you will, I thought, and suffered a blast of rage so pure and hot, I thought my innards would catch on fire. Raw and Aaz tore spikes from their own backs, holding them like spears. Zee snarled, digging his claws into the veranda stone.

"You will not touch her," he rasped—and a strange sensation sank through me, as though a hand was reaching into my body, pulling on the shadow entity coiled deep beneath my soul. I could not stop it. I tried, with all my strength, battling that inexorable draw of power and darkness.

You cannot fight this, came that whisper. *You gave your Kings a hand inside your heart. They own you now. You are their weapon, just as they were yours. Your heart, guided by their hearts.*

Confusion hit me, then horror. I tried to speak, but my body refused to listen. My body refused me *everything.* I just stood there, face impassive, eyes dull, *screaming* on the inside. Before, in the past, I had found myself unable to stop that darkness from possessing my body . . . but this time was different.

It was not the dark entity that possessed me.

It was the boys.

I was powerless and oddly removed, too. As if I were not in my own skin but hanging back at a distance, feeling the boys draw the darkness from me like a megaton tsunami, forcing it down a narrow path into a vein twisted with shadows gushing from my body . . . into their five hearts.

And all I could think was, *You little bastards tricked me.*

Zee, Raw, and Aaz shuddered, eyes fluttering shut. Dek and Mal crooned on my shoulders, trembling with pleasure. It was all I could do not to tremble alongside them. I knew what they were feeling, and not *only* because I had ridden that same wave of power.

I could feel their hearts.

Whatever they had done, their emotions were now mine. I wondered if this was what they had felt for the last ten thousand years: the heart of their Hunter, beating and loving and hating, like a ghost inside their chests. Confusing them, making them wonder if what they felt was real or someone else. Forcing them to pick apart their own hearts to be sure.

Eventually wearing them down, so that it didn't matter anymore if what they felt was real. It was all the same. Just one heart.

What they felt now was ecstasy. Rapture. Pleasure that bordered on agony.

I was in agony.

They will never let this go, whispered the darkness. *As much as they hated us, they loved our power.*

So we will let them play again at Kings. For now.

For now, while it amuses us.

Keep your fucking power, I snarled in my mind—but the darkness rested in my throat like the promise of a song, and I started to laugh. It was not my laughter. I was only a passenger, unable to stop that fierce wild sound from spilling out of my mouth—a sound shaped like a tongue tasting the air.

I scented anger and unease from the demon lords. I scented jealousy.

Zee and the others started laughing, as well: sharp, rasping sounds, like a chain saw born from a giggle. It sounded insane. It sounded like the boys were on the edge of doing something crazy. Which they totally were. I knew what that darkness could do to *me*. I remembered every death and act of destruction I'd caused while under its influence. I remembered the joy I'd taken in that death. Pure, beautiful joy.

I had resisted, though. I had fought back.

The boys had no intention of doing the same.

"Draean," whispered Zee.

Lord Draean slopped with blood, watching him with hard, bulging eyes. Five minutes before, he had been slightly overweight. Now his skin sagged, as though all the fat had been sucked out of his body. He had trouble standing, leaning over as if he was about to collapse.

Zee and the boys, however, seemed larger, sleeker, as though the rough edges of their skins were being polished away.

"Draean," whispered Zee, again, as Raw and Aaz edged forward, dragging those spikes through the stone floor. *"Draean, come to us."*

The demon lord trembled but did not move. K'ra'an and Oanu backed away from him. Only Ha'an remained, watching Zee, then me.

My legs moved. I did not lurch or stumble, but instead walked with grace, like a dancer, across the floor toward Lord Draean.

But it was not my own free will. I had not intended to

take that first step toward the demon lord, and once I started, I could not stop.

"Bring him," Zee said, and this time the power had faded from his voice but not the command.

I started reaching for Lord Draean before I even knew what I was doing.

I had some free will, though. When he tried to knock me aside, I punched him in the gut. He bent over, grunting, his blood-soaked shirt clinging to his now-jutting ribs. Up close, he smelled like a meat grinder. His eyes were horrible.

"I'm going to kill you," he whispered to me. "I'm going to eat your bones."

"You and a million other jackasses," I muttered, and grabbed the back of his neck, shoving him toward Raw and Aaz, who caught him as he staggered to his knees. Blood poured from his mouth when he hit the ground, as though the impact had jogged his guts loose.

"Power, you feel," Zee rasped. "Power, in *us*."

Draean laughed, wiping his wet mouth. "Fine. You have power. But what does that even mean? Nothing, Zee'akka. Nothing at all."

I smiled, and this time it was all me. "Do you want to die? Do you want your entire people to die?"

"Better than being *their* slaves," he said, as his left eyeball began sliding free of its socket. "Better to die in defiance than live at their whim."

"It was not like that," Oanu growled, slamming the tip of his tail into the ground. "We were not slaves."

"They owned us," K'ra'an said. "Is that not the very definition?"

"We were at war."

"Exactly," Draean stabbed his finger into the stones, and it crumpled as if his bones were turning to mush. "And where is the war now? Where is the purpose to all that power? Power is nothing without an eye on the horizon. A hunger. A need. No war, no need. And this world is *ripe*. This world is soft, and lush. We will feed a long time. We will make it last. And if it the Aetar come, we will fight free, with alliances of our own choosing . . . that have nothing to do with you. We have seen the consequence of your failure. All that great and *mighty* strength was not enough to save us. You were weak. You were *always* weak."

He glanced over his shoulder at me. "Nothing has changed. Except that now you must draw your power from a human. That is pathetic."

"She is the Vessel," said Lord Ha'an, softly.

"She is nothing but flesh and blood," replied Draean. "If that great power chose to inhabit a pregnant human woman, then I have no fear of it and no respect."

His words. His words hit me.

My world stopped. My entire world.

Draean frowned at me, spitting out several teeth. "Why are you looking at me like that?"

I tore my gaze from him, staring at Zee. He showed nothing on his face, but I felt regret pour into my heart. Regret and resolve. Behind those emotions, though, was the darkness and its hunger, spreading through the demon like an infection.

"You knew," I said, stung with a betrayal so deep I could hardly stand it.

"Got what we need," he rasped. "Leave us."

"No—" I began, but the armor tingled, and I felt a tug on my body that was familiar, and cold.

Just before I was forced into the void, Zee stepped forward and slammed his fist into Draean's chest. Bone cracked. Blood and other fluids gushed from the hole, as though his innards had already liquefied and were waiting for an outlet. The smell was terrible. I felt like I was going to vomit.

Which I did, moments later, when I fell through the void into the Seattle apartment, sprawled on all fours and holding my stomach.

Dek spilled onto the ground beside me, as did Mal. Both of them, hissing softly. I shoved them away from me, hissing back. Furious and hurt.

That darkness still oozed, an endless snake uncoiling inside my veins.

Emotions not my own continued to pummel me. Five heartbeats, filled with hunger and rage—and concern. I tried to push it all aside but could do no such thing. I could barely handle my own feelings.

I was pregnant. I was going to be a mother.

"Maxine," Grant said, behind me.

I burst into tears.

CHAPTER 19

I was still crying thirty minutes later, but the tears had slowed to nothing but damp eyes and the sniffles. So had the outpouring of that dark power, which was quiet now, resting. Whatever the boys were doing, it didn't involve any shock, awe, and destruction. Not yet, anyway.

I lay in bed, wearing nothing but my underwear. Grant was with me, his head resting on my stomach. Every now and then, he would hum. Occasionally, he drew in a shuddering breath.

"How could I not have noticed?" he whispered. "When I was healing you, after the fall. I should have seen."

"You were distracted."

"I should have seen," he said again. I didn't mind. I kept wondering the same thing about myself. Wasn't I supposed to be aware of these things? Shouldn't I have known I was pregnant?

Weren't the boys supposed to tell me—instead of tricking me into giving over control of my body? Weren't they supposed to give me some kind of warning instead of playing *demon knows best*?

How could I ever trust them again? Or was that a moot point now?

I rubbed my aching head and pressed a tissue to my nose. "Must be early on."

"Very," he said, in a tight voice. "Just a little light. Such a tiny little light."

I buried my fingers in his hair. Grant sighed and crawled up the mattress until the entire length of his body pressed against mine. His arms were warm, and very strong. I held him as tightly as I could.

Dek and Mal were on the floor, coiled around each other. Eyes closed. Pretending to be resting. I felt uneasy with their presence. On guard. Maybe they were there to protect me . . . or maybe it was to keep an eye on me for reasons that had nothing to do with my safety. I couldn't be sure.

The longer I lay here, though, the easier it was for me to sort their five hearts from mine. Zee's emotions were the strongest, the texture of them like a chewed fingernail dragged over sensitive flesh. Raw and Aaz, on the other hand, were as much twins emotionally as they were physically: a guitar wire strung between two posts, strumming constantly.

Dek and Mal did not share each other's emotions in the same way. Dek was softer. Mal harder. Like the difference in warm dark chocolate—and candy stored in the refrigerator, filled with nuts.

The irony wasn't lost on me. I had grieved losing my bond with the boys, and now I had a new one with them. Different. Not better.

Not better for me, anyway.

"I'm hungry," I said, and covered my face. "How can I even say that?"

"You're going to have a baby. Of course you're hungry."

"I don't know if it's my hunger or theirs." I peered at him between my fingers. "I'm scared."

"I'm terrified," he muttered, and gave Dek and Mal a flinty glare. "You two. Leave."

They raised their heads, looking at him as if he *must* be kidding.

"You abused her trust," Grant snapped. "This is not a game. She is not one of your toys."

Mal hissed, and the anger that flooded from him was hot and rough, and indignant. I didn't like it—it scared me, in fact—and I turned that anger back on the little demon by grabbing the clock off the nightstand and throwing it at him. Dek darted sideways, but Mal got hit in the head. I reached for the lamp next.

Mal hissed—and my arm froze.

I couldn't move. It stunned me all over again—and this time *I* was the one who was furious. I snarled at the demon, and Grant muttered ugly words beneath his breath.

Dek gave his brother a hateful look and bit his tail. Mal snapped at him, but suddenly I could move again. Instead of reaching for the lamp, I leaned against Grant's chest, trembling with anger as he wrapped his arms around me.

Regret poured into my heart—from Dek.

From Mal, I sensed the same, but to a lesser degree. He wanted to protect me but not here. This was more of the same, but somewhere, elsewhere, the demon lords were free—and that called to him. The need to *punish* them, and feel their fear . . . called to him. He *yearned* for it.

189

It wasn't just Mal I was feeling. Each of those five heart-beats was an earthquake inside me, a tremor filled with loneliness and hunger, and fury. Shaking me down, as though my heart had split into five fractured pieces.

Disconcerting. I felt lost in my own body. I felt possessed.

"I'm sorry I hit you," I told Mal, hearing strain in my voice and hating that. "But don't you understand why I'm upset? I'm *pregnant*, and you didn't tell me. Not only did you *not* tell me . . . you *did* something to me."

Grant's arms tightened. "Get out of here."

Mal gave us a long look and slid into the shadows beneath some magazines, disappearing as though a hole was in our floor. Dek hesitated, his little ears pressed flat against his skull.

"You, too," I said.

Dek sighed and grabbed a half-eaten teddy bear with his mouth. He dragged it over to me, placing it on the edge of the mattress. Stuffing leaked. A glass eye had gone missing. He nudged the broken bear into my hands and rested his chin beside it. His gaze was so mournful.

"What happened?" I whispered to him, not even sure what I was asking, just that some terrible heartbreak was bubbling inside me, and his was the kind gesture—that note of sweetness—that I needed so much.

Dek didn't answer me with a song, but his heart was gentle in mine. I scratched behind his ears and leaned forward to kiss his snout.

"Why can't you be less lovable?" I asked him, tears burning my eyes again. I wanted to hate him. I wanted to be angry with them all but just couldn't.

Not yet.

Dek gave me a toothy grin. I was taken aback by the burst of love that flowed from him: explosive and hot—and infected with the dark hunger drawn from the entity living beneath my soul. A strange circle of emotion and power, deadly and confusing.

Dek licked my cheek. Then, before I could say a word, he slid into the shadows beneath the comforter and vanished. I wanted to know where—on the other side of the world, with his brothers, on the moon.

Grant let out his breath. I turned, facing him.

We stared at each other. Just stared. Words were worthless in that moment. I'd seen television shows and movies where people cried and laughed, and had meltdowns in each other's arms, but that was fake, and this was us, and I'd found that more could be said in our silences than in colloquy.

He pushed a strand of hair from my face. "You okay?"

"I don't know." I wrapped my hand around his wrist, rubbing my thumb against his palm. Touching him soothed me, and so did the warmth that pushed through our bond.

"It's strange," I said quietly. "I feel them inside me. All five, right now."

"I can see the bond," Grant's gaze flicked from the crown of my head, down to my chest. "Five shadows. Five . . . hooks."

"Can you break them away from me?"

He looked so grim. "I want to say yes, but they're . . . deep in you, Maxine. It reminds me of our bond, only . . . more tangled. To get them loose will require extreme care."

"Extreme," I echoed. "What happens if you're *not* extreme?"

"You could lose pieces of yourself. Maybe. Remember, I'm no expert. This is only . . . instinct."

I trusted his instincts. If he said breaking the bond would be dangerous, then I believed him. But I didn't think I could live like this. Not forever. Not now, with a baby inside me.

The boys are guided by the strength of the Hunter's heart.

Those words. Those words I'd heard so often. Now it was *my* turn to be guided by *them*, but I didn't like what I was feeling. I didn't like all that anger flooding me, anger that was so close to hate it made my skin crawl. I was afraid the anger would become part of me, permanently. If I lived with the boys for ten thousand years, maybe it would. Perhaps that was what had happened to them, once upon a time. Maybe, in another life.

"I feel what they feel," I said. "It's all so close to me, I don't know what's real."

Grant held me tighter. "You know."

I shook my head. "The boys are angry and spoiling for a fight, like it's some grudge they've been holding. I wish I knew . . . I wish I knew if they felt that way while imprisoned on me . . . or if this just started with their freedom. Maybe those demon lords."

I hated the idea that all these years they might have been resentful of me, my mother, all us women . . . full of anger they could never express, for being imprisoned on bodies they could never escape.

Grant studied my eyes. "It must be strange to feel anything at all."

"What's strange is that their emotions are so familiar.

So . . . human." I reached behind me for that teddy bear, and flopped it between us. "I don't know why I'm surprised. Zee and the others have always expressed themselves through emotion. *Feeling* their feelings, though . . ." I had to stop, and fussed with the stuffing leaking from the bear's eye. "Makes me wonder if all demons share that . . . emotional vocabulary."

If they do, I thought, *then what really separates any of us?*

Grant seemed to read my mind—or maybe my own emotions were just that transparent. "Speaking the same language, emotional or otherwise, doesn't mean anything, Maxine. The boys shouldn't have done this to you."

"Gah," I said, squeezing the teddy bear's head. "I hate thinking about it."

"Okay." Grant gently loosened my fingers from the bear. "Let's think about how we're going to be parents."

Heat spread through me. I thought about my mother . . . and on the heels of that, my earliest memory of wondering who my father might be. Sitting in the station wagon at a gas station, watching some man carrying his son on his shoulders and thinking that was weird—because I didn't know any better. Asking my mother. Hearing the word *dad* for the first time.

"Most girls in my family never know their fathers," I said to Grant, feeling vaguely uneasy, and afraid.

He pulled me even closer. "That's not going to happen here."

I took his hand and placed it on my stomach. "No. It won't."

He briefly closed his eyes. "We need a plan."

"Yes," I said, then, softer: "Maybe I deserve this. I never

realized what it was for the boys, being imprisoned. I probably still don't get it. But if it's anything like this . . . I don't know how they stood it for all those years."

Grant gave me a hard, incredulous look. "You know what, Maxine? I don't care. I really don't. I want them back on your body, imprisoned. Short of that, I want to break the bond they've got sunk into you and make sure they can never force you again to do anything against your will."

"What if this is necessary? What if this is what it takes to control that army?"

"From what you told me, nothing's going to control them. They're not going to listen to Zee and the others."

"Not unless they terrify them. Or just kill them."

"If *we* killed them?" Grant asked bluntly. "What if? We could do it. I could. The Messenger."

"It's not just the demon lords. You take them out, you might kill an entire race."

"That's what they're going to do to us." Grant's gaze softened, troubled. "Don't think I'm saying this lightly, because I'm not. But I'm talking about survival."

So had Zee. So had Lord Ha'an. All anyone wanted to do was simply live another day, with food and peace, and safety. The problem was competing needs. The problem was uncertainty and a lack of trust, and solutions.

"I could have killed the Mahati," I said. "But they're just . . . people, Grant. Different, but not that different. I don't know what the others are like, but . . . genocide?"

"I'll do what it takes."

I pushed him away. "Zee said the same thing."

"Then we agree on something," he muttered, reaching for me again. "Maxine, don't. Come back."

I let him pull me close but didn't relax.

"I've always liked the name Lucy," he said.

"Shut up," I muttered.

"How about Agatha?"

"Be serious."

"Helga?"

I poked his chest. "Focus."

"I can multitask," he replied, capturing my finger. "Okay, none of those names. And I'm not ruling out killing those demons. I won't, Maxine. Neither should you."

"I never thought I'd hear you say that."

"I had a revelation today," he murmured. "And then another one, half an hour ago. My priorities have changed. I'm feeling particularly ruthless at the moment."

I rested my hand on my stomach. "Do you think all this is hurting . . . her?"

He was silent a moment. "I don't know."

"I wish my mother were here."

"I wish *my* mother were here."

Both of us snorted and looked at each other. Grant kissed my nose.

"I'm happy," he said. "I'm terrified, and beside myself. And I love you."

I gave him a crooked smile. "Are we going to be okay?"

"You bet." But something strained passed through his gaze, and he chewed the inside of his cheek. "There's something you need to see."

"I hate it when you say things like that."

"I hate saying it," he replied, and rolled sideways to pick up the laptop computer that was on the other nightstand. He flipped it open and set it on the bed between us. Minutes later, I was reading the news—specifically, articles relating to mysterious mass killings, all over the world. A small apartment building in Paris was the site of a horrific massacre, in which all residents had been found dead—dismembered, partially eaten. A cruise ship in the Mediterranean had radioed for help when nearly ten people had disappeared, with no evidence except for some bloody spots on the deck—and one severed head.

A nursing home in Montreal was missing five residents. Cadaver dogs had found bits and pieces of them in a nearby park.

"It's a big world," I said, quietly. "This is probably just the tip of the iceberg."

"So you *do* think it's those demon lords who are responsible."

"What I think is that they've been loose for two days, and they're starving—and ruthless. So yes, I'm sure they had a hand in it."

"It feels as though they're being discreet."

I thought about the earthquake in Memphis, wondering if that was still a coincidence. "They're arrogant but not stupid. I'm sure this is a scouting mission for them, a chance to iron out their future with Zee and the boys. Get a feel for what's changed in ten thousand years. Hell, from what I saw, they're probably fighting over what continent each of them will control."

"Are they vulnerable to guns?"

"Don't know. I think there's a difference in strength between the demon lords and those they rule."

"So? What next?"

A deep ache struck my heart, full of sadness. "First

thing we do is break this bond with the boys. Their intentions may have been good—"

Grant grunted.

"—but I won't be controlled. Not now. Not ever."

Because you are a Queen, whispered the darkness, from deep within.

Because I am my mother's daughter, I told it.

My mother's daughter.

My daughter.

It hit me, then. Finally, it hit me. Nothing I had ever felt before, in my life, compared to the determination and resolve that struck me, in that moment. Nothing. All my conflict slipped away, replaced by a straight road, a single path. It was a moment of pure, raw clarity.

Grant was right. Priorities had changed.

I was going to be a mother. I was going to have a baby.

And if I had to, I would kill the entire fucking demon race to keep her safe.

CHAPTER 20

I didn't like slipping into the void, knowing I was pregnant, but there didn't seem to be much alternative. We needed to speak with the Messenger about breaking this bond the boys had sunk into me, and there was only one way to reach her.

Before we left, though, I changed out of my blood-spattered clothes—and went to find Rex. Some volunteers pointed us to the warehouse basement, which was the first place I would have looked anyway. Secrets always seemed to end up underground.

The door was locked, but Grant had keys. Like most basements, it was usually dark, but when we looked down the stairs, a golden light was splashed across the concrete floor. I walked slowly, not wanting to rush Grant as he limped after me—closing and locking the basement door behind him.

The basement was large, filled with huge mechanical equipment from the warehouse's previous life as a furniture manufacturer. At the far end, well away from the stairs, a sagging couch had been set out—surrounded by Tiffany-style lamps and several plywood crates covered in sheets of glittery wrapping paper, like makeshift tablecloths.

Byron sat on one end of the couch, elbows on his knees. He had taken out his earring and was holding it between his fingers with a distant, thoughtful look in his eyes. Mary sprawled beside him, one leg propped on the back of the couch, a sword resting on her stomach. The blade had clean edges and an overdecorated hilt that resembled something out of a fantasy role-player's handbook. When I got close, I saw—sure enough—the word EXCALIBUR stamped on the shining flat surface.

"Grant's woman," said Mary—and then frowned, and sat up quick.

"Hey," I said, feeling nervous about the way she looked at me. "What are you both doing down here?"

"Mary had a bad feeling. So did Rex," replied Byron, tossing his earring on the crate in front of him. "They won't let me leave their sight."

"Good," Grant rumbled, as Mary studied my face and whispered, "Something wicked, something in the shadows comes."

Rex walked from a side room and stopped dead in his tracks. His aura shuddered.

"Fuck," he muttered, staring at me. "They bonded you."

I raised my brow, alarmed at how much he might say in front of Byron. "No swearing in front of children, please."

Byron's mouth softened into the faintest of smiles though that did nothing to erase the concern and confusion in his eyes. Rex crossed the room, watching me.

"You *let* them," he said, incredulous, as if just *seeing* the bond was enough to know exactly how everything had gone down.

Grant sighed, leaning on his cane, shoulder brushing mine. Quiet, warm strength. I soaked it in, listening to our bond—and the bond with the boys, which was still tumultuous, and disturbing. I felt violence from them—and had to steel myself to not be infected with those same emotions. If our roles were reversed, and *I* had been forced to live on *them* and share *their* hearts for ten thousand years, I could not predict how that influence might change me.

I gestured for Rex to come close. Grant and I led him to the stairs.

"The demon lords are loose," I said, trying to pitch my voice low enough that Byron wouldn't hear. "I just watched Draean vomit his guts out."

"Should I be impressed?"

"I need to know more, what their weaknesses are, the way they think."

"No," he snapped, "what you need to do is begin saying your prayers, assuming you believe at all in a compassionate God."

I reached for him. Grant beat me to it, grabbing Rex's collar and twisting that material around his fist. His eyes were pure ice, and his voice quiet as death when he said, "No jokes. Answer the questions."

I had a moment's déjà vu. It reminded me of when I was young with my mother, watching her on those rare, brief occasions when she confronted the demonically possessed in my presence. Specifically, I remembered a backwoods bar, dark, full of possessed men and women. A snowy day. A broken-down car. A trap for us. A test.

The demon stared as though my husband held a bazooka in his hand. "Let go first."

Grant's hand loosened, slowly, without apology. Rex tugged on his collar, giving him an uncertain look.

"I can't tell you much," he said, his aura turning gray as it hugged his skin with tiny nervous flutters. "By the time I was born, stories about the demon lords had been reduced to little more than old tales."

"They are not old tales to me," said a low, feminine voice.

Cool air moved across my neck. Rex stiffened, and so did Grant. For a split second, I forgot that the boys weren't with me, and almost told one of them to go investigate that voice. A strange sense of loss hit me, and vulnerability—all made worse by the intense, daggered emotions flowing through the bond.

I glimpsed movement in the deep shadows behind the old machinery—a massive irregular shape that was deeper and darker than any night. Red eyes glinted like tiny strokes of lightning.

"Blood Mama," I said.

"Hunter. Meet me outside in the parking lot."

WE found Blood Mama sitting inside a red Mercedes. Her human host was a redheaded bombshell; tall and shaped like an hourglass on steroids. Small waist, massive breasts. Her low-cut dress was red, and so was her lipstick.

The shadows around her head and beneath her eyes were purple and black.

Grant slid into the backseat of the car, and I got in up front. The interior smelled like a lemon had exploded. I rolled down the window so that I could breathe. It also gave me the illusion of room: her aura was huge, thunderous, and took up most of the front seat in a billowing, heaving coil of shadows.

Blood Mama gave me a long look. "Hunter. You always were a fool."

"I didn't come here for a lecture. Didn't *you* swear *your* fealty?"

"At least I knew what I was doing."

"So how does it feel?" I shot back. "Having their hearts inside you?"

"The same as it did before," she replied. "Disgusting."

"But you said yes. You were terrified not to."

"While you just have blind faith in their goodness." Blood Mama's lips peeled back in a grotesque laugh, and she glanced at Grant. "How do *you* feel about that?"

He gave her a flinty look. Blood Mama's smile did not fade, but it did grow strained. "They are butchers. You know that. You, with your eyes, can see that shadow."

"I see a shadow in you," Grant replied. "I think I prefer theirs."

Blood Mama's aura flared, and she closed her eyes. I said, "Tell me about the other demon lords. Tell me how this shit started."

"War," she muttered. "We were different, then. All of us. Not peaceful, but at peace. Our worlds were connected by a series of stable gates that led through the Labyrinth. We traded. We shared our cultures."

"Even you?"

She gave me a hateful look. "We had hosts, then. Not human. Other creatures that served our needs. We evolved together, our species beneficial to one another. They were the Puri and we were the Boha."

I let that sink in. "Lord Ha'an said that the demon kind did not always need to feed on pain."

"I hardly remember those days, darling." A smile touched her mouth, but it seemed self-mocking. "Those days are dead. The Puri are dead. All of them. I watched them burn, an entire world destroyed. Not just our world, but others. You think five clans were all there ever was?" Unexpected grief struck her eyes, and she looked away from my stare. "There were twenty worlds in our link. Twenty clans. Billions of lives, lost."

"Who killed them?" Grant asked.

"They have no name," Blood Mama whispered. "We never named them. We spoke of them as wraiths, or a wind made of light. A fistful of lightning, perhaps. No bodies. Nothing to fight. Just a . . . howl."

Chills struck. The darkness, oozing through me, stilled. As though listening.

"Zee and the boys," I said, touching my chest, my heart. "The boys summoned something to stop that . . . howl."

"Those Reaper bastards," she said bitterly. "Their world was farthest from any other. Few went there, few traded with them. Their kind were barbarians and slave hunters. They would send raiding parties through the Labyrinth to invade other worlds and bring back females and children. Sometimes to wed. Sometimes to sacrifice to the God they worshipped."

Blood Mama gave me a haunted look. "The God that is inside you."

It was very quiet inside the car. In my mind, the darkness sighed, and in a slow whisper said, *We were not the God of their vast temples. We were not the God of their dreams. But we heard that world, praying. And though we were too late to save more than a handful, we answered. We left the stars for that answer.*

A mortal is not a star, but a star does not dream. We had never known dreams.

We had never known the hunt, in flesh. We had never hunted pain. We did not know it could be sweet.

I closed my eyes. Grant's hand touched my shoulder and squeezed.

"It possessed Zee and the boys," I said, hoarse. "And then they gathered up the remaining clans, and turned you all into an army."

"An army based on their culture and their values. And all they valued was strength and an ability to fight. The Boha were worthless to them, but they took us in because they did not believe in waste." Blood Mama spat those words. "Once they had us, we all changed. It was slow at first. We didn't realize until it was too late. My kind did not need pain to survive. Just life. Ours was a peaceful symbiosis. No longer. The same with the Shurik. In the old days, they did not eat their hosts. They did not always take hosts, even. They ate plants and algae, and . . ."

She stopped, bowing her head. Her aura slammed against the window, the ceiling of the car, raging against the confines of her body. Lightning flashed inside those roiling shadows.

"All these years," I said softly. "All these fucking years. Why didn't you ever speak of this?"

Blood Mama gave me a grim, sidelong look. "Zee? Why not the others? *They* never told you."

"She's asking you," Grant said.

"This story is agony," she snapped at him. "It is madness. What we were, what we became . . . we lost *everything*. We lost our souls. Lord Draean? He was a swamp slug, a peaceful *nothing*. But after the war, he grew teeth. We *all* grew teeth. We had no choice, and now the Reaper Kings are reaping what they sowed."

I sat back, staring at her. "Lord Draean didn't seem keen on following the boys again. Nor did K'ra'an."

"There will be war," she said, simply. "I always knew there would be. Lord Ha'an is too loyal, and Lord Oanu, too predictable. Draean and K'ra'an always chafed at the yoke."

I looked back at Grant. "We need to stop this. I have to speak with the boys."

Blood Mama gave me a dismissive wave of her hand. "It is done, now. You are nothing but a thing they can use, Hunter. Your opinion means nothing. You might as well let me kill you." A cold smile touched her mouth. "It would solve so many problems."

No warning. No hesitation. The moment those words left her mouth, Grant's hand shot out, sinking through her aura into her hair. He did not pull on her head, but she froze at the contact, eyes widening in fear and shock.

"I can kill you with my voice," Grant said quietly, and the power that rolled off each word was immense, and terrible. "You've always known it."

"I also knew you were too soft," she whispered. "Too kind."

"Not anymore." My husband leaned forward, giving her a look that chilled me to the bone. "You will help us. You will protect us. You will do everything you can to keep harm from us. Your children will be our spies."

Each word swelled with power: ripe and lush, making the air shimmer with fleeting arcs of golden light. I had never seen light when Grant used his power, not like this, but it surrounded me like a soft veil made of sunrise.

But it wasn't just light for Blood Mama. She writhed in her seat, making a keening sound that cut me to the core. Her hands strained around the steering wheel, and her aura swelled, fighting at the bonds of her host.

"Stop," she gasped, but his voice drowned out hers, twisting, bending. Sparks of golden light flashed within her aura, burning through the shadows. Burning *her*.

"Grant," I said, as his voice dropped into that powerful, transforming hum. *"Grant."*

He released Blood Mama—with his hand, and his voice. The demon queen slumped forward, breathing hard, trembling. Her cheeks were wet with tears.

I stared at Grant.

He did not look at me. He leaned away, staring at the back of Blood Mama's head. Pale. Barely breathing. I recognized his eyes again. Without a word, he fumbled for the car door and stumbled out, half-falling on one knee. He started vomiting.

I did not leave the car. I exhaled slowly and focused again on Blood Mama.

"He altered you," I said. "Be thankful he didn't kill you."

"*I* should have killed him," she whispered, and gave me a hateful look. "You do it, Hunter. Do it, before he becomes someone you don't recognize."

"I'm a bleeding heart," I told her. "And I'll bleed out before I hurt that man."

Blood Mama shut her eyes. "You deserve what you get."

I waited a beat, then got out of the car. She drove away before I shut the door. It had started to rain, and I stood there, soaking in the open sky, listening to my heart pound. My heart, five hearts . . . and Grant's, deep in our bond.

He was sitting on the concrete, head bowed, rainwater sliding down his face and neck. I sat beside him and pushed wet hair from his eyes.

"I lost control of myself," he whispered. "I reacted from the gut, without thinking."

I was silent a moment. "What did you do to her?"

"I did what I said. She will protect us. Her children will be our spies. For all intents and purposes, she's ours." Grant could barely meet my gaze. "I crossed the line."

I put his hand on my stomach, and held it there. "What are we fighting for?"

His jaw tightened. "Life."

"Life," I repeated softly. "When this is over, I'll be there to help you sleep at night."

CHAPTER 21

THREE months after my mother's murder—back when I was twenty-one and still unaccustomed to the boys sleeping as tattoos on my body—I chased a demon into a Detroit car dump and realized that for all my training, all my knowledge, I just didn't have the stomach to punch out a ten-year-old kid—even one who was possessed and had murdered his baby sister in the backseat of a parked Chevrolet.

So I played coward. I let that demon run. I waited until nightfall. I made Zee and the others go hunting for me, and I followed, and only when the possessed boy was down on the ground, screaming in rage, did I lay my hand on him, gently, and exorcise the parasite out of his young, wounded soul.

I relied on Zee and the others, like that. I relied on them to protect my soul.

Now it was time for me to get my own hands dirty.

And protect *them*.

EASIER said than done.

When I tried to go to the boys, the armor refused me. Grant and I stood in the middle of the apartment, hair and clothing still damp from the rain, backpacks slung over our shoulders. I held my right hand in a fist, pressed against my chest. Eyes closed, I focused on those five heartbeats throbbing.

Five heartbeats, filled with anger.

I had felt their anger from that first moment of the bond. It had not yet eased. I was becoming used to it, but it frightened me. Feeling their rage didn't explain the cause.

But no matter how much I needed to see them, the armor refused to obey.

Or maybe it was obeying. Just them, and not me.

I started to grind my teeth. Grant raised his brow at me and reached into his back pocket for his cell phone.

"Hold on a minute," he muttered, and I peered over his shoulder, watching him dial Rex.

"Hey," my husband said, "I need you to do something for me. Find one of your kind. Doesn't matter who, just make sure the demon is bonded to Blood Mama. Tell the demon we need information about the Reaper Kings— what they're doing, who they're with. Everything."

I heard a very loud *fuck* on the other end of the line, then some equally strident, inarticulate mumbling.

"No," he replied, glancing at me, "I'm really *not* crazy. Just do it, Rex."

He hung up the phone in the middle of another explosive round of cursing. I crossed my arms over my chest. "Happy to help, was he?"

"He's having a bad day." Grant slid his arm around my

waist. "If we can't reach the boys, what's next? Trying to break this bond?"

I touched my chest, closing my eyes.

Talk to me, I said.

You do not wish to listen, replied the darkness, oozing through the bond with the boys. *You wish to hear only what pleases you.*

And you don't take no for an answer. Neither do I. Tell me what the boys are doing.

The darkness sighed with pleasure, a sound that I found perfectly chilling.

They are hunting, it whispered, and the center of my mind bloomed open like an exploding rose, revealing a red haze slashed with movement and coiled, tangled lines heavy with shadows that housed teeth and claws. I heard snarls. I tasted blood on my tongue. I felt an overwhelming, desperate hunger to *make someone hurt.*

It was a desire that was born from anger, but also pain and misery . . .

. . . and a terrible self-hate.

I leaned hard against Grant, breathless. *Take me to them. Please.*

The darkness did not answer me. Like a bird settling on a clutch of eggs, I felt that entity sink deep, deep inside me, back into its nest beneath my soul. Part of it remained in the bond with the boys, but not much. I could feel that. It was just a taste.

I opened my eyes.

"Maxine," Grant said, but I barely heard him. I was lost in that vision, in those emotions—the pain, and hunger for pain, forming the root of so much agonized rage.

"'Fear leads to anger, anger leads to hate,'" I muttered.

"Yoda, from *Star Wars*?"

"'Hate leads to suffering.'" I met his gaze. "Yoda knows his shit, man."

Grant's mouth crooked in a gentle smile.

❧

WE took the crystal skull with us.

I didn't know if there was much point to having it anymore, given that so many others had been destroyed—but there was always *maybe*. I lived for the possibility of *maybe*.

It was night in the desert. I looked up at the stars, and for a moment was lost, light-headed, thinking about hope and light, and thunder. My left hand tingled. So did my right.

We stood on the edge of the oasis. In front of us, deep amongst the palms, a small fire burned. I heard music playing. Beethoven. I carried a small backpack over my shoulder, filled with clothes, cash, and weapons.

"You know," Grant said, as we walked across the sand, "I once knew a man who named his daughter Sunday."

"No days of the week."

"Hello, Friday. Friday Kiss. Friday Cooperon. My girl Friday."

I kicked sand at him.

"Bessie," he said. "Bertha."

I shook my head and found myself touching my stomach—an unconscious gesture that took my breath away when I realized what I was doing. I glanced at Grant. He was looking at my hand. His gaze met mine, and even in the darkness of the desert night, I saw and felt his warmth.

We both heard a familiar chirping sound.

Dek poked his head from the sand at my feet.

A curious unraveling sensation filled me, almost as if my heart were a string coming untangled.

"You," I said, unsure whether to feel good or awful about seeing him. Had the boys felt me trying to go to them? Did they know what Blood Mama had told us or that Grant had altered her spirit?

"I tried to go to you," I said, unable to keep the reproach from my voice. "You kept me away."

I crouched, staring Dek in the eyes. "I don't think it was to keep me safe. I think you were hiding something from me."

The look in his eyes was haunting, though not nearly as poignant as his heart. I found fury and hunger in his pulse— but buried deep, overcome by a shuddering relief to see me. The kind of relief that came after a bad night, a bad time, when all anyone wanted was to be held, no questions asked.

So I held him—and felt held. More relieved than I wanted to admit to have him with me though it also served to highlight just how wrong, how dangerous, how vulnerable it made us all, in body and soul.

Mal appeared nearby. Grant picked him up and stared into his glinting red eyes. Both of them so intense, refusing to back down.

I touched his arm. "A lecture won't do any good."

"He deserves more than a lecture," muttered Grant, and dropped Mal. "Lying to you isn't protection."

Mal hissed at him. Grant kicked sand over his scales.

"That's my daughter," he snapped at the demon, and hearing him say those words made my gut clench with a hard, primal ache. "My wife."

"Mal," I said, crouching with my hand extended. He

bared his teeth one more time at Grant, then slithered to me, making disgruntled sounds. I felt anger roll into my heart, anger and shame, and that ever-present regret. Mal licked my hand, and I put him on my shoulder with Dek, who scolded him and bit his neck, gently.

I touched both their heads. "Where have you been?"

Dek buried his head in my neck. Mal remained silent.

I persisted. "You were hunting. I know it. Human or demon?"

Human or demon. As if one or the other would make a difference. As if one would be better than the other when both were bad.

Dek began to hum, but what I noticed first was that his breath smelled like blood. After that, I couldn't gather my thoughts enough to figure out what song he was singing. It didn't matter. My boys had been killing.

They've always been killers, I told myself. *You knew that. Only now they're not killing for you.*

I was such a hypocrite. Double standards, a mile long. But I didn't care about that. I wanted to know who had died, and why.

"There will be war," Blood Mama had said.

Grant reached for my hand, and we kept walking.

We found the Messenger at the fire's edge, which burned a safe distance from her tent.

No sign of her bonded Mahati warrior, though I thought he must be close. She sat in a meditative pose, legs crossed beneath her, spine straight as an arrow, and her palms resting on her knees. Her pale skin was golden in the firelight, casting deep shadows on her angular face. She watched us approach with no reaction save a slight frown.

"You are both a tangle of knots," she said. "Death would be easier than disentanglement."

Grant rubbed his face. "Do you have something to eat?"

Her brow lifted, and she winked out of sight. The cool night air filled in the space she had been occupying and swirled around me. My clothes were still damp from the rain. I might have felt a chill if it hadn't been for Dek and Mal coiled heavy on my shoulders.

Grant settled down in the sand, wincing as he straightened out his bad leg. I sat beside him, then couldn't keep upright, and I curled in front of the fire, staring at the flames. He placed a strong, warm hand on my ankle, while Dek and Mal—my little pillows—began purring.

"I think you all need to rest," he said.

"Just for a minute," I murmured, unable to keep my eyes open, my entire body aching and heavy with exhaustion. Just resting there, with Dek and Mal—and Grant—made taking one little nap sweeter than I could even say.

Inside my heart, my little demons went soft, quiet.

I fell asleep.

I don't know how long I really slept because I kept jerking awake for brief, uncomfortable moments—just long enough to assure me that we were still alive, that no one was attacking us, and that Grant was resting on his side beside me, staring thoughtfully into the fire. Dek and Mal were curled beneath my head.

Everything fine. Just fine. And then I would remember, too, that I was pregnant—and close my eyes thinking about names.

This went on, until finally, *finally*, I fell into a deeper sleep, one that held me down and kept me warm, safe.

I drifted, and smelled roses.

Bells chimed. Water murmured. I inhaled a breeze that made my heart ache with its sweetness, like dawn, or spring: a scent made for perfect days. I lay still, lost in that quiet. I floated. I opened my eyes.

I was no longer in the desert. I saw a stone arch. A vast balcony on my right, filled with silver moonlight. Roses covered the rail. Huge blooms. Soft petals. Crimson, not silver. Red as blood.

But it was all fake. In the shadows around us hung the night sky, as though the walls, the bed, everything, was nothing but a ragged illusion, a cobbled patchwork, between which were stars on the ceiling—stars in the crevices between the archway and the bed—stars in the folds of my covers.

A man sat in a chair beside the bed. I could not see much of him. Lost face, lost body, lost to those starlit shadows, a deep field of them, with the barest hint of spiral galaxies where his eyes should be. I wanted to see his eyes but was afraid, too.

"You're my father," I said, without waiting for him to speak, though my words sounded awkward and pained. "You tried to kill me."

The man leaned forward, though not far enough to reveal his face. I wondered if he even had a face. He touched my armored right hand. I managed not to flinch though it was difficult: His touch was fleeting, his large, elegant hand made entirely of silver metal.

"All separations are violent," he murmured. *"I would never try to kill you."*

"But you set a trap. You ripped the boys off my body. Why would you do that?"

My voice shook when I said those words. Grief and anger, burning through me with agonizing, brutal force. My head began throbbing. *The boys. My boys, gone.*

My family. My heart. Ripped away.

Now I was their weapon. Now I was the prisoner. Now I was at the mercy of their hearts.

The man sighed, and the sound was soft, like the breeze. Without seeing his face it was easy to imagine there was no man, no flesh and bone, but just a ghost, a figment of my imagination. A dream.

"We are all dreams," he whispered, and then: *"I had two reasons. I wanted you to learn that you can live without them. That when you have your own daughter, it will not be a death sentence. You can survive. You can live to be an old woman."*

He paused a heartbeat, while I soaked that in. *"You are not alive because of them. You are alive because of you."*

Before I could respond, he added, *"The second reason is that soon you will have a choice to make. I wanted your little Kings to have a similar choice. The same* freedom *to choose. It will matter, in time."*

I tried to push off the covers, but my arms were too weak. My legs wouldn't even move. I felt them—silk sheets rubbing my skin, an itch beneath my knee—but the overall sensation was one of compression, as though some great weight were bearing down. Holding me still.

Blood dripped from my nose. I tasted it on my lip.

"Why?" I asked, hoarse with fear. "Why does it matter?"

"Something is coming," he said, his quiet, deep voice floating from that field of stars. *"Ask Zee. Ask him to tell you what terrifies a Reaper King."*

216

CHAPTER 22

THE next time I opened my eyes, I was back in the desert. Words, ringing through my mind. More questions, too.

I started to sit up and stopped. Dek and Mal were stiff on my shoulders, staring to my left with quivering intensity. I followed their gazes and took a sharp breath.

On the other side of the fire sprawled an old man.

He was big. Not just fat, but muscular, with a barrel-chested heft that made me think of orators and mountain men. He wore loose, charcoal gray slacks, and a dark button-up shirt of the same color. His hair was streaked with silver, and his craggy face was familiar though it took me a full minute to figure out why.

It was the man from the warehouse, who had tried to save baby Andrew—and gotten his leg ripped off for his trouble.

He had his leg now, though. Right there in front of me, plain as day. He also had a new scar over his eye.

I looked for Grant and found him beside me, easing a thick sandwich from a plastic bag. He glanced at me, one eyebrow raised, with familiar, comforting wryness.

Only one person could inspire that particular look on my husband's face.

I studied the old man again, searching those eyes, the set of that mouth, looking for anything familiar. It was not until the man spoke, however, that I knew for certain.

"Sweet girl," said my grandfather, Jack. "It's good to see your face."

⊰⧟⊱

OLD Wolf. Jack Meddle.

He had so many names, and had lived so many lives—as a god, a legend, and ordinary man. I would never know his story. I would never entirely understand him.

I'd seen my grandfather a month ago, at the burial of his former body. Decades previous, he'd met my grandmother during her travels through Central Asia. He had known each of my ancestors, but somehow, in some way, Jean Kiss had been different from all of them.

They'd fallen in love.

A taboo. If the other Aetar ever discovered that Jack had interfered with my bloodline . . . *something* bad would happen. I didn't know what, but I'd seen how some of his kind worked, and it was ugly as hell.

He was family, though—the closest thing to a living relative I would ever have. Good to see him, though I might have been more excited had he shown up a few days earlier.

"I didn't expect you here," I said, unmoving.

"Or looking so comfortable." Grant handed me the sandwich, which he'd wrapped in a white napkin. "You need to eat."

I grunted at him. "I'm not hungry."

His gaze flicked down to my stomach and back up to my face. "Try."

I frowned and took the sandwich. I didn't look at what was inside, but that first bite tasted good—and fresh hunger roared inside me. I kept eating, and suddenly the sandwich was gone, and I was still starving. Dek and Mal made approving sounds.

Grant pushed another sandwich into my hands, his mouth twitching with humor. When he looked away at Jack, though, his gaze turned dangerous. "We could have used your help before now. *Long* before now."

Jack grimaced, and finally, in his eyes, I could see the man I had known, a man who had been born into so many lives, in so many different bodies, that the one he wore now probably meant very little to him, except as a shell for his soul: this skin of a man whom I'd first seen in the warehouse, and who had looked at me with mortal eyes.

Mortal eyes. A distinction I had learned to make only after spending time with my grandfather. It wasn't age but, instead, the depth of the gaze that gave away an immortal. All the things that soul had seen, and remembered.

Jack had witnessed the birth of stars. His eyes were pretty damn special.

He barely looked at Grant. Instead, he watched Dek and Mal with terrible wariness. The two demons returned his stare with similar suspicion—and cold calculation. He might be my grandfather, but he was also an Aetar. One of the thirteen who had imprisoned them.

"I felt Zee and the others go free," Jack said carefully, not taking his gaze off them. "It was terrible. Quite possibly one of the most wrenching sensations I have ever suffered."

"Tell me about it," I said, as Grant gave him a dirty look. I noticed the Messenger walking toward us from the shadows, her robes whispering. Even she looked at my grandfather with a raised brow.

Jack winced. "I'm sorry. That was thoughtless. I cannot imagine what you suffered."

No, you can't, I wanted to tell him, stung and feeling more than a little childish that he hadn't come searching me out. It was stupid. But he was my grandfather. I could get petty, if I wanted to.

I stroked Mal's tense body, feeling edgy because of him, despite him, some confusing mix of both that made me uncertain what was real, and what wasn't. "Where were you?"

"Indisposed. In a particular state of *being*, which did not allow me to come easily to you."

Grant opened his mouth. I touched his arm, and shook my head. "That body you're wearing . . . was torn up."

"He died," Jack said bluntly, scratching his new beard. "I happened to be nearby at that point and decided I had no time to be choosy about who my new host would be. I took over his fresh corpse, and brought the body here to be . . . healed . . . of its more severe wounds. I've also been making some additional modifications of my own."

The Aetar were masters at manipulating organic material with nothing but conscious thought. There was no telling what kinds of unseen "modifications" Jack had made. "You grew a new leg?"

"Attached the original. Some thoughtful soul had put it on ice, just in case. I stole it from a freezer."

I tried to envision that, then stopped. I really didn't want to know.

Grant looked at the Messenger. "We came to speak with you."

She had been watching me the entire time, assessing my body—up and down—with all the warmth a butcher might give a rotting piece of meat.

"Yes," she said, slowly, "I can see *all* her problems."

I frowned. "I didn't think there was a *list*."

Jack made a distressed sound and leaned forward. "Oh, my."

Suddenly, everyone was looking at me. I hadn't forgotten, either, that Dek and Mal were perched on my shoulders, aware of everything the others were saying.

I wasn't sure I wanted to test their loyalty when it came to this bond. I didn't need my heart broken one more time.

"Hey." I patted their heads. "Get lost for a bit, okay?"

As if *that* wasn't suspicious. Mal swung his head sideways, staring into my eyes. His little heart pulsed inside mine with misgivings.

He did not trust me. He knew why we were here.

I held his gaze, unflinching. "Mal. I won't pretend to know what you've experienced. But you've been in my heart. You've lived there. You know my faith in you. My trust. And maybe I did take it for granted, but I *still* trust you. So please . . . show me the same respect."

Just a little. Just enough.

Mal did not look away. A low growl rumbled through his chest, and his ears pressed flat against his skull, one little tooth bared. In his heart, conflict, shimmering into doubt, into pain, and that old, lingering remorse. Dek was carefully still, his emotions muted. I wondered, suddenly, if the boys were bonded to each other, if they could sense each other's feelings. I'd suspected they had some sort of psychic link but never considered until now what that might be like.

Finally, though, Mal relaxed . . . and slid through my hair . . . into nothing. Gone, in moments. Dek sighed and nuzzled my neck. Then he followed his brother *between*.

I let out my breath. All of us did, except the Messenger—who cocked her brow at me.

"Surely," she said, "you do not expect the Reaper Kings to *let* you break this bond."

"I won't know until we try," I replied, and held out my arms. "Do your worst."

"Er, don't," Grant murmured, giving the Messenger a hard look. Jack winced, rubbing his newly attached leg. He was very broad in this new body, husky, with muscle and fat. I was accustomed to my grandfather being lean as a dancer, with large, elegant hands. His hands were still large, but rough and coarse, with scars on his knuckles.

"How?" Jack asked me, his voice little more than a rasp. "How did it happen?"

"They tasted some of my blood. I . . . gave myself over." Jack exhaled slowly. "My dear girl."

"Don't. Just . . . focus on now."

I thought he would argue, but instead his eyes closed, and a strained grimace passed over his face.

"Lad," he said to Grant. "You know how deep this goes."

"Deep enough that I wasn't comfortable touching it without advice." My husband's gaze passed from Jack to the Messenger. "You and I . . . if we work together . . ."

The Messenger studied me with cold, detached thoughtfulness. "It is not a normal bond. Five souls, in hers . . . making themselves *part* of her soul. She is outnumbered. They are stronger than she, together. I see this in the threads that are knotted between them."

"It's strong."

"Stronger than anything I have ever seen."

"It is the bond of a demon lord," Jack murmured. "Only once could we break that, and we had no need to be careful. We hacked it apart with all the strength of our wills, and it was like chopping at the trunk of a thousand-year-old tree with nothing but a dozen small axes. Ugly, brutal."

I didn't want to imagine. I didn't want to think about what it would feel like to have those five hearts hacked from my soul. Again. "So, that's it? You won't even try?"

Jack tugged on his beard. The Messenger looked me dead in the eyes. "You do not want us to, Hunter. Not even your bondmate can aid you."

"There has to be something we can do," Grant protested.

"You are only a Lightbringer, and wild-born. Powerful, yes, but not a god." She looked at me. "There is no path to freedom, Hunter, unless the Reaper Kings release you. *That* would be safe . . . though it is unlikely to happen. You are a slave now. Make peace with it."

She suddenly seemed bored and gave Jack a look of cold deference. "Maker. Praise be your light. I will go and fetch refreshment for your new body."

"Ah," said Jack, uneasily. "Er . . . thank you, my dear."

The taller woman's gaze darkened, a faint scowl tugging on her thin lips. We watched her vanish into thin air.

"Awkward," Grant said with a careful glance in my direction.

Jack grunted, scratching his beard. "I need to shave."

I rolled my eyes. "Well, don't let *me* stop you."

"My dear—"

"No," I snapped, and there was too much of a snarl in my voice for comfort, too much of that simmering anger inside the boys, moving through me. I could resist those emotions, with effort. Right then, I didn't want to make the effort. "That's it?"

Jack seemed taken aback. "No. But I need time to think. None of this should ever have happened. Not their release. Certainly not this . . . new bond." My grandfather nearly choked on those last words. "How did they get loose?"

I stared at him. I'd come here under the assumption that there would be a fix, an answer. Some kind of reassurance.

Being told I was screwed was *not* comforting. At all. And the idea of telling that story, reliving it, made it even worse.

I pulled the crystal skull from the backpack and held it up for Jack to see. He sucked in his breath, staring with the sort of stunned, horrified shock that I would have expected from a terror victim. Not him.

He did not blink or look away, and though that jolt didn't fade, for one brief moment—so brief, it might have been my imagination—I glimpsed hunger behind his gaze.

"Where," he said, slowly, "did you find that?"

"A demon was told in a dream to give it to me. I thought, maybe, you had something to do with that."

Jack's gaze flicked to mine. "No."

"We found several others. The boys destroyed them."

He flinched.

"There were bodies, encased in stone," I added. "In the desert, beneath a ruined city."

Jack swallowed hard and appeared ill. "Yes."

"Who were they?"

"Don't," he whispered. "Don't make me say it out loud."

I stared at him. "There's something else you should know."

He visibly braced himself, expression so grim. Grant cleared his throat, glancing at me.

"You tell him," I said, unable to say the words out loud. It was too personal and new. Maybe it was the same for him. He had to take a breath and hesitated, with a look on his face just as raw and intense as what I was feeling.

"I'm going to be a father," he said in a soft voice, with utter seriousness and solemnity—that is, until a smile spread over his face. "A father."

Despite everything, all the horror, the danger, seeing that smile was like being infected with joy. I laughed out loud.

If Jack had appeared stunned at seeing the skull, *this* news seemed to hit him like a rocket in the gut. He stared at us. No smile. No words of congratulations. I kept expecting him to say *something*, but as the silence continued, my own smile died. So did Grant's. I hated that. I really did.

"Is there a problem?" I asked, my voice sharper than I intended.

Grant leaned forward. "He's scared."

I waited for Jack to disagree, but that didn't happen. All he did do was slump his shoulders, rub his new beard, and look at us with tired eyes.

"I'm scared *for* you," he said, but from the way Grant looked at him, I wondered if that was entirely true.

I tried not to grit my teeth. "Jack."

"I'm *also* happy for you," he added, glancing at my frowning husband. "I'm happy that you are going to have a baby."

Glass shattered behind me. I whipped around—but all I found was the Messenger staring at me, bottles crushed in her bare, bleeding hands. Her eyes were so dark.

"You," she said slowly, "are with child?"

I tensed. Grant pushed himself up on one knee, a look on his face I had never seen.

"I will kill you," he said, "if you even *breathe* wrong around her. I will destroy you. I will rip you apart."

The Messenger did not stop looking at me. "Maybe you should."

I flexed my right hand. "You want to do this now? I'm ready."

She went rigid. Jack said a sharp word. The language was coarse, unfamiliar, but the Messenger flinched and closed her eyes.

"You told me there are no gods," she whispered in a tight voice.

"About this, there is," he said. "I am your God, when it comes to that child. You will not harm her."

"The offspring of a Lightbringer . . . and the Hunter, with her power . . ." The Messenger drew in a deep breath and dropped the shards of glass into the sand. "I will return with more drinks," she murmured, and vanished again.

Grant did not relax. Neither did I. I was filled with the somewhat twitchy desire to sink my teeth into hot, soft flesh. Made me want to swish out my mouth with ginger ale.

"Jack," I said, nauseated—and hungry.

"Tell me your story," he replied, quietly. "Hurry."

⌘

THE Messenger returned almost fifteen minutes after I started talking, but she did not say a word. She set down bottles of chilled water from wherever she had fetched them, then sat a short distance away, sinking into a meditative pose and closing her eyes. I glimpsed movement on the edge of the oasis: the Mahati, walking gracefully in the night amongst the palms.

I told Jack everything, starting from the rose. He listened carefully, but his focus remained on the carved skull, which he placed a good distance away from him.

He gave no impression that he wanted to touch the thing. In fact, he seemed wary, a sentiment I shared. I was glad I didn't have to look into those empty eyes. The rest of the skull was hypnotic enough, its smooth surface reflecting the fire so that it seemed flames burned deep inside the crystal.

"Those demon lords," he murmured, almost to himself. "I never knew their names. When we broke their bond to the Reaper Kings, it disoriented the entire army, especially them. Just long enough for us to raise the prison walls."

"You didn't try to kill them?" Grant asked.

"We couldn't," he said with a faint look of surprise. "The bonds they share with their individual clans make them incredibly strong. Maybe not as strong as Zee and the others, but very nearly immortal. In hindsight, we should have struck those bonds, as well, but our focus was on the Reaper Kings."

Jack met my gaze with discomfort—but some defiance, too.

"The boys are not innocent in this, my dear. No matter how much you care about them, don't forget that. Their army killed billions, and destroyed civilizations that were . . . precious and remarkable. They would have killed more had we not stopped them." He hesitated, looking down at his scarred, battered hands. "Not that the Aetar didn't do the same, elsewhere. Perhaps it was justice. All of us, punished in different ways."

Justice. Punishment. *Billions dead.*

Another lifetime. Different hearts.

How much can be forgiven? How can the extinction of worlds be redeemed? Where is the redemption in mass murder? Is there such a thing when the crime is so immense?

And yet, I was contemplating killing an entire race of demons. Out of self-defense, yes. But still. It would be murder. It would be extinction.

I didn't expect redemption for that. Just survival.

I drew in a deep breath. "Tell me about the crystal skulls."

Jack hesitated, staring at the skull in front of him. I tried to imagine him with the same bone structure—sharp teeth, huge eyes—but it was too alien, and he was too human.

"Each of us involved in building the prison had one of these skulls, attuned to our particular identity. This was mine. I'm shocked to see it, though. I threw the damn thing into the Wasteland."

That surprised me. "Nothing escapes the Wasteland."

"*Almost* nothing," he reminded me. "But this artifact?

Found in a toolbox in a basement in Texas? That defies understanding."

I thought about the other skulls the boys had destroyed. "Why would you have tried to get rid of it? Why, *any* of you?"

"Because they made us too powerful. Each skull, carved and polished from stones cut from the Labyrinth." Jack stared at the skull, and, in a soft voice, said, "We thought we were strong before, but when we focused through them, when we focused on our desires . . . it was like being fed by a star. Frightening, and beautiful. Truly, we *did* feel like gods."

The Messenger's mouth tightened. I pressed my right hand against my leg. "You felt like gods and gave up that power? There must be more to that story."

"You think?" he murmured.

"I know," I said. "Who made the skulls? The Aetar?"

Jack stared into the fire, and the fall of flickering light cast shadows that made him look tired and thoughtful, and grim. "No. That is beyond our abilities. We only discovered the Labyrinth because the Lightbringers knew of it. Before that, we were nothing but drifters in space. We drifted so long until we found that home world, we forgot where we came from, or why we even left."

Something told me that wasn't entirely true. Grant's gaze hardened. "How did the Lightbringers discover the Labyrinth?"

"I don't know," Jack said simply. "The Labyrinth is a crossroads between space and time, but it takes a particular manipulation of energy to open its door. Energy is what your kind does, lad."

"And that?" I pointed at the skull. "If the Aetar didn't make it, who did?"

Jack grimaced and said nothing. Grant glanced at the Messenger.

"He is called the Tinker," she said, ignoring the older man when he gave her a stern look. "Even the Lightbringers knew of him."

"That old?"

"What is time in the Labyrinth?" she replied with a hint of disdain. "Time means nothing, there."

"You make it sound as though he lives *inside* the Labyrinth."

"He is the only one who does," Jack finally said, still not looking at me. "You travel through the Labyrinth, but you don't remain."

"Why not?"

"It will not let you," said the Messenger, as if that was the most ridiculous question she had ever heard. "If you do not open a door of your own choosing, the Labyrinth will choose for you."

"So how do you know what door to open?" Grant asked.

The Messenger frowned. "You see its light."

I closed my eyes, thinking of roses and starlight, and a man with silver skin. "Who is the Tinker, and why is he different?"

"We don't know," Jack said. "Neither did the Lightbringers. He's a ghost. Few have seen him in the Labyrinth, and only from a distance. No one has ever spoken with him. Trust me, we tried. Some of us even hunted him, thinking . . ." He stopped, shaking his head. "Thinking to possess him."

"Familiar story," Grant said coldly.

I touched his hand. "If you don't know how to find him, then how did you convince him to make those crystal skulls?"

Jack hesitated. "We . . . prayed."

"You . . . what?"

"If you have a need, sometimes the Tinker answers, with gifts." My grandfather looked profoundly uncomfortable. "He made seed rings for the Lightbringers. He made our crystal skulls and left them where they would be found. He made the armor that your ancestor discovered and that you now wear."

"And you don't know how he does it."

"Some would call what we do magic," he said in a subdued voice. "But to us, it is just an ability, another kind of science. What *he* does, though . . . is so far beyond our capabilities . . . that *we* call it magic."

I had to soak that in. "You've never spoken of him."

"He is an uncomfortable topic for my kind."

"Because the Aetar can't control him."

Jack studied his old, gnarled hands. "Yes."

I wondered what else my grandfather wasn't saying. "He made the rose that broke my bond with the boys. I didn't ask for that."

"I know."

"And you're wrong. Someone *has* spoken with him. Someone did a lot more than that."

Jack looked me dead in the eyes. "I know that, too."

Silence fell around the fire. Grant and I watched him. He watched us back. All of us, so still, lost in the desert hush and the crackle of flames burning between us.

The Messenger stirred, losing some of the stiffness in her spine. "Who is this person who spoke with the Tinker?"

My grandfather closed his eyes, and his chest sank inward as though he were hollow and brittle. It was so him, all of his movements and gestures, that I found myself forgetting his was a new body. I could see only his spirit.

"Someone very special," he murmured. "Someone very dear."

My heart seized when he said those words, swallowed up in an ache that reached down into the pit of my stomach. My mother. My mother, so special and dear.

I'd never understand her, no matter how much I wanted to. That killed me, all those wasted years. I'd loved her, learned from her . . . but in the end, I'd resented her, too. I still couldn't forgive myself for that.

But the ache in my chest deepened, and I realized suddenly that it wasn't because of anything *I* was feeling.

It was the boys.

I hardly had time to react. A sharp stabbing pain lanced my ribs, making me gasp. It hit me again before I could recover, and I doubled over—breathless, in agony. I felt as though I were being cut open with a dull saw—and I expected to see blood when I checked my hand.

Nothing. Clean.

Grant grabbed me around the waist, hauling me back against his chest. "Maxine," he said, voice throbbing with power. "Maxine, listen to me."

"Something's happening to the boys," I managed to gasp out. "Jesus."

Jack scrabbled across the sand, picking up the crystal skull. "We need to break the bond."

The Messenger rose to her feet, staring past us into the desert. Her hand fell to the crystal chain looped around her waist, and it fell free into her hand like a whip. I twisted in Grant's arms, panting with pain, and glimpsed movement in the night, at the edge of the oasis.

I didn't know what I was looking at. An earthquake, maybe. The desert, rippling like the surface of a wild, heaving ocean. A violent hiss cut through the air, accompanied by an oddly sweet scent: vanilla and orchids.

"Demons," she whispered.

CHAPTER 23

❦

*"T*HE *unfamiliar will stun the eye,"* my mother once said. *"You'll waste time trying to make sense of it, and that time might get you killed. So don't think, baby. Don't try to make sense of anything. Just react. Move."*

Move.

The demons were small and muscular, shaped like slugs, with no visible eyes and no heads except for open mouths filled with endless rows of razor-sharp teeth glistening wet with slime. Their bodies formed a massive wave that undulated toward us with breathtaking speed. Everywhere, surrounding us on all sides—hundreds, maybe thousands—spilling from the desert sands into the oasis.

The darkness had been quiet—but it stirred, deep inside, flowing into that new bond I shared with the boys. Heaving through us all with a cool, muscular pulse that felt like a worm sliding around my vital organs, straight into my throat. Sickening, and more than ever before, frightening. I had no control over it. Neither, I thought, did the boys.

Shurik, whispered the darkness, in my mind. *A swarm has been primed.*

I had no idea what that meant. All I could think about was Lord Draean and that golf ball–sized lump traveling beneath his skin, eating his host from the inside out.

That piece of shit was trying to kill me.

A cold, clenching anger hit, followed by disgust and indignity. I didn't know if those were my emotions, and I didn't care. Inside my head, I heard my voice, the darkness, the boys, all whispering, *How dare he, how dare he strike me, our Queen, me, our heart, how dare he swarm his filth and blood, we will have blood in death, his death, his—*

"Oh, damn," said Jack, voice trembling. "We need to run."

"No," I said, overcome with hungry, vicious fury. "Hell, no."

"Maxine," he protested, but I snarled at my grandfather, all the pain in my side fading beneath the pounding rage pouring into my heart. I burned with rage. I burned.

Yes, whispered the darkness, and that old, hard smile crawled up my throat. Only this time, it was me—me, or something like me—and not the force living beneath my soul.

"Grant," I snapped, and he let me go, his eyes glinting golden as he said one word—one endless word that was primal and throbbing with power. The Messenger had already begun singing, her voice melding with his, forming a wall of sound that made the hairs stand on my skin.

My right hand flexed, tingling all over, and the armor flashed with blinding light—transforming, answering my need.

Moments later, I held a silver whip. Light as air, delicate, etched with coiled lines shaped like roses. It shone with a soft glow that rippled each time I breathed—as though the whip breathed with me. A chain connected the grip to my armor, chiming like small bells.

I leapt toward the Shurik, sweeping the whip over that first wave. It flashed light, slicing through the small, fat bodies and spattering blood into the sand. Cries rattled, hisses breaking. All I felt was satisfaction. I wanted to kill them, more than anything. I wanted to taste their flesh, drink their blood. I wanted to hear them scream.

I had a baby inside me. My daughter. My husband behind me. My love. My grandfather. If I ran, if I didn't fight now, there would be no hope.

And I had hope.

A tall figure glided from the shadows at a full, leaping run: the Mahati warrior, attacking the swarming Shurik with the sharp tines of his fingertips, stabbing and crushing, snarling as the demons encircled us. But there were too many, and as quickly as we killed, more took their places.

One of the Shurik leapt into the air and sank its teeth into the Mahati's leg. Instead of biting and letting go, it swung its body hard for leverage and started burrowing directly into his calf. He screamed, and the Messenger's voice broke. Without hesitation she lunged after him, slashing her own whip at the swarming Shurik.

Her weapon did not cut through the demons as mine could, but merely knocked them aside. Grant stepped closer to me, gaze cold and determined, all the muscles in his throat straining as his voice grew deeper, even more inhuman. Power rippled over my skin. Power shimmered in the air. His voice rolled through the night—twisting down with an incredible, surging strength that flowed over my skin like an exhale from a hurricane. Our bond pulsed with light. My bond with the boys pulsed with darkness.

The Shurik slowed, faltering. I didn't know what my husband was doing to them, but those closest stopped completely—all the demons behind them bumping up against each other, milling as though confused.

I glanced back at Jack and found him standing still with the crystal skull clutched to his chest. It glowed with a faint light.

"Go," he said in a strained voice, without looking at me. "He's done it."

I didn't know what *it* was, but I waded through the Shurik, who trembled and gasped for air with those hideous mouths—but did not bite me.

Grant's voice dropped to a low, steady hum. The Messenger made the same sound when I reached her, but she was bent over her bonded Mahati warrior, who lay half-sprawled in the sand. Five Shurik were embedded in his legs, torso, and shoulder. Their fat bodies wriggled slowly, jutting from wounds that oozed blood. Ready to eat him from the inside out.

That could have been me. One heartbeat, one distraction. The Mahati was strong, fast, but he had been overwhelmed.

I realized, finally, what Lord Ha'an had meant when he said the Shurik would have massacred his people had Zee and the boys not intervened.

I'm looking at what will happen to humanity, I told myself, nausea rising through my disgust and anger.

The Messenger's voice did not falter when I crouched beside her, nor did she look at me. The Mahati's gaze was wild, his chest heaving with pain. When the Messenger touched his leg near one of the embedded Shurik, he flinched—but did not fight her.

I grabbed his wrist, hard with muscle and warmer than I expected. "We need to move you."

"I will do it." The Messenger stood and picked up the fallen Mahati. He was her height, and bigger, but she slung him into her arms as though he weighed nothing. Her expression was curiously vulnerable.

I lingered behind as she carried him from the Shurik swarm, turning in a slow circle and studying the demons surrounding us. So damn many. Overwhelming numbers. I got the creeps standing there, but I wasn't even sure they were alive anymore. Not one of them moved.

And then Grant fell silent, and I was certain.

I walked from the swarm, silver whip dragging across dead demons and cutting them as easily as a knife through water. I felt a certain dull satisfaction, but it was shallow and cold. Much like my anger. Not just mine, but the boys.

Lord Draean tried to assassinate me. Those Shurik didn't wander here on their own.

But where were the boys? Had they not felt I was in danger?

Or were *they* in more danger than I?

The Messenger was on her knees, yanking a dead Shurik from the Mahati's torso. It made a wet sucking sound, and blood gushed from the wound. The demon stifled a groan, cracking open his eyes to watch as she laid her hands on him and hummed. Jack stood nearby. He didn't look at me. He faced the dead swarm, clutching the crystal skull, gaze so far away and remote I wasn't certain he was still inside his body.

Grant was pale, expression stark, hard, as though he had been standing within a terrible wind that had buffeted him raw.

"You okay?" he murmured.

"Fine," I muttered, barely able to speak past the rising thunder in my chest—those five hearts pounding around mine, filled with fury and hunger—and shock. My side began aching again.

"I need to go to the boys," I said, grim. "I have to understand what just happened."

Grant leaned on his cane, staring at me. "You're crazy."

"I'm taking the bull by the balls." I looped the whip into my hand and crouched, poking one of the dead Shurik: bloody, slimy, and shaped like a turd. I wanted to squirm and pull a heebie-jeebies fit but gritted my teeth and stayed where I was, trying not to imagine it eating its own young, or the inside of a human being.

I glanced up at Grant. "How did you stop them?"

He could not hide his regret from me, or his pain.

"I changed them," he said, hoarse. "I shifted their light. They were being driven by an instinct to kill and feed. It was the same for all of them. I transformed that instinct, in the same way I affect Blood Mama's parasites."

And Blood Mama herself, I almost heard him thinking.

"You cut their bond with the Shurik lord," Jack said in a tight voice, finally looking at us. "You stopped the flow of energy."

"If you want to call it that," he said with particular weariness. "It wasn't my intention. I altered their souls into something so different from what they were before that whatever the bond held on to no longer existed. It disoriented them, and when they were weak . . ."

He stopped. I reached for his hand, watching his jaw tighten as though he was trying not to be sick.

"It was too easy," he murmured. "Killing them was like cutting a string."

Jack stared with haunted eyes. "You'll have to cut many strings before this is done, lad. You're a weapon now . . . and doing things my kind never could."

Grant tensed. The Messenger's healing hum faltered, and she looked at the old man. All of us did. I felt annoyed with my grandfather and deeply protective of my husband.

I squeezed his hand. "Would that work on me?"

He immediately shook his head with a vehemence that bordered on horror. "I would have to change you, Maxine. I would have to transform your soul so radically, you wouldn't be the same person. Even then, I don't know if it would work."

"You could put me back."

"You're not a box of Legos. A soul is energy, and that energy forms a pattern. Once you shift the pattern, you can't just rearrange it. Not the way it was. Something would be lost."

"Something's going to be lost anyway."

Grant leaned in with hard eyes. "Not like this. We'll find another way."

I rocked back on my heels, frustrated and troubled. Not just with his answer but with myself, and my creeping sense of disloyalty—as though I were betraying the boys.

My side ached even harder. I gritted my teeth, swaying backward from the others, breathing long and deep through my nose. My chest felt too full, swollen with a hard knot of emotion that seemed to buzz through me with unsettled, wild power. Made me feel trapped. Shoved into a small, terrible cage. My right hand tightened around the whip so hard, my fingers ached.

I tried looking at the stars, the desert, anything to alleviate my claustrophobia. Instead, I felt dizzy, and a strange keening ache spread from the boys into my heart. I bent over, holding my chest as that ache was followed by a wash of rage and shock, and despair. Our bond felt sick with fear. Pain splashed against my skin, long, dragging cuts that sank into my nerves like fire. I looked, but found no wounds. The pain was real, though. Too real.

"Maxine," Grant said with concern, staring at me as though he could see the wounds. I reached for him, but before our hands met, I felt a cool rush of air over my back. Jack cursed, and the Messenger stiffened. Her Mahati warrior snarled, struggling to sit up.

I turned, and found three men behind us.

The tallest, standing in front, was young, tanned, and extremely good-looking. Vaguely familiar, even. I was certain I had seen him on television or in a magazine. Of course, I was just as certain that whoever that young man *had* been, he was likely as good as dead. His eyes gave him away. No one else could have those cold, dead eyes.

"Draean," I said. "I thought Zee might have killed you."

A mirthless smile touched his stolen mouth, but that faded as he turned in a slow circle and gazed upon the dead Shurik swarm at his feet. The men with him, also young and handsome, did the same. Shock filled their eyes. One of them spat, as though ill. Between them, they held an iron chest, which nearly slipped from their hands.

"I did not believe it," whispered the demon lord, reaching

down to pick up one of the dead Shurik. He pressed the slimy corpse to his cheek with disconcerting tenderness and closed his eyes. "I cannot even hear their songs, in death."

A lump squirmed down the side of his throat. Similar knots moved beneath the clothes of the men with him: down a thigh, across a chest.

I let the whip uncoil and drag through the sand, light and quick, and deadly. The hissing sound it made brought Lord Draean's attention back to me, his eyes flickering open with hate.

"How?" he whispered.

I swayed forward. Grant moved with me. So did Jack, though I did not look at them. I felt their heat, like a wall at my back. I listened to the Messenger's robes rustle as she rose from the Mahati's side.

"How?" I whispered, fury rising inside me, a terrible killing rage that was mine and dwarfed even those five hearts racing. "Because we're stronger than you, mother-fucker."

Lord Draean bared his teeth. "Strong? You are human. You are cattle. I have eaten more of your kind than your dreams can hold. I have suckled mountains of bones. I never met strength in any human that I could not over-come."

I smiled and planted my foot on one of his dead Shurik. I pressed down hard, and guts oozed from its mouth. "Your corpse is going to end up on a stick, roasting over my fire."

Lord Draean threw back his head, laughing. Blood drib-bled down the sides of his mouth, seeping from the corners of his eyes. He tossed down the body in his hands and stomped on it, grinding in his bootheel.

"Human whore," he said, with disdain. "Whore to old Kings who are useless and broken. I will savor your skin."

Grant stepped forward. "You'll do no such thing."

Draean gave him a sharp look. "What is in your voice?"

"Transformation," whispered my husband, and the power in that one soft word was lush and thick, rolling around us with an almost physical presence. He ended that word on a hum, a rippling sound with so much weight I felt as though I were listening to a thousand hands pulling, pulling on the air, on my body, on the ground beneath my feet.

"What," Dracan began, then backed away, as though truly startled. "No. Your kind are dead."

Grant leaned hard on his cane, eyes flecked with gold. Jack swayed close to my side, holding the crystal skull—which glowed between his large hands.

"No," murmured my grandfather. "The Lightbringers are not yet dead."

Draean seemed stunned. "You. The Wolf."

Jack bowed his head, and the crystal skull exploded with light.

White light, starlight, blinding and cold as a winter. A blast of freezing air hit me, and I flinched, staggering back as the light from the skull slammed into the demon lord and his men. Screams tore from their throats their sagging, melting throats—which split open like ripe fruit, gushing blood. I watched in fascination and horror as their flesh melted, dropping away in wet chunks that seeped foul-smelling bile. All those men—Lord Draean—liquefying in their clothing.

And from that liquid dropped three squirming slugs.

One was larger than the others, the same color as a muddy ruby, pulsing with bright orange veins that glowed as though lit from within by fire. Long crimson teeth gnashed, and a long tongue snaked out, the tip shaped like a spoon. Ugly as hell.

I lunged forward, cracking my whip down like silver lightning. Draean was impossibly fast, darting sideways— but the very tip of my weapon sliced off part of his side, and the cry that rolled from him was shocking—and shocked.

Before I could bring down my whip a second time, the Shurik who had accompanied Draean attacked. I danced aside, heart pounding, watching teeth flash—and heard a sharp cry behind me, sharp as a thunder crack. Grant.

Those two small bodies writhed in midair and dropped. Dead.

When I looked for Draean again, he was gone. He had run.

I stood there, breathing hard, adrenaline pouring through me—and a fierce, ugly smile touched my mouth. My smile. Not the darkness, not the boys. All that viciousness was mine alone, and it felt good.

I looked back at Jack and Grant. "We have a chance."

Neither man smiled back. My grandfather's eyes were haunted, his skin shining with sweat. His grip on that crystal skull was white-knuckled, and when he looked down at the artifact, an expression of pure revulsion and dread passed over his face.

Grant was steadier and gave me a faint nod, determination in his eyes.

The Messenger strode past us toward the chest that the

Shurik had dropped. She circled it with a frown. I joined her, and all the ferocious energy pouring through me prickled and grew quiet. I had a bad feeling, suddenly. Inexplicably bad.

The chest was unlocked. I hesitated, then lifted the lid. My knees buckled. My heart.

Zee was inside. Broken and bleeding.

CHAPTER 24

I dropped to my knees, unable to breathe. Searching my heart, my soul, for those five heartbeats. Precious heartbeats.

All of them were subdued, quiet. No emotion leaking through.

I didn't know what that meant. Were they unconscious? Near death? How the hell had this happened?

"Zee," I whispered, dragging his sharp, small body from the chest. I hardly knew where to touch him. Black blood oozed from multiple lacerations that looked like flog marks. His throat had been partially cut, as had one ear. He had a gash in his side the size of my fist. It was in the same spot where I suffered that dull, persistent ache.

He was limp and unresponsive, a jumble of angular limbs and claws that dangled, flopped. I held him close, whispering his name. He didn't even twitch. My only consolation was his slow heartbeat inside my chest—but even that was ragged, dull.

"Grant," I said, hoarse.

My husband grunted with pain, thumping down beside

me and wincing as his bad knee popped and cracked. "Give him to me."

I shook my head, hugging Zee closer. "Just tell me what you see."

"He's mortal," Grant said, after a moment.

❧

MORTAL.

Even the stars are mortal, said my mother, one clear night in a campground in Yosemite National Park. *Everything dies, baby. Some things just take longer to get to it.*

Except the boys weren't supposed to die. Not my boys. I counted on them like I counted on the rain falling, or the world spinning round and round. Some things you took for granted. Some things just never gave out.

I fell to Texas, with Zee in my arms.

It was dusty and hot. Late afternoon, maybe. Grant let go of my arm, and I ran to the house, unsure what I was doing, just that moving, moving forward, was all that mattered.

I veered from the living room, taking the stairs two at a time until I hit the bedroom we'd been using. The covers were still rumpled, books scattered on the nightstand and our clothes on the floor. I staggered to the bed, arms aching, and half fell as I laid Zee down. I stayed there for a moment, trembling.

"Zee," I said.

Still no reaction. He looked as small as a child, and vulnerable. His blood seeped into the covers.

My heart filled my throat. The sound of a cane floated from the hall, and Grant limped inside, stopping at the bed.

"This can't be happening," I whispered to him. "Nothing hurts the boys."

Grant hummed a little. "My power still slips over him."

I pushed myself off the bed and retreated toward the door, never taking my gaze off Zee. "I'll be back."

I staggered down the hall, one hand braced on the wall. My mother had kept a first-aid kit in the bathroom, and I'd replenished it during our first week in the house. Old habit. Accidents always happened.

I found the box, but I had to take a moment to catch my breath, and leaned on the bathroom sink. My side ached. My skin stung. Those five heartbeats, so damn quiet. I tried reaching for them but got no reaction.

So I reached for the darkness. I stretched through my soul, seeking out that presence. I found it in moments, coiled, quiet.

Too quiet. I jabbed that entity with a sharp mental finger, uncaring what the consequences might be.

I'm not stupid, I said, furious. *I know bonding to me was supposed to give the boys access to you. And you gave them power. I felt you in the bond. You delighted in the hunt.*

The darkness stirred. *Yes.*

I gripped the edges of the sink so hard my fingers hurt. *So what happened? You couldn't protect Zee? All that power, and you couldn't do even that much?*

Silence. Long, thoughtful, silence.

They control you, it whispered finally. *Not us. Never us. What little we gave them was a gift. A taste for times past.*

I frowned at those words and caught a glimpse of myself in the mirror.

Someone else looked back.

I froze, unable to breathe or blink. My face was the same, but my eyes were black as pitch, black as the night sky, flush through with shadows. Even the bathroom light did not reflect in my eyes—as if there was nothing *to* reflect. No surface. Just an endless void, a limitless darkness. A place for light to fall, where it would never be found.

"Stop," I said, and though I heard my voice and watched my lips move, nothing sounded right.

Nothing can contain us if we do not wish to be contained.

"You lie," I replied, watching my empty, soulless eyes.

Lies are weakness, and we are not weak. Once, they invited us. Once, we chose them. Now, we choose you.

Why?

Because you do not want our power, it murmured. *And that is something we have never known. We have never known the heart of light.*

The heart of light. Somewhere, deep, I thought I might know what that meant . . . but the thing inside me was still beyond my comprehension. An entity so old, so powerful, so beyond mortal . . . that I was just as alien to it . . . as it was to me.

I closed my eyes, afraid to look at myself. *Why didn't you help them?*

To remind them of their place. To remind them that they cannot take for granted the long shadow. This is no longer their hunt to lead. And there must be a hunt. There must be death. There must be rebirth.

I bowed my head and took a deep breath, then another, filling my lungs until it hurt. I was terrified to look at myself, but I forced up my chin.

My eyes were normal again. I stared at my reflection, shivering, afraid to look away even for a moment. When I bent to pick up the first-aid kit, I moved slow and careful—and when I did leave the bathroom, the back of my neck prickled—as though someone watched me from the mirror.

Someone like me. Another me. A woman with eyes that could swallow the light of a star.

Grant wasn't in the bedroom. I thought I heard him moving down the hall. He would take one look at me and know something else had gone wrong. I didn't want that. I didn't want anyone to know what I had just seen. I had many nightmares, but that one . . . my eyes, the mirror . . .

I blinked hard, dragging back my focus. *Zee.* Zee was in trouble. All the boys were. That was here, now, immediate.

Blood had stopped seeping from the little demon's wounds, but the cuts were no less wicked, deep enough to require stitches. I found a needle and thread and tried to close the slash in Zee's throat.

The needle refused to pierce his skin.

I wasn't surprised, but it frustrated me. I tossed the needle back into the first-aid box and grabbed bandages and gauze. Only a handful of his wounds could be wrapped. Many deep cuts were on his dark, scaly back.

"Turd," I kept muttering, as I tried to bandage his wounds. "Little fucking Shurik turd."

The next time I saw Lord Draean . . .

When I was done bandaging Zee, I lay down, curled in a ball and facing him. It had been a long time since I'd had the opportunity to just . . . look . . . at Zee. He almost never slept. Not like this. Deeply unconscious and unaware, and so vulnerable. So . . . defenseless. A million thoughts crawled through my mind—memories from childhood, memories from the past six years, little moments of kindness, his quiet.

I thought, again, of what Blood Mama had called them. Barbarians. Slave hunters.

I recalled that dream, too, or vision: that man in the shadowed room, that room of starlight and roses, telling me to ask Zee what a Reaper King feared.

I covered his clawed hand with mine and closed my eyes. I didn't think I would sleep. There was no way. No way at all. I wasn't even tired.

But the next time I opened my eyes, the bedroom window was dark with dusk, and a blanket had been spread over Zee and me. I began to sit up, alarmed. I was an idiot. Might as well just paint a target on my back.

"No," Grant murmured, behind me. "Don't be hard on yourself. I was here the entire time."

I glanced over my shoulder. My husband was seated in the overstuffed armchair beside the nightstand. His cane was in his lap, along with a tin whistle held loose in one hand. I was afraid for him to see my eyes. I touched my face and steeled myself before looking directly at him.

I breathed a small sigh of relief when his only reaction was a gentle, tired smile. "Jack and the Messenger are downstairs. Nothing new to report."

"What about Zee? Any changes?"

He shook his head. "You're going after the others, aren't you?"

"I have to."

"Not without me."

I wanted to tell him no, but my heart crawled up my throat, and I could not speak those words.

"Thank you," I said instead.

"You're my wife," he replied, but behind those words, in his eyes, I knew what that really meant was, *You're my friend, and I love you.*

The hall floor creaked. Jack appeared in the doorway, holding a steaming mug and giving us a hesitant look. I was surprised to see that he had shaved. His face was broad and creased with wrinkles, but there was a certain character there—a particular set of miles—that seemed to suit him.

"Might I come in?" he asked. "I made you tea."

"I appreciate that." I felt uncomfortable around him and didn't know why. I didn't like it. Jack was my grandfather. We were family.

Family with secrets, and lies.

I glanced down at Zee. No reaction. I was still looking at him when I reached out, blind, for the tea—and flinched when Jack clasped my hand instead. He did not speak at first. We simply looked at each other. I was afraid what he would see in my eyes, but his were fathomless.

"Sweet girl," he said, gently. "I *am* sorry."

I felt like a cynic when he said that. There was so much he might be sorry for, including things I probably didn't yet know about.

"For what?" I asked, as Grant leaned forward, watching him.

"Everything." Jack handed me the tea, and backed away from the bed. "All those millennia ago, during the war, the things we did to survive . . ."

His voice trailed away, perhaps because he had been staring at Zee . . . and that was too much of a distraction.

I needed my *own* distraction. "How did it feel to use the skull?"

"I never wish to use it again. It felt too good. And it will draw the wrong attention, using that level of power, again and again." Jack hesitated. "The breaking of the prison on your body would have been enough, alone, to draw others of my kind here."

"We always knew that would happen."

"Only now they will have weapons, and numbers. No simple scout like the Messenger."

"Fine." I said, grim. "Are you coming with me when I rescue the boys, or staying?"

"Coming, of course." Jack looked affronted. "I am your grandfather."

I tried to stand but felt too dizzy. The mattress sank beside me, and Grant laid his hand on my knee.

"Rest," he said.

I started to shake my head, and Jack touched my brow with his fingertips. Something cool moved through me, like a breeze, wiping away my fatigue and light-headedness

I caught his wrist before he pulled away. "Who was she? The first woman of my bloodline?"

Jack froze. "I don't think we have time for this."

We might not have time later, I did not want to say. "Please."

Slowly, carefully, he pulled free of my grip. "Her name was Eiame."

"Eiame," I echoed, and felt a quick pulse in Zee's heartbeat, deep within my chest. "Why did the Aetar choose her?"

"She was genetically groomed. Endowed with extra strength, endurance, perfect immunity—"

"That wasn't my question," I interrupted. "Why *her*?"

Jack's jaw tightened. "She was a sex slave. The others thought she would be easily controlled."

Grant made a disgusted sound. I sat back, staring. "A . . . sex slave."

"Don't look at me like that. Those were different days."

"Really? Because it seems to me that in ten thousand years, nothing's changed. Humans still use each other in despicable ways. They probably picked up the habit from you assholes."

"Maxine—"

I held up my hand. "Okay. So she was a slave, and convenient. Was that really it? Or did she piss someone off?"

"I told you. They thought she would be easily controlled. She was very young and very *kind*. Docile, obedient . . ." Jack stopped, closing his eyes. "Eiame was pleased to serve her gods."

Grant gave him a scathing look. "Did she feel the same way afterward?"

Jack swallowed hard. "I don't know. She fell into a coma. We had to artificially impregnate her, in the hope her offspring would be able to handle the bonding process without the same shock to her system."

I almost regretted asking about her in the first place, though I was glad to know her name. "It worked, I assume."

My grandfather glanced away at Zee. "When I look at him, I still see a monster. I see a devourer of worlds."

"You've felt that way all these years?"

"Every time I see them. I never forget, dear girl."

"Do you forget the murder of my world?" Grant asked

quietly. "A murder you participated in? Do you forget that you enslaved an entire race and bred them for those Aetar games of flesh?"

Jack looked at him. "No. I am a monster, too, lad. I know that's what you think of me."

Grant held his gaze and did not deny it.

"Just as my kind will find you to be a monster," added my grandfather in a soft voice. "You and Maxine, both."

"So we're all our worst enemies," I muttered, sipping tea. "What's your point?"

Jack looked at Zee again. "There is no such thing as true redemption. Even if, by some miracle, you find forgiveness in the eyes of others . . . you never forgive yourself."

Grant slumped back in his chair. "Did you come up here to help or just make us all feel miserable?"

Jack walked to the bedroom door. "I came to deliver tea. And to tell you that some demons are downstairs, waiting to speak with you."

CHAPTER 25

I stopped at the foot of the stairs, staring at my mother's living room, and felt my brain explode. The only way it could have gotten weirder would have been to find the demons in front of me sitting on the couch, sipping soda and watching television.

Actually, it *was* that weird.

Lord Ha'an sat on the floor, propped up against the front of the couch. He looked exhausted. His long fingers were covered in curling blades, strapped to his hands like gloves. Each serrated tip dripped with blood. All of him, bloody, as though he had splashed through buckets.

Some of that blood was his. I saw gashes in his side, across his chest—round holes that looked chewed through. His chest rose and fell with shallow breaths. His eyes were closed.

Beside him was Lord Oanu, also slathered in blood— fur sticky, armor scored with deep scratch marks. I watched him place an experimental paw on the couch cushion, and push down. His ears twitched. So did the tip of his tail. He was wounded: his flanks appeared gnawed on, as did his underbelly around the joints of his armor.

The couch sagged beneath his massive body. He sprawled with a sigh, nearly hitting Ha'an in the head as his massive paw dangled off the cushions.

"Oanu," I said, but even though his ear swung toward me, he did not—or could not—lift his head to greet me. His eyes closed in moments and stayed closed. I would have said he was dead if not for the faint rise and fall of his chest beneath the armor.

Blood Mama stood near the stairs, dressed in a crisp trench coat and stiletto heels. Her host was no redhead but a brunette with curls, a pouty mouth, and a beauty spot on her chin that was less of a mole than a mountain. She did not appear to have engaged in any battle—though her aura carried a hint of deep purple, a color I had never seen in those thunderous shadows.

I stopped beside her. "What happened?"

"War. I told you. It has started."

"They're demon lords. I thought they were invincible."

"A demon lord is only as strong as the bond," she replied, with a cold look. "The Shurik and Yorana joined together and launched surprise attacks upon the others. The massacres weakened Ha'an and Oanu." A cold smile touched the corner of her mouth. "Oh, how I grieve for their losses."

"Zee and the boys."

"They came to help Ha'an and Oanu but had no army to draw strength from. These two demon lords had not yet bonded to them, and so they lacked their combined power." Blood Mama's smile deepened. "Apparently, their bond with you also failed . . . and they were overrun. Captured."

I tried not to let that pain show on my face, but it was too much of a struggle. "I thought they were bonded to you. That should have helped."

Her smile faded. "Grant . . . changed me . . . too much. It severed the bond. I suppose I should thank him for that, but I cannot."

"You have your freedom."

"No," she said, giving me a dark look, "I do not even have me."

I held her gaze, refusing to think about the implications. "Where are the rest of the boys?

"My children are searching for them."

My right hand flexed into a fist. I could find them. I knew it.

Grant came down the stairs and leaned on the rail above us. His gaze swept over the living room and the two demon lords sprawled on the floor and couch. Both seemed to be in a deep sleep. It reminded me of Zee.

He glanced down at Blood Mama. "You brought them here?"

She stiffened at his voice but did not turn. "I hate all the demon lords, but I hate these two less than the others. They need refuge. No place else in this world can offer them that."

That almost sounded like a compliment. "Where are the rest of their people?"

"Scattered. Hiding."

"On earth?"

Blood Mama's aura flared, but color shifted from deep purple to violet, flowing into obsidian shadow. I saw no flashes of red lightning. I saw power, but it was calm, sleek. "Remote places. Deserts. Jungles. Mountains."

"They'll feed."

"They will feed," she said, looking me dead in the eyes. "They will feed their children as you would feed yours, Hunter. Can you live with that?"

I frowned. "What about the Shurik and Yorana?"

"They will also feed," she murmured, walking to the front door. "They will be careful at first until they learn more about the weapons of this world. Until their numbers grow. And then they will stop being careful."

Grant joined me at the bottom of the stairs. "Blood Mama."

She twitched and stopped. "What do you want from me now, Lightbringer?"

"Do you hunger?" he asked. "For the pain of others?"

Finally, she turned to look at him. "I hunger for your death."

"That's because you want to hate me. Not because you *need* to."

Blood Mama snarled at him, but it didn't hide the moment of uncertainty that flickered in her eyes.

The front door opened. The Messenger strode inside, whip in hand, a low hum rolling from her throat. Her Mahati warrior followed and strode across the living room to Lord Ha'an without a second glance at the rest of us. He fell down on one knee, examining the other demon's wounds, then flashed the Messenger a hard look.

"Why would I?" she answered his unspoken question. "He is the enemy."

The Mahati bared his teeth at her. I flicked my hand at the Messenger. "Can you heal Ha'an and Oanu?"

"They are healing on their own," she replied coldly, and

glanced at Grant. "You can confirm this. Watch the threads of their light."

"I see it," Grant said. "They're receiving energy from elsewhere. The bond with their people, perhaps. That must be why they're sleeping. They're letting their bodies recover."

"Is that what Zee is doing?"

He hesitated. "I don't know. It seems different with him."

I chewed the inside of my cheek and strode across the floor to Ha'an. The Mahati warrior stood as I approached, as though ready to defend the demon lord. I held up my hands in a conciliatory gesture, and his low, rumbling growl faded—slowly.

Jack appeared in the doorway of the kitchen, holding the crystal skull.

"They were awake when they arrived," he said in a strangely quiet voice. "I didn't realize that their bodies would require such a deep sleep in order to recover. Seeing them wounded . . . shocked me."

Something about the way he stood there made me uneasy. I stepped between him and the couch, glancing down at the skull—those glinting holes for eyes, so many rows of sharp teeth. I thought about large, silver hands fashioning the crystal in a workshop filled with roses—and for a moment, could see it so clearly in my head, I wavered.

"Old Wolf," I said, mouth suddenly dry. "All those years ago, did you ever think to destroy the clans in order to get to the demon lords?"

"We tried," he said. Grant eyed him, limping to the middle of the living room where the Messenger stood, fingering her iron collar and watching Jack. "We stitched together nightmare beasts to hunt the demons. But they were strong, then, and well fed. Their numbers were vast, dear girl. In the millions."

Jack's hands tightened around the skull. "It seems only a fraction of those numbers survived. I never imagined I would say this, but the demon lords are weak now. They can be killed."

I walked to him. "No, Jack. Not these two."

My grandfather, who had always seemed like an elegant, gentle man, stared at me with impossible indifference and grim resolve. "Don't be sentimental. Don't be lulled into thinking you have a connection, an alliance, with any of the demon lords. If you let them recover, and survive, you will have to fight them. That, or let their people kill. Can you do that? Can you live with yourself?"

"Jack."

"Think of your daughter."

I placed my hand on top of the skull. "I have seen the children of the Mahati. If you kill Ha'an, you will kill those children."

"They're demons," he whispered, though I saw the pain in his eyes.

"Jack," I said gently. "We're all demons, in our own way. We're all human."

Jack retreated, and I followed him, one hand still on the skull.

"We're going to do a lot of killing," I said, incredibly saddened by that certainty—as well as the old conflict and pain in my grandfather's eyes. "Demon lords will die, but not these two."

His gaze flicked past me. "You've never seen their armies kill, my dear. You've never heard the screams from the slave pits, and smelled the cook fires upon which humans roast."

Doubt crept. He was right. What was I doing? I had seen the Mahati eating human flesh. Now, they—and the other clans—were hunting on this world. Whose side was I on?

Jack tried to step around me. I blocked him. I moved without thinking, and that decided it for me. My instincts said no. My heart said no. Despite the risk, and danger—no matter what I had been taught about keeping this world safe—everything in me resisted these murders. Even the attempt.

There had to be another way. I couldn't live with myself if I didn't try. And if I was wrong . . . I would never forgive myself.

I glanced back at Ha'an and Oanu but found myself meeting Grant's gaze instead. I wasn't certain what I saw in his eyes, and it frightened me. I could fight Jack, but if my husband decided to kill the two demon lords . . .

Inside my chest, a heartbeat flared.

Zee.

Confusion trickled through the bond. I held on to that feeling, searching for the other boys—but their presence continued to be muted, dull. Having their hearts in mine had been disconcerting, but not feeling anything—all over again—was worse.

I turned, just in time to see Zee fall from the shadows behind a chair. His bandages were still in place, but his limbs flopped in all the wrong directions as he attempted to sit up. I crossed the living room, falling down on my knees beside him.

His eyes opened. Nothing but red slits, corners crusty with dried fluid. I held my breath as we stared at each other, listening to—feeling—his heart reassert itself.

"Maxine," he whispered, and our bond sparked with surprise—resignation—and then despair.

"Babe," I said in a soft voice.

He brushed his claws against his bandaged throat. "Lost strength. Power . . . refused our call. Should not have been."

Zee struggled to sit up. It was painful watching him. Strained, labored, without his usual deadly grace. Shame filtered through our bond, along with resentment and fear. We met each other's gazes, and he stilled.

"My heart," he rasped. "My heart in yours."

I said nothing. Zee continued holding my gaze, red eyes glinting too bright.

"Thought answers were in blood," he whispered. "Thought . . . together stronger than apart. Wanted to protect you."

"You wanted power," Grant said, with a hard edge in his voice. "So you took it."

Zee gave him a long look. I touched his face, forcing him to look at me. "We're going to get the others. You need to stay here and rest."

"No," he rasped, and his heart pounded harder, with fear and remorse. I closed my eyes, searching for that hard, coiled presence resting deep inside.

Help him, I said. *Help them all. Give them the strength they need.*

No response. Not even a tickle. Which meant all the strength they needed, the only thing that was going to power us through this day, was me. Me, alone.

Grant placed his hand on my shoulder. "I know what to do now."

I didn't ask questions. I dragged Zee in my lap. No protests, no struggle. He flowed against me, a tangle of sharp, bandaged limbs.

"Little king," I whispered, and he sighed.

I closed my eyes as Grant pulled a tin whistle from his back pocket and began playing a twisting, riddling melody that lilted and tugged, swelling with long, sweet notes that flowed through me, sinking warmth into my bones. Light filled my heart, a light that fell on those other five hearts, all of which twitched and pulsed and throbbed beneath that heat.

His music twisted and made power. Power that flowed through me, into my bond with the boys. Zee trembled in my arms, releasing his breath with a hiss. His skin rippled beneath my hands.

I opened my eyes, watching him rip off his bandages. The ragged edges of his flesh began knitting together. Heartbeats gathered strength. An awakening burst from them, a noise of confusion and fear—but also relief. Even the darkness came awake, basking in that light, whispering to itself with pleasure.

And deep in my belly, deep as anything, I felt a spark.

The tin whistle faltered. Grant stopped playing.

"I felt that," he said, with a wonderment that made me smile.

Zee tumbled out of my lap, tearing away the rest of the gauze. The wound in his neck was mostly gone, as was the gash in his side. The cuts over the rest of his body had completely faded. A little shudder raced through him, and he tilted up his head, staring into my eyes.

"Don't even think about telling me not to come with you," I said. "And don't force me, Zee. Don't."

His little shoulders sagged. "Trying to keep you safe."

"It didn't work," Grant said, slipping the tin whistle into his back pocket. "You need help."

Zee looked past us at Ha'an and Oanu, who continued to sleep—and then his gaze skipped to Jack, who watched us with the crystal skull still in his hands. They stared at each other.

"Meddling Man," whispered the little demon. "Circle comes around."

"It always does," replied my grandfather with particular weariness. "I was so afraid you would destroy us all if you ever went free."

"Might happen." Zee tilted his head, looking up at Grant and me. "Or maybe our circle done. Maybe our hunt, done. Power shifts, Meddling Man. Power changes."

"That was what frightened us the most, even more than you." Jack looked at me. "The unknown. The untested. You never know what power will do to the heart. Whether it will grow stronger, brighter . . . or burn out."

"I'm burning," I said to him. "I'm burning to get the hell out of here and find the boys."

But even as the words left my mouth, I heard a booming sound outside the farmhouse and an immense hiss that traveled through the walls like a rising storm. The sound grew so loud, the window rattled, and the floor began shaking.

I ran to the window. It was dark out, pitch-black; but the thumping, the hisses, was accompanied by shrieking wails that made my teeth hurt.

"I know those sounds," Jack whispered.

"Shurik and Yorana," Zee rasped, flexing his claws. "They come."

CHAPTER 26

I stepped onto the porch—left hand on my hip, right hand hanging loose and ready. It was difficult to think past the hisses and shrieks, and the rumble of movement that churned through my chest in a thick vibration. My first instinct was to run, but my heels dug in, and my right hand shimmered with light.

The armor transformed. A sword filled my hand, familiar and light as air. Runes covered the hilt and blade, coiled lines and knots that resembled roses.

"Can't see who's coming," I muttered, as everyone followed me to the porch.

"I can," Grant said in a tight voice. "Looks like they plan on overwhelming us with sheer numbers."

"How bad?"

"Earlier, in the desert, was a drop in the bucket."

"They want to kill us," Jack murmured. "They know we're a threat to them. The only threat on this world, perhaps . . . and all of us are here, gathered in one spot like a prize."

"Draean and K'ra'an cannot resist," Blood Mama said.

"If they kill Zee, an Aetar, a Lightbringer . . . and the precious Vessel . . ."

"I get it," I snapped. "Why haven't they done away with the boys?"

"Will want you to watch," Zee muttered. "Our Queen."

I glanced down at the demon. "Are the others in that mess?"

"Yes," he rasped, and I grabbed his shoulder, looking back at the Messenger. "If it becomes too much, take them out of here." I looked at Grant. "Sever those bonds if you can. Make them yours. I'll be back with help."

"Maxine," he said, but I was already gone.

I seemed to drift far longer than usual within the void, but this time the emptiness did not seem so vast—or empty. I did not feel alone.

You will need us, whispered the darkness, rising through me, stretching my skin with power, igniting my bond with Grant. *You will need us for this hunt.*

I did not answer. But I didn't fight it, either.

I fell into the field below the hill where my mother was buried. I could see the farmhouse, glittering like a jewel in the night, but from here to there—the ground rippled and shook with the endless forced march of thousands and thousands of small bodies—the Shurik, wiggling and undulating across the ground. Amongst them, taller demons, elegant and graceful, carrying swords across their backs and giant spears.

Marching, marching, toward my mother's home.

It looked so small and vulnerable, a tiny light under the clear night sky, heavy with stars. One moment, one heartbeat, one tiny me—lost, lost in what was going to be another battle, another sacrifice—of blood and life, all of which seemed to be never-ending. If I lived through this, another fight would come. If I lived through that, there would be another battle.

Right then, more than anything—that little house represented peace. Peace and safety.

And it hurt to see. It hurt, because it made me afraid I would never have peace. That my daughter would never know that life, or even the promise of it. That I would be fighting until she was born, fighting afterward, teaching her that the only way to live was one hard kill after another.

I glanced at my mother's grave and saw the silhouette of the oak tree against the night sky. I saw the gentle waving of its branches and leaves, and at its base, clumps of bushes heavy with gooseberries, which my mother loved to eat because they were sour. In my heart, I felt such regret, for everything.

A cry went up. I turned in a slow circle, keeping that farmhouse beacon alive at the corner of my eye. Everything I loved was down there. Everything I was going to love—inside me, now.

I'm tired of this, I told the darkness. *It's always the same. I don't want to fight or kill.*

You must hunt, it whispered. *You must hunt to live.*

I'll hunt peace.

Peace comes after death, and death is a long song you are not ready to sing. But when you are ready, it added, *you will not sing it alone.*

I felt a snap inside my soul, and power poured through me. More power than my mind could comprehend. I felt as though I were hemorrhaging a nuclear bomb, or the core of a star, shooting off sparks into my blood.

And it all poured into my bond with the boys.

Zee shuddered, crying out. Somewhere close I heard other cries, familiar in their rage, echoing the rage inside my heart. I started running, Zee loping in front of me, growing sleeker and bigger, slashing his claws over the Shurik who tried to leap at us. I could barely think past the tsunami raging through me, and if that power had not been channeled through the bond into the boys, I was certain I would have split apart into a million little pieces.

My vision blurred. My running feet hardly seemed to touch the ground. I moved with more grace than the wind, and each scent, each sound was electric and wild. Thunder raged through my chest, thunder and fury, and I began to lose myself to those emotions, swinging the sword as though it were an extension of my arm—biting into flesh, bone, releasing blood and death. I did not see who I killed. I tried not to care.

I kept that farmhouse beacon at the corner of my eye.

"Zee!" I shouted. "The others!"

Even as I spoke his name, I saw the boys inside my mind, in my heart: wrapped in massive chains and borne down by iron hooks that pierced their bodies to anchor them to stone. Raw's chest had been impaled, while a thick iron spear, serrated with barbs, penetrated Aaz's entire jaw. Hundreds of needle-thin spikes pierced Dek's and Mal's long bodies.

But they were awake. Fighting. Hearts pounding inside mine.

We are together, I called to them, through our bond. *Boys.*

Resolve washed down the link—five points of light

burning within the darkness. Five stars, smoldering around the star blazing inside my own heart, our light merging into shadow, into power, into fury.

My vision flickered. Darts around me, streaks of flesh and screams. Air moved against my body. I glimpsed Shurik throwing themselves at me—turning to ash before they could touch my body. Chaos, everywhere. No organization. Just lives thrown away.

Raw fell from the shadows, snarling. Aaz was close behind him. Covered in blood. Immediately set upon by a group of Yorana bearing whips that they rained down with screams. Raw and Aaz charged into demons. Dek and Mal writhed into sight as they skipped through shadows, so quickly it was as though they were flying—in and out—and each time they emerged, it was to rip open another throat.

I didn't care about the blood, or death. My boys . . . my boys were alive, and here.

Their hearts were frenzied, hammering with wild hunger and abandon. They killed, and each kill excited them even more, working them into a heaving, deadly mob of muscle and darkness, and death. I felt them. I was there, with them, as they killed, swept up in the same bloodthirsty excitement. I stopped fighting. Stopped moving. Eyes closed, my entire being lost in the brutal lust for the kill.

It was euphoric. It was terrible. I was possessed, and I didn't know if I cared because the emotions and power pouring through me were bigger than I, an avalanche sweeping my soul into a little hole where a small part of me wailed in horror, while the rest was overcome by five hearts not my own.

My vision split. I saw in my mind a sea of bodies, pushing and pulling. Each demon aching to retreat, but unable to because of those bonds—those bonds to Draean and K'ra'an, who threw their people at the boys . . . and farther away, the farmhouse.

The farmhouse. My beacon. I had to protect it.

I focused on the demon lords and fell into the void.

Moments later, I stood on a distant hill, behind two tall figures. I was not myself—but maybe I was, maybe—and I swung my sword without warning or hesitation, cutting into K'ra'an's side.

I could have sliced him completely in half, but something stayed my hand. Me. Part of me still with mercy.

He cried out in shock, twisting to face me, clutching at the sword in his side. He made another sound of pain—smoke rising from his palms where he touched the gleaming metal. The fury and disbelief in his eyes faded into horror as he looked deep into my face.

"Already dead," I whispered. "Or not. Depends on you."

"You will kill all my people," he said in a trembling voice, as purple sweat oozed down the red skin of his face. "For what? There are many humans to spare."

The darkness inside me heaved with laughter.

"Not the point," I whispered.

K'ra'an bared his sharp teeth. "Then, what?"

"I am your Queen," I hissed, those words rising from deep within. I didn't know if they were my words. I was too lost. I was spinning inside, and my actions, my voice—I could not say who spoke: the darkness, or me, or the boys.

Zee, Raw, and Aaz fell from the shadows, landing with solid thumps that made the ground shake. Mal slid onto my shoulders, hissing, while Dek coiled around my feet.

"And they," I added, *"are your Kings."*

"No." K'ra'an spat blood at my feet. "Even if you are the Vessel, I will be *free*. We gave too much. We *sacrificed* everything, for *them*. No more."

"No more," I echoed, and chopped off his head.

Deep inside, part of me screamed when I did that.

And somewhere else in my soul, the part mixed with the boys and the darkness, there was only satisfaction, and pleasure.

A job done.

Survival ensured.

Screams rose around us, cries of horror from the demon army that twisted and rattled the air, rising into shrieks—

—that were suddenly silenced. Complete, dead, silence.

I turned to look at Draean. He was staring at K'ra'an's corpse, blood streaming from his eyes and nose, a rattling choking sound in his throat.

"It could be different," I whispered. "You *were* different, once. Peaceful."

"No," he said, tearing his gaze from K'ra'an to look at me, with resolve and resignation, and hate. "If you let me live, I will hunt you. I will catch you. I will enter your womb and consume your child."

I swung the blade, right into Draean's neck.

He did not cry out or flinch, though his gaze remained on me even as I struck the blow. His head rolled down the hill. The rest of him collapsed beside the other demon lord.

Zee crouched, digging his fist into the dead man's torso. I heard a sucking sound, and then he pulled out his arm— revealing a large, wriggling Shurik slug in his fist.

The darkness moved through us all, strong and powerful. Zee stared into Draean's eyes in perfect silence—then ripped him apart in one sharp yank. He tossed the pieces aside. I heard more screams rising, voices high in pitch, spiraling higher with despair. I tried not to listen. I tried not to imagine an entire race dying from the loss of a single bond.

The boys and I stared at the dead demon lords. We stared at each other. I looked past them at the farmhouse—up at the stars—and started to sway.

Those stars were moving toward me.

And then they were in me.

❧

I opened my eyes and found myself resting on a bed of stars and silver roses. Zee was curled against my side, while Raw and Aaz huddled along my back. Dek and Mal shivered beneath my head.

The darkness was quiet. My soul was quiet, though it felt wounded, too, with a particular lightness that made me feel as though an important part of me might just float away.

I saw a man sitting amongst the stars. He was turned from me, staring at something in his hand. I tried to sit up but couldn't move.

When I looked again, though, the man was beside me. I still could not see his face, but his body was encased in silver, skin etched with runes and designs that seemed to tell a story—one so tangled, I couldn't make out the details.

"Who are you, really?" I asked softly, wishing I could see his face and trying instead to see what was in his hand.

As if he could read my thoughts, he turned his palm and showed me a jagged lump of crystal.

"I am a dreamer," he replied. *"There are songs in your world about that sort of thing."*

"My grandfather calls you the Tinker." *I want to call you father,* I did not add.

"Old Wolf. A man of many secrets." His hands covered the crystal. *"Make a wish."*

I raised my brow. I didn't have anything to wish for . . . though as soon as I had that thought, Grant filled my mind.

"Ah . . . the Lightbringer. I thought you might like him."

"What's that supposed to mean?"

"His mother did not find your world by accident."

"You helped her?"

"Do not be offended. All I did was open a door. Life took care of the rest."

I frowned, disturbed by the notion. "Tell me again who you are. Tell me *what.*"

He rubbed his hands over the crystal lump, silver skin flashing in the starlight while those intricate etchings flowed like water up his arms, down his ribs. *"I was a man. I am still a man, in some ways. But something found me, long ago, and I was . . . transformed."*

"What found you?"

"I do not know. Just that it was power, and light. A presence born at the beginning." I sensed a smile in his voice. *"It is the opposite of what is in you."*

A chill swept over me. I tried to sit up, but my body refused to move.

"The opposite?" I asked. "I want to get rid of it. It's terrible. It's violent, and awful."

"It is just power . . . and power requires a strong heart to guide it. I would much rather you bear that burden than anyone else. Your mother agreed."

I wanted to hear about my mother, but my irritation was stronger. "So you both planned everything, is that it?"

"Not everything." He stopped rubbing his hands, and his shoulder tilted toward the bed I rested upon. *"Zee'akka. Raw'akka. Aaz'akka. Dek'akka, Mal'akka. Wake, little Kings."*

Their eyes flashed open, alert and suspicious. All of them sat up, spines cracking, muscles rippling beneath their skin. Dek draped protectively over my chest as they stared at the silver man, the stranger.

My father.

"You," Zee rasped. "Star Man."

"Me," he agreed. *"You have a choice to make, all of you. And it will be solely your choice, offered just this once."*

Zee's shoulders tensed. "Speak it."

"You can remain free, without bond to Maxine. Or you can live again on her skin, as you always did, before I intervened."

The boys gave each other uneasy looks. Zee whispered, "What purpose, this offer?"

"You were possessed by an unnatural force for over a millennia. And then you traded that possession for a prison upon a woman's skin. Woman, after woman, who possessed you all.

"So. I offer you freedom or the prison. Think about it. You have as much time as you need. A thousand years, if need be. This is the Labyrinth, after all." He leaned forward, and pressed something into my hand. *"Rest. Dream."*

"No," I said, distressed by what he had offered the boys. "Don't I have a say?"

"Not this time."

"That's heartless."

"I still have a heart, Maxine. You are in it."

I wanted to protest, but the stars had begun to move. I closed my eyes, dizzy.

"Your daughter will be beautiful," he whispered.

THE next time I opened my eyes, there were no stars—just a blue sky that stretched forever, and sunlight that was golden, young, and crisp against the green leaves of an oak. I turned my head to the left and saw my mother's grave.

I ached all over. My head hurt. A round, hard object was in my hand. I tried to sit up, and stopped.

I was covered in tattoos.

CHAPTER 27

WHEN I was thirteen, I ran away from my mother.
It was stupid. I knew that at the time, but I needed space. I needed freedom. We had never been apart, not in any significant way. Always on the road, my life spent in cars and hotel rooms—libraries, if I was lucky—with only a glimpse in passing of kids my own age. Waiting, at night, for my mother to come home from killing the things that hunted humans. Knowing one day I'd join her.

That was the price of being her daughter.

One morning, we drove to some fast-food restaurant to buy breakfast. I told her I had to go to the bathroom. All I did was walk out the side door and keep going.

Beautiful day. Shining sun. Cool, crisp autumn air. We were in Denver. I walked to the gas station next door and caught a ride with a woman who had a golden retriever in her backseat. The dog liked me. I'd never spent much time with one.

His name was Puck. The woman called herself Chari. For three hours we drove to Laramie, Wyoming, taking back roads that wound through a raw country filled with stone and grass, and hills that looked like jagged teeth. We listened to seventies rock on the radio, and when the reception turned to static, we talked about life.

Chari, to put it mildly, was all about peace and love. To call that an alien concept was an understatement. Not that I was already some coldhearted killer. I wasn't one of those kids who stomped on ants. I was all about peace and love, too.

But I also knew there was a cost—and a lot of people in the world who didn't believe in compassion. Who would take a woman like Chari and turn her inside out and find everything good and cut it from her, piece by slow piece.

Someone needed to protect her. Someone needed to protect them all.

Chari bought me a sandwich when we reached Laramie. She was reluctant to leave me, but I told her I had an aunt who lived in town and that I would be fine. I'm pretty sure she knew it was a lie, but she also believed in minding her own business—in addition to all that peace and love. She gave me her phone number in case I needed anything.

I wandered, for the rest of the day. Freedom was okay, but I was still alone.

I had just enough money in my pocket to buy a pair of used cowboy boots at a pawnshop. A little big for my feet, but the leather was soft, and I could feel all the miles of another life in the soles. I liked that. The old man who sold them said they suited me and that I'd grow into them.

Near sunset, I found a spot near the train tracks that ran through town and made myself comfortable.

Dek and Mal located me less than a minute after the sun slipped below the horizon, their purrs broken with concern. Zee followed, moments later. Full of reproach, and silence.

My mother caught up several hours later.

I was ready for anything. My mother was not a woman to be fucked with. Never mind the demon-hunting. In New York City, I had seen her crush a man's face with her fist, just for grabbing her ass. She was, in my mind, the most dangerous woman in the world.

But all she did was stand there, staring at me. I didn't budge or look away.

"You're all I have," she said, finally—and that wasn't what I expected to hear, but it hit me harder than a slap.

It *was* a slap.

But I needed that. I needed that day in the car with Chari. I needed to be reminded of why my mother lived the way she did, and that the price of being her daughter wasn't just isolation . . . but a duty. An honor, even.

My mother and I had to be hunters, killers, so people like Chari could have their peace and love.

We had to fight because no one else could fight like us.

No one else could bear the cost.

⚜

THREE days after the boys made the decision to return to my body, and five days after the battle at the farm, a red Corvette drove down the old dirt driveway, causing a dust storm and thumping some major bass.

It was near sunset. I was sitting on the farmhouse porch drinking an ice-cold ginger ale, listening to Johnny Cash, and reading a book of baby names. So far, I hadn't liked any of them.

The boys tugged on my skin. My heart ached when I felt that. With sadness, maybe. I was still working that out.

Grant limped onto the porch, leaning hard on his cane. "What now?"

"Eh," I said. "Probably a demon."

He nudged me with his hip. "Given all the other weird things that have happened, what are the odds we'll have a boy?"

I just looked at him. He grinned, holding up his left hand. "Don't hit me."

I grunted, glancing more closely at his hand and the new ring he wore. It was a wide, thick band of clear crystal, the interior of which was filled with an intricate, knotted design similar to what currently covered my armor—and my father's skin. I knew it had some meaning, just as I knew the repeated motif of the rose probably had little to do with actual roses. Until I had the opportunity to speak with my father again, I was content to simply call it beautiful and mysterious.

Much like the ring itself.

Grant followed my gaze. "Nothing has happened if that's what you're wondering."

"Hmm." I put down the book of baby names as the Corvette spun into the front drive. "I'm suspicious. You'll probably start time-traveling, or speaking in tongues."

He laughed, but it sounded nervous.

Grant and I walked off the porch as the Corvette's door swung open. Blood Mama stepped out. Her host wore a sundress that showed off an indecent amount of pampered leg, and her ample bosom heaved. Her purple aura danced like a wild storm.

"I'm done here," she said, without preamble. "I've made it known to my children that they are to watch the borders of this land. If there are any . . . excursions . . . you'll be informed. You do realize, however, that you're insane? The clans will not tolerate living in such close proximity. Not here. Not for long."

"This is several thousand acres," I said.

"We used to colonize entire *worlds*," she replied. "Perhaps you should find us one."

"Maybe I will," I shot back.

Grant cleared his throat. "For now, I just want to find enough livestock and building materials to get them started."

"And the Shurik and Yorana? You think they'll listen to you?"

Grant frowned at her. "They'll have no choice. I hold their bonds."

I shoved my hands in my jeans pockets and looked down at my boots. My husband was now a glorified demon lord.

He couldn't explain how he had done it. At the moment I had killed K'ra'an—and Zee tore Draean apart—the bonds with their clans had swung loose, and Grant had grabbed them. Grabbed them, made them part of himself. Just an instinct. Not much different from the bond we shared except this was less intimate. Like two small suns burning in his chest. Not uncomfortable. Just warm.

And powerful. So powerful that Jack had speculated Grant might now be immortal. Or, at the very least, the most powerful Lightbringer ever to have lived.

I wasn't entirely sure how my grandfather felt about that.

Jack was gone, with the crystal skull. I didn't know

where. He had not said good-bye, and his absence made me uneasy. I thought—I was certain—it had everything to do with the demons who would be living on this land. Demons he had tried to murder ten thousand years ago. Demons he would have murdered five days ago if I had not stopped him.

Maybe he would be proven right. I didn't want to think about that. Ha'an and Oanu both knew I had protected them from Jack. Apparently, their comalike state didn't hurt their hearing. As a result, they both felt they owed me. Enough to play by my rules.

And my rules were simple: No feeding on humans.

Blood Mama started to get back into her car.

"Wait," I said. "When this first started, all I heard was the gloom and doom. Your children, hiding. Your children, contemplating *suicide* because they said it would get so bad."

"And you think," she said softly, "that we exaggerated?"

I stayed silent. Blood Mama gave me a bitter, surprisingly pained smile. "For once, Hunter, I envy you. I envy your innocence. I hope . . ."

She stopped and looked down. "I hope you never learn what could have been. I hope none of us do. To see the full nightmare of the old army unleashed . . . millions strong, and ruthless . . ."

Blood Mama visibly shivered, her aura sucking down around her shoulders. "Perhaps we all changed, being apart from the Reaper Kings and their influence. Perhaps some of us . . . became more as we were, before the old war. I would not have imagined Ha'an and Oanu agreeing to your terms so quickly, otherwise. But they were a peaceful race, before the Reaper Kings took them. We all were."

She grimaced, and without looking at us, got back into the Corvette. Grant and I retreated to the porch as she drove away.

"She ordered the murder of my mother," I said, watching the cloud of dust as she sped off. "How come I want to . . ."

Forgive her, I almost said. But I couldn't bring myself to say those words out loud. Because she *had* ordered my mother's murder, along with the murders of so many of my ancestors. Me included, had things been different. I could not let myself forget that.

Grant slung his arm around my waist. I looked out at the horizon.

Sunset had come.

⊰⊱

LATE that night, the boys and I ran away. I did not know where we were going. I let them choose.

It was dark where we landed, except for the stars. I looked up before I looked anywhere else, and the sky was alive, and when I held my breath, and held my heart, I thought perhaps I heard a song, somewhere, in my soul.

The night was spectacularly clear, and the air tasted thin. I looked around, but all I saw were an odd set of ruins where the stonework was precise and seemed to have been part of some odd-looking interlocking structures.

"Where are we?" I asked, as Dek licked the back of my ear, and purred.

"Puma Punku," Zee rasped. "Ancient city. Built by Aetar when they first come to earth. Home to them, many years."

Raw and Aaz loped along the ruins, while Mal dropped from my shoulder to explore a nearby hole. I patted Dek's head and joined Zee on top of a stone block, facing the horizon while the wind blew through my hair.

We were silent, together. That had never been unusual. But now, instead of it being easy, there was tension in the air. I felt . . . vulnerable around him now. Off balance. Power had shifted, then shifted again. Everything was different. It made me sorry and sad.

"Wait," Zee whispered, and leapt off the stone, bounding across the ruins with his sleek, effortless grace. I touched my chest as he ran, and it took me a moment to remember that I could not hear his heart. I felt empty again, inside.

A short distance away, he stopped—and started digging. Raw and Aaz joined him, all three working together until they pulled a surprisingly small bundle from the dirt. As Zee ran back, parts of his body seemed to melt inside the shadows, distorting his size—and the same was true for Raw and Aaz, who flowed in and out of sight like ghosts.

Zee laid the bundle down at my feet. I heard clicking sounds inside the ragged layers of cloth, which were threadbare, filled with holes and loose fibers. He stepped back and looked at me.

I knelt and pulled apart the bundle. The armor tingled, sinking warmth into my bones—but I did not stop. The boys gathered around, watching. I tried to be gentle, conscious that whatever I was touching was old—but at a certain point, I just had to pull. The fibers split.

I found bones inside. An entire human skeleton, jumbled together in a messy pile. Raw and Aaz sniffed the bones and snarled. Even Dek and Mal backed away, as though uneasy. Purrs fell into silence. I stared into empty eye sockets, and shivered.

"Who is this?" I asked.

"First mother," rasped Zee. "First heart."

I sat back, stunned. "Eiame? But . . . why is she here?"

"Know where every mother buried," rasped Zee, giving those bones a sad look. "Bones, lives, hearts, resting in all four corners. This where we caught and made."

Caught and made.

Raw pulled a six-pack of beer from the shadows, but no one drank or ate. We just sat, solemn and quiet, looking everywhere but at each other.

"Zee," I finally said. "Why did you . . . come back to me?"

Dek licked the back of my ear. Raw sighed and shoved a beer down his throat.

"We thought . . . thought we had to be same," rasped Zee, after a long moment's silence. "Same as before. Same in heart. Same hunger. Same fire. Same . . . hate."

He studied the woman's bones. "Learned we not same. Realized . . . don't have to *be* same. Were Reaper Kings, but Reaper Kings of *then*, not Kings of *now*. Know what love is now. Ten thousand years taught us human heart. To live with human heart. To *have* heart."

Zee looked at me. "You, our heart. You, our nest. All, us, together."

"It's a prison."

"Not prison," he rasped. "Redemption."

I stared at him. I stared at all of the boys, who gave me sad smiles. I remembered what it felt like to feel their hearts in mine, and so in my heart I poured every warm feeling, all my love, and imagined it trickling inside them like the sun.

Zee's shoulders sagged, and he crawled into my lap. Raw and Aaz joined him, and, moments later, Mal slithered onto my shoulder beside Dek. I touched my stomach, and imagined a little soul, a lovely little light.

We looked at the stars.

"Where's your heart?" my mother once asked me. *"Where's your heart, baby?"*

"Here," I whispered. "It's here."

Two Stunning Works
From *New York Times* Bestselling Author
MARJORIE M. LIU

ARMOR OF ROSES

⊰ **A Hunter Kiss Novella** ⊱

When demon slayer Maxine Kiss investigates a grisly murder, she finds herself involved in a conspiracy dating back to World War II—and a secret mission that her grandmother may have carried out for the US government, one that involves the mysterious armor of roses . . .

THE SILVER VOICE

⊰ **A never-before-published Hunter Kiss short story** ⊱

On their honeymoon, Maxine helps Grant explore his heritage through memories locked inside a mysterious seed ring, leading him to the silver voice and secrets his mother kept hidden from him—until now.

Available together online!
Also includes a letter from Marjorie!

M992AS1011

From *New York Times* Bestselling Author

MARJORIE M. LIU

A WILD LIGHT
-⩥ **A Hunter Kiss Novel** ⩤-

Obsidian shadows of the flesh . . . tattoos with
hearts, minds, and dreams. By day, they are my
armor. By night, they unwind from my body
to take on forms of their own—demons of the
flesh, turned into flesh.

"I adore the Hunter Kiss series! Marjorie Liu's writing
is both lyrical and action packed, which is a very rare
combination."
　　　　　—Angela Knight, *New York Times* bestselling author

"Readers of early Laurell K. Hamilton [and] Charlaine
Harris . . . should try Liu now and catch a rising star."
　　　　　　　　　　　　　　　　—*Publishers Weekly*

M935T0811

From *New York Times* Bestselling Author

MARJORIE M. LIU

DARKNESS CALLS

Demon hunter Maxine Kiss wields her living tattoos to fight the darkness and the predators that threaten the earth. Now she's on a mission to rescue the man she loves—but her only chance to save him could end with her lost in her own darkness.

"Readers of early Laurell K. Hamilton [and] Charlaine Harris...should try Liu now and catch a rising star."

—*Publishers Weekly*

M499T0609

Also Available from *New York Times*
Bestselling Author

Marjorie M. Liu

THE IRON HUNT

"The boundlessness of Liu never
ceases to amaze."
—*Booklist*

Demon hunter Maxine Kiss wears her armor as
tattoos, which unwind from her body to take on
forms of their own at night. They stand between
her and her enemies, just as Maxine stands between humanity and the demons breaking out
from behind the prison veil. It is a life lacking in
love, reveling in death, until one moment—and
one man—changes everything.

penguin.com